The Memory Jumper
Copyright © 2022 Amanda Michelle Brown

Library of Congress Control Number: 2022909090
ISBN 979-8-9850102-3-7 (paperback)
ISBN 979-8-9850102-4-4 (hardcover)
ISBN 979-8-9850102-5-1 (ebook)

This book is a work of fiction. Names, characters, places, and incidents either are the product of the author's imagination or are used fictitiously. Any resemblance to actual events, businesses, companies, locales or persons, living or dead, is entirely coincidental.

Cover design by MAD Studio

Published by Lost Island Press
San Jose, California
www.lostislandpress.com

For Diana Cockrell,
who taught me how to write

And for my mother, Rebecca Brown,
who taught me how to love to write

THE
MEMORY
JUMPER

THE
MEMORY
JUMPER

Lost Island
P R E S S

AMANDA MICHELLE BROWN

Don't speak
Don't breathe
You are not free
The questions are rhetorical
You should've known that

Take on the facade
That it's okay
You have no other choice

Your cage is large
Be grateful

There are others worse off than you

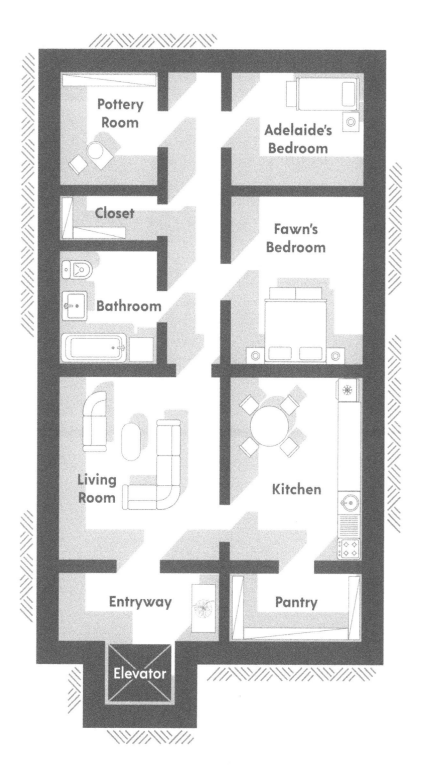

ONE
ADELAIDE

I t takes me a minute to remind myself that the red paint dripping from the table isn't my own blood. It glows unnaturally in the light of my single white LED lantern.

In moments like this, the best thing to do is just remain silent. *If you don't move, they can't see you.* I think I read that about a dinosaur.

"What did I tell you about painting in your room?" The woman in front of me speaks words of rabid fangs, the light from my lantern spilling across her face and making it just as harsh as the murderous look in her eyes.

Disappear. Disappear. But I'm still here.

"I'm sorry, Fawn. I'll take my stuff out to the kitchen next time." My voice gets lost in my terror, and only squeaks come out. This irritates her more. She towers over me, both in actual height and presence. She's a rhinoceros; a tiger; an elephant; a…cow? Why did I think of that? The thought makes me want to laugh, which makes me want to smile, which makes me actually smile for just a second.

Too late. She's seen. "You think this is *funny?* Destroying the furniture I bought for you?"

I close my eyes. *Furniture I technically paid for.* I breathe in and out. I start another list of animals Fawn is like. A weasel; a bear; a…it's pointless. No animal compares to her.

I almost wish she'd hit me, just to get it over with. But Fawn's game is primarily in the mind. It's a poisonous, invisible game that makes me sometimes wonder if I'm a tinge insane. It's a symptom-less sickness.

Instead, she tosses the rest of the paint tubes, palettes, and paintbrushes off my desk.

I retreat inside my mind. I wonder if normal humans can do this. Just because I'm a Memory Jumper doesn't mean other people don't lock themselves inside their minds during stuff like this.

I wonder what's going through Fawn's mind.

She leaves me to clean up the mess. The red paint mixes with blue, green, and a little ochre.

Good. No blood.

I'm curled up in a corner of my room, the farthest corner. The farthest corner in the farthest room in the house. I pretend it's my safe corner, but that's a lie: Fawn's bedroom is right next door. There is no safe place here.

My room is smaller than Fawn's, but I don't need lots of space anyway. Everything is beige: the walls, the floor, the bookshelves, the bed. To make it less…well, *beige*, I've taped pictures of places I want to travel to one day over my walls. I also personalized the bed frame with my own acrylic paint doodles to liven the place up; Fawn was not happy.

The floors are cold, hard concrete, just like the walls, so I always wear socks. I have a stash under my bed, which Fawn declares makes me the definition of *messy*, but I like them under there because they're easily grabbable.

And I love my shelves: they hang from the ceiling, bursting with books. Right now, a few books are missing: I currently flip through a novel about the Titanic, my electric lantern lighting each page. I touch every face in every picture. These are my friends.

I switch to browsing a field guide about sparrows. These are my friends too.

You know what all these pictures show? What they speak of? Mothers. And something called maternity. Lots of the books I've read talk about mothers. Well, Fawn is the closest thing I have to that. She's only a couple of years older than me, but I've always known her as my mother. She's provided for me and guided me; she's installed herself as the mother figure of my life.

Not that I call her Mom.

A knocking sounds from above me. It's the hollow thunk of someone pounding on metal. I wait for the familiar rhythm: *thunk, tap-tap, thunk, tap, thunk, stomp*. My heart rate rises, but I think I'm okay. Fawn should be calm by now after some time away from me.

All my life, I've lived underground in this box we call home. The only way out is a teleporter, which I make my way to right now so I can let Fawn back in.

Since our home was previously a safe house, the teleporter has an added safety mechanism: it stays hovering a floor above us until the user gives an audible signal (a password, really). That way, if someone were to ever discover us, they couldn't actually get into the house.

I walk into the entryway, which is anything but welcoming. A single glowing light bulb casts its harsh white light across a lone table, on which sits an obviously fake orchid. The only saving grace of this display is the fact that I made the vase in which the flower sits.

I take great pride in my pottery, a hobby that Fawn's been kind enough to allow me to do. I have all my supplies in what was supposed to be a closet. A couple of times a week, I go in there and make plates, bowls, vases, and jewelry holders. She sells them in the city, and we get a little extra money through that. I love it because it makes me feel in control for once.

But I wish I could be the one selling my items. I want to run a booth, to help people pick out the perfect gift for their loved ones or wrap it in colorful tissue paper.

I press a button on the wall and wait like a loyal pet. I always have to wait and say *hi* or else Fawn will throw a fit.

How many times have I pressed this button and wished that I was the one inside the teleporter instead of being stuck in here? I'm not allowed outside because of my value. If everyone knew about my powers, they'd be flying at me fast as mosquitoes on standing water. People would try to kidnap me, misuse me.

I don't want that. And neither does Fawn.

The teleporter opens with a cheerful ding. Fawn's eyes meet mine, calculating, measuring, evaluating—always stripping the subject of all its coverings, revealing motive and areas of lacking.

I've never met someone with eyes that are so exactly described as circles; it's like those old-timey cartoon characters. I think Fawn was their inspiration, except her eyes don't make her look goofy. Fawn has only three modes, two of them more common and nastier: a cold, aloof innocence and a shrinking, empty anger. Every now and then, there's a flicker of a woman who actually cares for me as a daughter. And those are the moments I live for. She is an expert actress when anyone besides me sets foot in the house: you'd think she's the kindest, most thoughtful woman in the world.

Just another one of her games.

But when I Memory Jumped into Fawn's mind when I was five, she couldn't let a good opportunity pass her by. I don't remember what I saw, and I have never Memory Jumped into her mind again. She doesn't let me.

At first, Fawn thought I was some kind of witch…but she was a single woman with hardly any source of income. So she began selling my service.

I can't blame her, and I don't. At least, that's what I've been telling myself for years.

If you tell yourself a lie enough times, it'll eventually be nothing but the truth.

Fawn nods at me as she steps out of the teleporter with an elderly woman. Her brunette hair is perfectly parted down the middle, so dark it's almost black. Her skin is a light type of sunkissed brown that I can never attain because I'm kept away from the light; I can't ever remember being outside in my eighteen years of life.

I'm glad she has a client; she can't be mad at me in front of a client.

The woman sways a bit, her face shrunken in wrinkles, her eyes clouded over with time. She doesn't say a word as Fawn grabs one of her arms and helps remove her from the teleporter. I grab the woman's other arm.

We cross the entryway and enter the main room, a modest area with much-loved cream sofas. Light spills in from above; there's a skylight cleverly concealed by a pond on top of it. I remember when I was younger and Fawn would press the emergency button, which covered the skylight and sent us into darkness. She'd tell me to be deadly silent; that someone was hunting us. I breathe a little more heavily thinking about it.

One wall is made entirely out of one big screen. I often change it to picture lofty mountains, sparkling oceans, or dense jungles. The pictures move, and sometimes I am lucky enough to find a scene that actually shows people milling around a busy street, or animals walking around nature. But our blind customer does not need to be impressed by any visual stimuli, so I leave it at its current view: the Rocky Mountains mid-winter, carpeted in icy white that looks so plush and delicious I want to both roll in it and eat it at the same time.

I wonder what a mountain would feel like.

"Ms. Dahlia, this is my—my daughter, Adelaide." She says *daughter* like it's a bad word. She doesn't bother going over our origin story again: how, fifteen years ago, she was babysitting me when riots broke out across our country, Frelsi. Anti-Memory-Jumping groups executed coordinated attacks on known Memory Jumpers, killing thousands in what became known as The Memory Wipe.

She took me to a Memory Jumper safe house and stayed with me, waiting for my parents to come for me.

But they never did.

And we're still hidden away in that same safe house to this day.

I smile politely at the woman. "Nice to meet you."

The old woman turns her head toward me. I wonder if she'd mind knowing she's being recorded. Fawn has cameras here in the living room, in my bedroom, and in my pottery room. I try to forget about that. "Nice to meet you, doll."

"Ms. Dahlia has Alzheimer's and will eventually lose her memory. She has already lost her husband. She would like you to erase all her memories: except one."

I've had clients like this before. Clients who have diseases that will terminate their memory or their lives. Clients who simply want to live in a beautiful memory. I don't quite understand it myself; how could one memory be wonderful enough for it to be replayed over and over again?

I always feel a bit guilty about these tasks. It's hard to destroy something to feel right. But it's what Ms. Dahlia wants.

And Fawn has made me do far worse things.

"Which memory would you like to keep?" I ask. Ms. Dahlia reaches into her clutch, an antique thing made of granny-approved patchwork stars and stripes. A memento of our old government. She retrieves a piece of paper, crumpled a bit from its journey but still legible.

"I had my nurse write this down as I dictated."

I take the paper and read it. My heart warms at the words; I curl the paper in my hand, tilting my head.

"This is a good choice," I say. Ms. Dahlia smiles as if my approval has cemented her decision.

"Thank you, Miss Adelaide."

I stick the note in my pocket and wipe my hands on my jeans. I always get sweaty palms before Memory Jumping. In fact, I get sweaty palms before anything involving my always-bound-up nerves. I'm always aware of what will happen if I fail.

"Are you ready, ma'am?" Fawn asks. Her voice sounds patient, but she's as tense as a coiled-up slinky. Fawn likes to get them in, get them out, quick.

"Yes. Yes." The old woman runs her pointy, crinkly finger along the stitches of a proud star on her purse. "And all the details are planned out?"

"Absolutely." Fawn can't just bring Ms. Dahlia back to the nursing home in a stupor. If the old woman were to wake up and only remember one thing, questions would be asked. That's why Fawn has special contacts, Buddy and Perkins, that can *deliver* people when their conditions have been…altered.

Their kind, the Visionaries, have been persecuted by the government just like Memory Jumpers. The twins get mad when people dismiss their gift as *fortune-telling*. They are specialists in realities. They can show you the reality that you are currently on the path to, as well as alternative realities. But it's ultimately up to you to decide which one will actually happen.

Fawn connected with them in the black market years and years ago, adopting them as brothers almost. Of course, she lunged on their gifts just like she had with mine.

But they don't ever see the real side of her. As far as they know, we are a mother and daughter Memory Jumping for income. After my Jump, we must wipe our clients' memories for safety purposes; there's nothing sinister about that.

As far as they know, they're just bringing the clients back to their previous location for a clean transition back into normal life. Buddy and Perkins also help us with groceries on occasion, reveling in *taking care* of us and feeling needed.

I love Buddy and Perkins. They're brothers so similar you'd think they're twins. Both are slightly overweight, with a marvelous sense of humor and a bit of stubble on their copious chins.

I guess they're a type of henchmen, but the best and kindest kind there is.

"All right, Ms. Dahlia." Fawn looks at me. She can see the nervousness in my eyes, I know it. I give her a thumbs up so she won't snap at me later about chickening out. "Thank you so much for allowing us to help you."

I place one hand on Ms. Dahlia's temple. My hands are always cold, so the old woman gasps a little as they meet her warm forehead. But she doesn't beg me to stop; at least *she* doesn't chicken out.

I close my eyes and focus, really hard. I dig into the core of my brain, the epicenter, imagining a pinpoint. The world fuzzes out, becoming blurry. I can't feel my hands or legs anymore. In fact, I can't feel anything except a sizzling in my soul.

Then comes the actual Memory Jumping. I target the center of Ms. Dahlia's brain and then focus my energy on catapulting myself there. The feeling is sharp but not unpleasant. I travel through her brain in a blur of black and white and occasional colors and feelings. I finally land in one of her memory locations.

I have read all about memory in my science books. Most is theory; people hardly know how it's stored, where it's stored, or why certain memories fade away. And there is certainly nothing about Memory Jumping.

I never think of myself as peculiar until I see the look in my Jumpees' eyes. The funny thing about people is we all think we're normal until we meet other people. Then we realize that this quirk about us is abnormal, and that not everyone thinks the way we do.

And that not everyone can Memory Jump as easily as they can whistle.

Sometimes, people think we're using black magic. One guy ran out when I placed my hand on his forehead, screaming like the devil himself was on his tail. I saw myself a little differently in the mirror after that.

I jolt back to the task in front of me. I need to search for the memory. I decide to try the bottom part of Ms. Dahlia's memory first, the long-term. A golden door appears, shining and certain. Then it shoots out, far away from me, and other doors visualize along a long corridor. My feet reappear, then my legs. Soon I can see and feel my body again.

I'm in Ms. Dahlia's mind.

Almost every door is different in some way. They are all labeled, neat and tidy. Not everyone's brains are like that. I have been in some brains that were the most disheveled, disorderly things. It's a good thing I can search for memories when I need to, or I would've been in there for the rest of my life.

Ms. Dahlia's memories, at least here, are ordered alphabetically by the people involved. There are simply names, no explanations as to whom the people were. I stick my fingers into my back pocket and retrieve the piece of paper.

I would like to forever remember the moment I knew David Watersby loved me. We had been just friends up to the time, but one night we went to the movies. We were supposed to go with a group, but they all canceled last minute, so it was just me and David. I was watching the movie when I felt something, and I looked over...he was just staring at me. And I don't mean in a strange way, or even an unmeaningful way.

I swear, when a man looks at you that way, you know he loves you. There's not a doubt about it. It's written all over his face.

You'll know you're at the right memory because you'll see him driving a white, sleek Stinger. I was wearing a blue headscarf and a white linen dress.

I pass a couple of *B* names and continue down the hallway, searching for the *D*s. There are a whole lotta *C* names, that's for certain.

I finally locate the *D*s, and Daniel is one of the first. I open the door and see opaque images floating everywhere. They're all from Dahlia's point of view, tinged with her emotions.

In one, she hugs a younger man tightly, her eyes scrunched as little droplets of water fall down her cheeks. Tears drip down my own cheeks as I melt into the memory. In another image, Dahlia sits on a couch, having a serious conversation with the man. A thread of dark purple worry snakes through the memory, which makes me curious. I put my own feelings away and get back to my job. I find a memory in which Dahlia wears a white dress. She looks out the window at a white Stinger vehicle, a rugged and popular jeep-like car.

It's time to do my job.

I close the door. This is the one I need to save. I could destroy all the doors at the same time, but it always takes a bit of time for me to get up the courage. I'll just start out with one; maybe do another one; maybe three.

I don't know why this is so hard for me. Memory Jumping is what I do. It's what I was made for.

But something about destroying someone's memories, even if it is their choice…it doesn't feel right. Maybe it's because deep down inside, I know that memories, even painful ones, were made to be kept. They're what shape people into who they are.

Before I wimp out, I turn to the door next to this door and rip off the doorknob. It does not come off easily, but it releases with less effort than an actual doorknob. Golden flickers and flashes swallow the door, turning it into shining sparkles.

From amidst the burning destruction, I look at the name-plate again.

And realize I have made a terrible error.

TWO
ADELAIDE

D*avid*, it says. *What?* I look at the other door; its nameplate says, *Daniel*. Wait…I pull out the piece of paper and reread it. Dahlia's husband was named David. And I just destroyed the David door.

Ugh! I'm so stupid! I always get the names David and Daniel mixed up. My cheeks flush and the heat pounds against them. It's just like Fawn says; I'm such a ditz.

I destroyed the wrong memory.

The door isn't completely gone yet. I grab the side that is still visible and push away the flying sparks, but my hand goes right through them, and they keep eating away at the door like voracious termites.

I bend down to the ground where I threw the doorknob. I pick it up and press it against the door as if it will magically reattach itself.

"Come on, come on, come on," I mutter and start sweating. Again.

The light gnaws at the hole where the doorknob was,

removing it from existence. Then, with a final flash, the door disappears.

Forever.

Oh wow. This is bad.

I just destroyed the *only* memory Dahlia wanted to remember forever.

I know what Fawn will do if she finds out—

I reopen the Daniel door and enter. The memories float through me, slipping and sliding around, new ones showing up every few seconds. I pull the closest one towards me. The memory expands and plays. A door opens and Dahlia walks out onto the front porch to see a young woman (her daughter?) and her companion pull into a driveway, driving the aforementioned Stinger. The girl gets out of the car, waves to the guy, and walks onto her porch.

I fast-forward the memory and Dahlia talks to a man. They are in a living room.

"I don't want her with that boy," Ms. Dahlia says.

"Dahlia…" The man starts, but I stop listening.

That girl in the car was Ms. Dahlia's daughter. I misinterpreted the memories I saw. Badly. I drag my hands over my face, moaning. David was Ms. Dahlia's husband. . . Daniel was her daughter's boyfriend. All the names starting with *D* float around in a mass, and my mind spins.

Yup. I deleted the wrong memory.

"It's done?"

I try not to wince at Fawn's question as I sit on the couch, fresh from my Memory Jump. My shoulders hurt and my lungs cry out for more air. Memory Jumping usually leaves me a bit tired; the longer I stay in there, the more winded and disoriented I become. "Yup." Oh, it's done all right.

I wrestle with something deep inside pressuring me to tell the truth.

"Grace," Ms. Dahlia whimpers. Fawn's head shoots toward her, and spikes of dread fire up my cheeks, rendering them hot...and telltale red, I'm sure. I had hoped Dahlia wouldn't say anything; that she would just sit there in the memory, not saying a word. Then Fawn would never know.

But this memory is too emotional for Dahlia to stay silent.

"No...no."

Fawn's perfectly drawn-on eyebrows shoot downward, and I run my hands over the couch cushion, fingers twitching in anxiety. "What is she talking about?"

I don't say a word. I don't have to, because Dahlia keeps muttering and sniffling.

"Who the heck is Grace?"

I dig my nails into the soft flesh of my palms. I go deeper and deeper, and the stings drown out everything else. Then I shove my hands underneath my legs and will Dahlia to shut up.

I have messed up before, but never this bad. This is an epic failure. A destruction of someone's future.

"We can't have her babbling like this at the nursing home. Too suspicious." Fawn glances at me. I force myself to keep her gaze, try not to blink. Fawn is too worked up to notice my suspicious activity. Her mouth grows tighter. "You need to go back in and fix this."

As much as I hate going into people's memories, I hate altering the memories even more. There is just nothing right about that.

"Fawn...I—"

"Listen, Adelaide, I know it hurts your conscience. That's

okay. But just see what your conscience thinks tonight—tomorrow—next week, when your hair is all over the floor."

I bite my lip. Fawn tells me almost nothing about my parents. But one time I was able to drag out of her that my mom would always keep her hair super long; in fact, she said I look so much like my mother, it's eerie. I'm such an average person. I don't have any freckles for a cute fairy look, no dark and romantic eyes, no long legs or dainty hands. My eyes are even average gray. My hair—brown and long and wild—it's my *thing*, my connection to my mother.

I can't lose my hair.

That's the thing about Fawn. She has this uncanny ability to pinpoint the things in life that mean the most to you, however silly or inconsequential. Then, slowly, painfully, she pries them away.

I can't mess up again. But I can't tell Fawn that.

"And listen, we can't let Dahlia live in misery the rest of her life." Fawn looks so pretty when she smiles, even if the smile is as fake as my life.

I place a hand on Ms. Dahlia's forehead and close my eyes. I center in on her brain…and Memory Jump.

I find the Daniel door. I turn the knob and enter, feeling like a thief of the worst kind.

I would remake Dahlia's memory of the moment she knew her husband loved her, but I'm not powerful enough to create the emotion of love. I've been able to synthesize anger, sadness, pain, and grief. Even happiness sometimes, when it's rooted in something shallow.

But love is the most powerful emotion of them all. It's the core of what a human is. If all other emotions were to be destroyed, but still love existed, we'd all still be able to survive. In fact, we would thrive.

I'm going to have to work with what I have.

I pick through a few of the memories playing inside of the Daniel door. There is a memory of Dahlia arguing with Daniel, apparently because he didn't bring her daughter home by curfew. I fix this by adjusting the clock. Another memory is Daniel kissing Grace right in front of their house. Dahlia turns to her husband. Their pain leaks into me, a feeling like empathy and yet beyond it. I change the memory to Daniel leaving without so much as a hug.

Then there is a memory of the day Grace married Daniel. A thin veil of solemnity overshadows the heaviness of sadness despite these strong emotions. And yet Dahlia showed up to the wedding.

I jab my finger at the memory and my finger dissolves into it. My body soon follows, and I find myself inside the memory. The feeling is a bit like entering a room that has metallic streamers in the doorway, a shivery kind of transition feeling.

I am at the back of the room. No one can see me. I can manipulate the memory just as I want to; this isn't actual reality, rather a bunch of chemicals and neurons. It is always possible for a memory to be incorrectly stored. I tell myself all this, trying to make myself feel less guilty.

I pinch my fingers and fling them to my right, fast-forwarding the memory. The pastor asks the young couple if they are willing to accept each other in marriage.

I insert doubt in the girl's mind; make her pause as Daniel, the pastor, and the audience watch her. She glances up at Daniel. Her eyes trace his features. Suddenly, she can't remember why she fell in love with him. Did she even love him?

"No." The word hardly takes up a second, but it blasts across the room like a sonic boom. At first, everyone is silent.

"No," Grace repeats. "I don't know what I'm doing. I'm sorry."

Whispers ricochet around the room like bullets in a saloon. The feeling of relief that washes over Dahlia is so potent, it's like what I imagine diving into water must feel like.

I leave Dahlia's mind, and when I readjust my eyes, I am back in the living room sitting on the couch. I stand up and join Fawn, who stands tense as an irate rattlesnake.

"Did it work?" My words wobble. I am so upset I failed, terrified Fawn will punish me. I try to read her.

Fawn doesn't say a word. She watches Dahlia. The old woman's lips move back and forth, up and down in inaudible words. Then…a tear trickles down her face and conceives a smile.

"Grace," she whispers. Then, she's silent. I wait a few more very long seconds, willing her to stay quiet. Fawn slaps me on the back, a small smile on her face. I flinch, more used to accusing gestures rather than congratulating. I'm afraid she might startle Ms. Dahlia, but she remains mute.

"Stupid old woman," Fawn says. I think the old woman is beautiful, sweet, and lovely. I want to leave with her.

I dare a glance at Fawn. She stares at me like she can see into the very roots of my soul. Her eyes are aloof, but meaningfully so. Something hides behind those wooden irises. I bet she won't tell me what's so embedded into her mind.

Her eyes harden, eyebrows shooting down in degradation. "Stop trying to dig into my mind."

I drop the line I had automatically attempted to connect to Fawn's brain.

"I didn't mean to."

Her eyes harden and her eyebrows shift. "Wait…how did you do that without touching my forehead?"

I honestly didn't even notice I did that. I shrug. "Not sure."

Fawn stares at me as if I'm an alien she wants to dissect. It makes my skin wriggle.

"Wipe her." I hate this part of our job. Our clients don't always know we will wipe their memory of us, but we do it anyway. Fawn says it is for our protection. *Protection, protection.* She uses that word so much.

No one ever even remembers what I do for them. The only thing people want in life is to remember, or to be remembered.

Fawn walks away without another word. I delete Dahlia's memory of meeting us, noting the sweet tinge in the air. When I get back to reality, no time has passed so I follow Fawn. I have to walk fast to catch up with her; she can speed walk like no one's business with her long, skinny legs. As she walks, I mentally give myself a high five for making her hair look so good. It's shoulder-length, but I managed to wrestle it into a really cool fauxhawk style. Her almost-black hair makes it look even more intense than it would on a blonde or a redhead.

Well done, Adelaide, I congratulate myself. No one else will ever be able to give me a compliment, so I must shower them upon myself.

"When are Buddy and Perkins coming?" I ask.

"Within the hour. I paged them and they'll bring Dahlia back to the nursing home."

Fawn doesn't turn back to talk to me but keeps walking: I've been dismissed. The speed of her voice matches her walking pace.

I retreat to my room, grabbing my lantern from a hook on the door before entering. The hook is above a screen, which Fawn uses to lock and unlock my room. It can also convert our house into hiding mode in a matter of a few taps. There are probably more capabilities on there, but the unspoken rule is that I don't mess with it.

I circle around the room, turning on other lanterns with a tap. One tap gives a soft glow, two a decent shine, and three makes my bedroom nearly all visible. Sliding across changes the light quality from white to more warm.

I notice with a sigh that my bed isn't made; the covers are all twisted up like an uncooked pretzel, with my favorite fluffy white blanket piled on the top like whipped cream. I usually don't forget to make it in the mornings, but this morning I was particularly nervous.

Fawn's voice comes through a security camera in the corner of my room. I like to forget that it's there. "What are you laughing at?"

"Just myself."

She scoffs; it comes out really grainy through the sound system. "Come out here and socialize—Buddy and Perkins are here."

I bolt out of my room to the living room. Buddy and Perkins are there, wearing black like they think they're cooler than they actually are. They tower over Fawn and me, bald heads impressively shiny. Perkins has told me he's six foot two but Buddy is only five eleven—I think both are lying.

I wrap Buddy in a big hug first.

"Hey, what gives?" Perkins yells, wrinkles digging into his forehead as he frowns. "Is Buddy your favorite or something?"

"I chose him *at random*," I say, letting go of Buddy and heading over to Perkins.

"I don't want your hug anymore." He flinches, and I giggle. Perkins doesn't really mean it, and I know that. He continues his drama for a couple more seconds before finally opening his arms, and he gives me a hug too.

"All right, Buddy," Perkins says, pulling away from me.

"Hey, did you guys bring me that magazine I asked for? And the shoes?" Fawn asks.

"No, we don't buy *trash*," Perkins says. Fawn rolls her eyes, a smile lighting up her face as she laughs.

"My magazines aren't trash, they're inspiration!" Fawn retorts. "Queen Colette's dresses are gorgeous. I'm not a fan of the queen herself, but her wardrobe overrides that."

I remind myself of the snippets of information Fawn has shared about the queen occasionally. From Fawn's snippy comments, I gather that the queen is a quiet, almost invisible woman. And those two things go directly against any character qualities Fawn owns.

"We'll bring you an issue next time we stop by," Buddy promises. "And we're having trouble finding the shoes. They don't have the size you asked for. But we'll keep looking. We're going to have to go through the black market; everything in The Switches are too expensive."

I love hearing little tidbits about The Outside. I take each one and store it in my memory, along with the images I see in peoples' memories, creating a half-formed picture of The Outside. I've gathered that The Switches are a group of markets. Sounds innocent enough, but Fawn has painted a dark picture of The Outside.

I grew up with her warning me about the power-hungry, bitter people who killed my mother, who was a Memory Jumper just like me. I've met a decent amount of people and while some of them could easily be killers, there are others— like Dahlia—who are nothing but fragile daisies with lovely eyes and innocent smiles. Could the people like Dahlia outweigh the evil ones?

After The Memory Wipe, a massacre of my kind, King

Wesley bowed to public pressure and made Memory Jumpers illegal. He had just inherited the throne from his father, who had built Frelsi out of the ashes of a resurfaced America after The Insurgence over fifty years ago. The throne couldn't afford another angry mob.

So he banned my existence.

He made me a sin.

"We better get going with Dahlia," Buddy says.

I want to ask Buddy and Perkins to stay for a while, but it feels a little devious to play a game of cards while Dahlia is out sleeping on the sofa.

"All right, Perkins." Buddy turns to me. "We'll see ya later, Adelaide."

I wave goodbye and retreat back to my room, emptiness settling inside of my stomach.

I smooth out the covers and fix the blanket on my bed. I have thirty minutes until I need to make dinner, but I want to do some reading before then.

I plop onto my bed and fly up a bit in the air before thunking back down. My hair is a silky curtain and it spreads over everything like another blanket. I run my hands through the brunette strands closest to my face and my fingers catch a few knots. I pull myself back up and walk over to my dresser, littered with various history novels, and find my brush. I also dig up my book of useless facts. It's my most valued possession.

It's so thick and heavy. One of my clients gave it to me when I was eight years old. The client was such a wonderful man, perhaps the person's brain I most enjoyed jumping into.

His name was Oscar, and he was absolutely brilliant. I never told Fawn, but before I completed his task, I toured his cavernous intellect.

When Fawn walked out of the room to get him some tea ("...with a little bit of lemon juice, please," he had requested endearingly), I admitted to him how I had looked around his memory. He simply laughed, a deep and thick laugh that made his belly jump up and down. And then he told me he would bring me a book the next time he came.

He never came back.

But Fawn got the book from him somehow. Inside, there was a message for me. It said, *Knowledge is freedom. Oscar.*

I asked her why he didn't come back. Fawn, as usual, gave me little details. She said he *was busy* and didn't have time to *play around with little girls*. But she gave me the book anyway. It was one of the nicest things she's ever done for me.

I look at it now as I tug the brush through my hair.

USELESS FACT #45
Men process women's voices in the part of the brain that they process music.

I've read all these facts countless times, but they still fascinate me, particularly the ones about the brain.

Soon, it's time to prepare dinner, and I head to the kitchen. The kitchen is my safe place—Fawn rarely enters. In here, it's my rules, my recipes. And tonight, my recipe is chicken parmesan. Fawn took a look at the calorie count for the sauce and nearly gave up the ghost. She always does this, despite being nearly a foot taller than me and still a solid kind of thin. But then, after I cook, she'll smell the delicious scent and scurry into the kitchen like a little weasel, complaining the whole time.

I survey the kitchen—observing my mini culinary kingdom fills me with such joy. I love my little gingham hand towels; I love organizing the refrigerator *just so*. I love the calendar on the wall, random photos of cows marking each month. Fawn brought it back for me from The Outside earlier this year.

I whip around one way to turn the stove on, feeling like I'm dancing as I circle the other way to swipe the plastic off the container for the chicken. A jaunty dance beat pumps from the living room. Fawn must be doing her old lady workouts.

I start to chuckle, recalling an image of Fawn huffing whilst squatting with a five-pound weight. The sound is strange; these walls don't hear much laughter. Sometimes I join Fawn for her workouts, and then there is absolutely *zero* laughter: we're both in too much pain.

I place the chicken in the pan, then drown it in herbs. I glance at the clock on the wall. The minute hand has just left the five.

I make sure my chicken is safe, then walk over to the refrigerator to grab some vitamin water. I look back at the clock.

I make my way to the living room. Fawn stands there, watching the moms and old ladies on the wall doing some complicated dance routine.

"Here's your water," I say. She jumps, probably burning the most calories she has for the past fifteen minutes.

"It's 5:06."

"I'm sorry; my hands had chicken on them."

Fawn leaves her workout to pat me on the head. "Sweet girl. I'm just trying to teach you life skills. Punctuality is godliness."

Number one, when will I ever need to be punctual? Fawn

has made it clear I'm never leaving this place. I won't ever have anywhere to go. And, two, its *cleanliness* is next to godliness.

I take a deep breath. She grabs the water from my hands and dismisses me by staring back at the television.

At dinner, she dives into the chicken. It's gone in six minutes flat, and then she complains I put too much sauce on there and added an extra 300 calories. She never tells me my food was good. Instead, her wolfing the food down like a rabid pig is my compliment. And her not biting my head off for barely scorching something is another form of a compliment.

She chooses now, as I'm digging into my own meal civilly with a knife and fork, to tell me about a new client.

"He's extremely important. His name is Paul Green, and this job has to do with *the monarchy.* He'll be coming in the next couple days to debrief us."

I tug at the collar of my bright yellow shirt, which suddenly feels as if it's shrinking.

"Okay."

"No. No, not okay. Addy, you don't understand." She only calls me Addy when she's really annoyed with me. My knife slows. Today was going so well; she hadn't snapped yet. I thought she'd make it through today without a meltdown.

I stare at a spot on the sleek white table where Fawn dropped a bit of sauce. I'm gonna have to clean that up later. "This man…he could change our lives."

I look into her eyes and give her a smile and a nod so she can't say I'm ignoring her. Then I shove a bite of chicken in my mouth. It's too big.

"You'll have to go outside to do this right." The chicken attacks the side of my cheeks, then slips down my throat. I swear, it's trying to kill me. I cough and splutter and almost die.

"What day is it?" I ask, smacking my chest.

"Why?"

"You're lying. It's April Fool's. How will we get back down without someone to press the button?"

Fawn grabs one of my hands, yanking me toward her. My knife jumps ship and clatters on the ground. "Buddy or Perkins will stay down here until we come back. And stop that. I don't lie to you, and I won't ever."

"Can you please tell me about my parents then?"

Fawn rubs her thumb over my hand. "That's not lying. That's wisely choosing to withhold information. Trust me, you don't want to know."

I laugh. I've read all the philosophers and their thoughts on moral issues like lying. Not giving people information is lying, period.

I pat down a piece of my bangs that always wants to stick straight out. "*But I do want to know.*"

"No, you don't."

If I were any other girl at any other table with any other parental figure, I'd say it. *I mean, I'm the Memory Jumper here. But it seems that you're always pretending you're reading my mind.*

But, as usual, I hide the truth inside of my aching frame. Because the aftermath of a sassy comment isn't worth the one moment of satisfaction. She'll just yell at me, call me names, and send me to my room.

Fawn's eyes go back down to her empty plate. Her fingernails shine in the light coming from the suspended light bulbs above us. Her nails are so long that they could dig a grave, always perfectly painted. She keeps them long, too. I've never painted my nails in my life.

I'm not sure about this new client, this *Paul Green*.

All I'm certain of is the color of Fawn's nails: ominous, fiery red.

Her favorite color.

USELESS FACT #97

It's impossible to remain angry at someone you truly love. Anger lasting for more than three days indicates that you don't really love them.

THREE
QUEEN COLETTE

T he butterfly bobs through the air, a red admiral on an invisible ocean. I'm worried about it; someone must've left the door open to let air circulate through the castle, and this unsuspecting insect waltzed right in.

It'll never escape now.

I'm not in the Great Room anymore: the world melts away, and I see his face.

Green.

Paul Green.

I was the butterfly; he had promised to open the window of this castle and let me out.

But—

I snap back into the real world. Everyone else has their eyes trained on the man at the head of the table: my husband.

Intense, dark, cold. So unlike Paul's. King Wesley's empty stare trains itself on my face, but I look back at my flying friend. My dinner guests melt away once again. All I notice is the buttery light descending on the butterfly's wings, the way the insect flies in a strange bouncing motion, as if constantly catching itself before it falls to its death.

Like me.

"Colette." I pull my eyes away from the entertainment, focusing on the blonde woman to my right with the garish forehead and surface-level personality.

"Yes, dear?" I answer.

"Is Adam excited to pick his wife?"

I'm caught in a poisonous flashback. My mother told me my beauty was a gift, a bargaining chip for a struggling family. But the only thing my appearance ever gained was the attention of the next king of Frelsi. And he needed a quiet, uncomplicated woman at his side.

And that woman was me.

Then Paul became entranced by my beauty. My marriage was no obstacle for him. And, shunned by my husband and empty on the inside, craving love, it wasn't an obstacle for me either.

Will my son treat his future wife the same way my husband treats me? Have I created a monster? I set my fork down as my hand trembles. I hide my hand in my lap and draw a smile on my face.

"Yes, he is."

"How are the preparations coming?"

As if I cared about the colors of tablecloths and the luster of candelabras. I'm only decorating my own cage.

I pull the corners of my lips up into what could pass for a smile. "Splendidly. The china is simply stunning—just wait until you see how white they are. I've never seen anything like it."

Perhaps if I spend more energy on things that don't matter, I'll forget the heavier things that do. I look for my butterfly friend. My eyes sense motion in the corner of the room, but what I see makes my heart falter.

The butterfly has found the panel of windows that border the ceiling. They're massive and confusing.

The butterfly throws itself against the unseen, never giving up hope. It repeatedly backs up, then plows back into the glass. Over and over and over again. Every time it hits the glass, I know it's such a tiny little vibration, but I feel as if the whole earth is shaking.

Crash. Crash. Nausea overwhelms me; I clench the napkin on my lap, the luxurious linen-like burs on my perfectly manicured hands.

"I—I'm sorry." King Wesley's eyes still watch me. Always watching, always calculating. Always waiting. "I must—I must powder my nose."

I shove my chair back much too gracelessly for a queen, then launch myself out of the room.

I must get away from here.

Must get fresh air.

Must find a place where I can breathe, where I can be myself again.

Where has Colette gone? Tears fall from my eyes as I stumble towards the nearest bathroom to hide. Colette is gone, replaced by a butterfly who traded freedom for a golden cage.

It's all my fault. It's as if my husband knows—knows the terrible things I've done. And this is my price to pay.

I wonder if my child would hate me.

That night, I toss and turn in bed. It's too hot, too stuffy. I throw myself out of my bed and head towards my balcony doors. They're covered by cream tapestries, which I whip apart in a frenzy. I yank the doors open, and a rush of breezy night air whispers across my body.

Where is my child, the one I gave away to hide my secret? I try to push the thought back. It's easier to pretend during the day, easier to be put-together and proper. But, in the darkness and loneliness of the night, I remember what I have done.

In the moonlight, I remember the young man who looked at me in a way Wesley never had. Who actually loved me, who wanted me.

I remember those fleeting months when my heart started pumping again. The color returned to my cheeks, my hair stopped falling out, and I didn't have to talk myself out of bed every morning. But interest quickly turned instead to lust. And I broke the vow I had made with my husband.

When I told Wesley I was pregnant, he knew the child wasn't ours. I honestly didn't know what he would've done if Paul Green hadn't been there himself to blackmail us into keeping the child. After all, Green had plenty of blackmail fodder: an adulterous queen would've made national news and embarrassed Wesley in front of every other world leader. He also had the letters I'd sent him, physical proof of my infatuation.

So Adam was born. I loved the child, because I knew he was the product of love. Maybe not true love, but it was far truer than any other love I'd had. Of course, Wesley was cruel to him. And I simply didn't exist anymore.

Maybe it was to get back at Green. Maybe it was to stake his ownership of me. But two years after Adam's birth, I was pregnant with Wesley's child.

I shouldn't have told Green about it. I don't know what kind of madness came over me. But my loyalty to Green won out. Green of course saw it as an assault on our pact to install

Adam as king, and he demanded that we keep the growing child in my belly a forever secret.

I always figured he was the only man who had ever made Wesley back down, and my respect for him only grew.

I retreated to a corner of the castle for the next year. Wesley told everyone I was deathly ill. In actuality, I had never been so happy. It was as if Wesley shunned me. He allowed few people to see me, to know my actual condition. And, to protect the secret, I wasn't allowed outside of the castle. I rarely saw my husband, and I began to actually feel free.

Dare I say it? I didn't struggle letting Mason go. He was the child of myself and my tormentor. He was a symbol of so many things, least of all love between husband and wife. When I handed him to a maid and told her to find a suitable home, I felt nothing.

And I returned to being queen.

Now, I look across the town and wonder where my child is. I feel a tinge of pain, because Mason is the rightful king of Frelsi. Yet my own bastard child will get the throne.

Yet Mason is half Wesley. And no one with even a table-spoon of that man should have any power.

And yet Adam has cups and heaps and pounds of Wesley, just by living in his shadow every day.

"I'm so sorry, Mason," I whisper into the breeze. I believe it carries my message out to him. And I believe he hears it and has already forgiven me. He likes his freedom, anyway. "You don't want this life."

I fall asleep on the balcony, drenched in moonlight. My maids tease me the next morning at how unqueenlike it is. And I can't help but agree.

I haven't left my son's side for four days now.

Wesley hasn't been here once. But I guess that's to be expected: Adam isn't his real son anyway.

"Please tell me what is wrong with my son," I plead to the doctor, who is dressed in spotless white. We're outside of Adam's room so he won't hear our hushed, worried tone. I don't want to give him any reason to fear.

"We don't know," he says. "Believe me, if we knew, you would be the first to be told."

I shut my eyes tight. I can't lose my boy.

"We're wondering if…it's something outside of science."

My eyes fly open, and I take a step towards him. "What kind of something?"

"We've been noticing a steady pattern across this city regarding health over the past ten years," the man says, coming around the hologram so I have a clearer view of him. He adjusts his thick white glasses and sighs. "We get cases of inexplicable comas, accompanied by other symptoms such as unusual brainwave patterns and even brain damage."

My finger circles the soft fabric of my shirt collar. But what I *want* to do is tear the fabric, thread by thread. Maybe that would ease the anxiety swelling in my soul. "What do you mean brain damage?"

"I'm not saying this is what it is, ma'am." He strokes his sad, patchy beard. It's a coping mechanism: he is on edge. Everyone in the castle knows how unstable I am right now, and they all treat me like a lion cub growing stronger and less predictable each day. His eyes watch me carefully. "Some doctors have thought that perhaps it's Memory Jumper activity."

I keep my face frozen. He can't know how he has lassoed the truth, a great dripping thing that oozes blood from my heart every day of my life. "Those are illegal."

"But there are reports of illegal Memory Jumping every now and then." *I should know.* He lets his guard down a little, his shoulders dropping. "And we've found some documentation linking Memory Jumper activity with symptoms like your son's."

I bring my hand to my head, dragging in a deep inhale. *Breathe, breathe.*

"Is there…will he…"

"We need to do some more tests, but there is no reason to believe that he cannot come back from this."

Without Adam, there will be nothing keeping me at the castle. There would be nothing tethering me to life—except that's not true. The unforgivable thing holds me captive to this life, to this castle, to this coffin where I wander as the living dead. I'm so far past hoping, I can't even imagine what I want my life to be.

"Fine. Fine, look into every avenue. Scientific or not."

I am a mouse in a corner, an antelope at the last watering hole.

And every cat, every crocodile, every carnivore alive is watching me.

Waiting to descend.

FOUR
ADELAIDE

T here. It's finished. I lean back on my stool, bumping
into the door of the room because my pottery room
is *that* cramped. It's more like a pottery closet.

I run my fingers against each other, the clay slimy but
satisfying. The pot I've created reclines on my pastel green
potter's wheel. I lean a bit to the right to see it from another
angle. It has such character, as do all my creations. This one
has a poochy belly and an extended upper lip.

One day someone will display a tulip or a sunflower in my
creation, and that brings me joy.

I clean up my supplies, saving leftover clay and discarding
the overly goopy pieces, then cover my new pot and add it to
my growing collection, which all dry on a repurposed bookshelf. Fawn will bring my creations into town tomorrow to fire
and glaze them in a real kiln.

I hang my apron up on a peg on the wall, an apron that
Fawn sewed for me about five years ago when she got on a
sewing kick. She was very good at it, and I still have three or
four dresses in my closet that she designed for me herself. My

little apron is made of jean, a fabric long gone out of style but still a retro favorite of mine, and has dainty daisies embroidered all over it.

I take one last look around the tiny room to make sure everything is in pristine condition. Fawn must not have any reason to end my pottery days.

I find my adopted mother leafing through a clothes magazine in the kitchen. She looks so serious, even in this activity that should bring her joy.

"I made another pot." Her eyes don't leave the pages of her magazine. I need to ask her about my jewelry, too, which is bad because she's going to throw a fit at buying supplies for my latest project: outer-space-inspired jewelry. My next project is a pair of Saturn earrings.

"I didn't see your schedule on my desk." Fawn has me write up what I do every day, so I don't *waste time.*

"Sorry, the creativity just attacked me and I—"

"The schedule will be on my desk in five minutes."

I nod. "Right."

I go back to my room and grab the first piece of paper and pen I see.

7:00—wake up and get ready
7:30—make coffee
8:00—start school
12:00—make lunch
12:30—eat lunch
2:30—start on pottery

Prepare dinner at 5:30…eat dinner at 6:00…I also want to do a new cover of one of my favorite songs from the 1960s. If I must be positive, living underground for eighteen years gives one ample opportunity to learn lots of instruments. I can play piano, guitar, violin, and I even dabble in tambourine.

"We only have one client today, by the way." Fawn's voice coming through the speaker makes me hop out of my seat.

"Is it Paul Green?" I ask into the speaker.

"No," she answers, offering no further details. "P.S., one minute."

I scribble down some more activities, then do a mad sprint back to the kitchen. There's my workout for the day.

Fawn surveys the paper. With a red pen, she makes changes and adds a few things. Clean my room; clean the bathroom; lots of cleaning, and she's marked it for before I start school. Great. I'm going to have a super slow start to my day

She also marks our client's visit for two hours instead of one, then sets my schedule down. Good, it's been approved.

"Would you get me some jewelry wire and tiny Styrofoam balls?" My heart leaps as I voice my request. I'm already compiling a list of reasons to give her when she begins interrogating me.

"Didn't I just buy you some?"

"Yes, but I'm getting more and more orders every week. I've already used all the wire you got me for the orders I have."

She's quiet. It's like she didn't hear me. I wait a respectful ten seconds, staring at her. Maybe if I stare hard enough, she'll turn into a big bright red *YES!*

"Sooo is that okay?"

She licks her finger and then turns another page. "I have to think about it."

What is there to think about? It's Styrofoam and metal. My lips plow into one another, and I nod, then spin around to get out of here before I say something I'll regret.

I head to the bathroom to start on cleaning. I'm like a little bird, content as I spot-check all the mirrors per Fawn's demands. After I'm finished, I continue on with my schedule, following it loosely. Fawn rarely checks to see if I'm actually following her dictator-like timetable.

Our client's visit interrupts me, and I huff when Fawn calls me into the living room. I was finally starting school for the day.

I enter the living room and find two men with Fawn. One kneels on the floor, cowering, and a chill rushes down my spine. My breath leaves me, and panic threatens to scoop me up in its paralyzing arms. He wears a suit, but it's obvious that he's been in a scuffle due to the dirt that powders his knees. He stares at the floor, dejected.

The man beside him grips his elbows. He has a fluffy mustache and fluffy eyebrows, together probably thicker than his skinny frame. Yet he's clearly in control of the other man. He chews on something.

Something that isn't gum.

"Adelaide, this is Mr. Jackson."

I can't even greet the man. Something is not right here. I name his shaking companion Oliver.

"Jackson needs our assistance in clearing this man's mind."

Why can't I always have clients like Ms. Dahlia? Why can't I always be the hero?

Fawn sees it as income. There's no morality to it. It's a way for a mother and her daughter to survive; what can be wrong with that?

"Mr. Jackson, please let Adelaide know your specifications."

The man grins to reveal gnarled teeth. "Remove his family from his mind. Any memories of them, any bits and pieces. You can add in things too, right?"

Fawn takes a swig of her mango kombucha before answering for me. "Yes, sir."

"Add in some villainy. The man has too good of a conscience."

"That's a character trait," Fawn says, swishing her drink around. I'm always amazed at how to-the-point she is with scary characters like Jackson. I'd be on the floor shivering with Oliver if I weren't with Fawn. "Adelaide works with memories, not personality."

Jackson sneers, chomping on his tobacco as if grinding the retort between his jaws. "And I'm paying how much for this?"

Fawn grins, in control. Always in control. "You can leave anytime you want to. I also have all the paperwork associated with your visit. When was your parole up, again?"

And, just like that, Fawn has the upper hand. Jackson adjusts the tobacco in his mouth, the corners of his lips lowering in a glare. "Well, Miss Fawn. Aren't you the researcher?"

"Do you want her to do this or not? Or did you also want dinner?"

Jackson snorts. "Fine, fine. Let's get on with it."

I walk over to Oliver. He hasn't looked up once. It's as if he hopes the earth will cave in from the power of his stare and he'll disappear. Or maybe Jackson will.

I'm sorry.

I'm so, so sorry.

I'm just as much at Fawn's mercy as Oliver is at the mercy of this Jackson character. She may not have her hands clenched around my elbow, but her fingernails constantly pierce my heart. Her presence constricts every fiber of my being.

Neither Oliver nor I are free. The method just looks different.

I place my hand on Oliver's forehead. He pulls his head back, and Jackson grabs Oliver's head with both hands and holds it.

"What are you going to do to me?" He finally screams. I've heard so many grown men scream. It's a sound I'd like to remove from my own memory.

"Shut it, Oliver, you miserable—"

I've Memory Jumped before Jackson can finish the insult. There's black, then I'm shooting a short distance into Oliver's memory.

He fights me; his memory is thick, and I have to really plow through.

When I finally am in his memory, nausea overwhelms me. It's that feeling when you're in a nightmare and don't realize it; when dread sweeps over you in snowdrifts before you realize it was only a dream.

My legs won't move. I half urge them to, the effort weak. What would happen if I just stay in here forever? Time stops when I'm Memory Jumping anyway. No one would ever know.

I dismiss the thought. I'm stuck. No waking up from this terror.

I think of his family and close my eyes. Wind sucks toward me like a vacuum cleaner as the family memories come to me. I rip off the doorknobs and will my brain to stop thinking. To stop going in circles, trying to get me out of my situation. There is nothing I can do except go on.

My eyes jolt open. The doors disappear in flames. I only half see children with peanut butter smeared across their faces; a young wife whipping a picnic blanket in the air, lassoing the clouds above her; a baby reaching for a mobile with twirling turtles.

Don't think, don't think, don't think.

The deed is done. I exit the man's memory and reappear in the living room, on my knees, shoulders heaving from effort and mental exhaustion. Jackson finishes the insult he had started when I Memory Jumped, and the words snap through me.

Fawn pats me as if she doesn't even see my pain. "Great, great. Jackson, will you need assistance from my men?"

Jackson scratches his stomach and clears his throat with disdain. "No. I can take care of him myself."

Fawn doesn't lose her cool. "No problem. That'll be—"

I don't care how much we made. I don't care if Jackson builds us mountains of gold.

All I'll see are mountains of guilt, blood, and haunting eyes that see me as a devilish tool in the hands of a stunning young businesswoman.

I'm in a mood for the rest of the day. Fawn dismisses me to turn on a Pilates workout and I take refuge in the far corner of my bedroom, cradling a gnarled copy of *Nicholas Nickleby*. I don't deny that it smells like it's been through a couple of owners unconcerned with personal hygiene, but it's worth the exposure. I grip my knees to my chest when the evil head-master approaches the helpless Smike with a whip; I marvel at Nicholas's bravery when he throws himself in front of Smike.

The image transforms into my earlier Memory Jumping client. Jackson grins, his words and intentions whiplike enough. Oliver, a crumpled Smike, begs silently for help.

I should've stepped in front of the whip; I should've—I wish I had—I could've—

I shut the book, and the sound slaps through the air with

condemnation. I wind up to toss it across the room…but then I stick my finger amidst the final pages.

It's a story. Just words on a piece of paper. Powerful, colorful, realistic…but still only words. Which means it has a good ending. It must. Charles Dickens owes it to me.

My eyes scan the pages until I find my promise: yes, Smike and Nicholas escape the headmaster and the evil uncle. And yet even the end is tinged with sadness.

Is there truly no ending that is a hundred percent happy?

I make my way to the kitchen and prepare dinner on autopilot, whipping together some kind of stir fry. I'm not hungry enough to eat my portion so, after serving Fawn, I store the rest in the fridge.

"Why aren't you eating?" Fawn sits in a chair at our kitchen bar, eyeing me. The way she says it makes it an insult, not a question of concern.

I close the refrigerator door. "I'm not hungry."

"Why not?"

As if my life couldn't ever possibly make me sick enough that I wouldn't have an appetite. I just shrug, the words lost. "I dunno."

She grunts. My answer has been denied.

"I'll eat something later," I offer.

"If you eat, you eat now."

We're spinning around in circles. Like a…what's that thing called? Ferris wheel. Like an out-of-control Ferris wheel. She's in the bucket on the top, I'm in the one on the bottom. No matter what topic we're talking about, we're never in the same bucket. She can't hear me from up there; I have no voice down here.

I'm too upset to say anything. Thankfully, Fawn lets it slide and retreats, probably to her room.

I love washing the dishes. Most things in my life are dirty

or become dirty, so the ability to clean at least one thing is a welcome chore.

I remove the cups from the bar, then the single fork and two plates, placing them in the sink. I douse the sponge in soap and fizz it up between my hands, then grab a plate and scrub. I focus all my emotions—the tangled, the messy, the painful—into cleaning every single area on the plate until I'm certain I could lick the plate without any regrets.

My gingham towels are wet and dirty, so I set them aside to wash later and dig out a different dish towel. It's one I picked out for Fawn for a Mother's Day long ago. I must've been six and had questionable taste since the towel is illustrated with yellow ducks wearing paper hats. It's not exactly Fawn's style. I can't remember if she liked it or not.

I put the dishes away, slowing my movements to make the task last longer. I don't want to go back to my room all by myself. I want to do things that matter instead of reading books in my room all day, praying for a life better than the one I live.

I can. I can, I can, I can. The words remind me of *The Little Engine That Could.* Buddy and Perkins used to read that story to me. We'd make trains out of marshmallows and see who could get the most boxcars before giving in and eating the fluffy goodness.

Don't live in the past, I coach myself. *This is your present.* And yet sometimes the only way I can keep going in the present is to remember the past. Or to plan the future.

I scoff. If I had the book of my life, I could flip to the end like I did with *Nicholas Nickleby.* I'm afraid of what I'd read. And yet here, now, I resign to the hopeless *The End.*

Adelaide can never be free. Today and tomorrow are both the same: a battle I cannot win, a war that is slowly whittling my soul into something hard and numb and unrecognizable. Nothing will ever change.

And I need to be okay with that.

I wake up to terrible music pumping through the house. It's some combination of saxophones and synth and…I moan— then moan again because I hate when Fawn does this. It's like a declaration. Whatever I'm doing doesn't matter enough for me to give it my full attention.

Then I realize something else, something worse: I woke up late.

I bolt to my desk and hurriedly draft a morning schedule, then snatch it up and run out to the kitchen to start on breakfast.

"Adelaide?" My name is a knife through my heart.

"Yeah? Uh, yes?"

"Don't worry about breakfast, I already made myself something."

The wind from the living room fan could knock me over. She almost never cooks. "What?"

"I'm not repeating myself." Well, there's a bit of the Fawn I know. But why—what—how?

She appears in the kitchen, looking like an overly sugary sorbet in her bright pink sports bra and orange leggings. Despite her sweat-doused skin, you could still slap her on a magazine cover. She pulls out the rubber band holding her hair up in a ponytail and her brunette tresses sit gloriously.

Not fair.

"Hey, so we have that…*life-changing* guy today right? Paul Green?" I decide to use Fawn's strangely perky mood to my advantage and milk her for information.

"Yes!" she chirps. "He's *very* well-to-do. Let's just say I did my research on him, and his prices got bumped up to reflect his financial situation."

"Oh yeah?"

I soak in Fawn's comments. Money means nothing to me. I'll never see it. And the things I want cannot be bought anyway.

This whole strange conversation calls for waffles. I need sustenance. I pull out ingredients, Fawn's glowing hopes pricking my back.

"Is this your schedule for the day?"

"Yes."

"Add *Make a cake* on there. We'll need to celebrate!"

She flits out of the room—note that word, *flits*. Dinosaurs like Fawn don't *flit*.

I keep replaying the conversation as I complete my waffles. There's nothing more pleasing than opening the waffle iron and scooping out a perfectly carved waffle.

I garnish the masterpiece with swoops of syrup, strawberries, and then chocolate chips. Yeah, this sugar rush will definitely help my nerves.

I can hardly focus this morning. I've got the jitters, and I'm peeved that they make me incapable of finishing any schoolwork.

Flowers and clouds and butterflies float through my mind, realities that are so close yet so far. I wonder what our guest will be like, and what he'll want...but most of all, I wonder how he could change my life so much.

FIVE
ADELAIDE

"Adelaide, this is Mr. Green." A man sits on our white leather couch, a polite distance between him and Fawn. The man is large and makes the sofa look minuscule. His thick arms drape over the back of the couch, and he wears a dirty charcoal gray shirt with black pants. I'm quick to notice the gun holstered in his belt. But the strangest thing about him is his green headscarf, hiding everything except his mouth and two eyes narrowed in either suspicion or annoyance.

"I'm sorry we have to meet under such conditions," the man says. "But I must keep my identity a secret…at least until later when I know you can be trusted."

It's been Fawn's life's work to keep my identity a secret. My *existence* is a secret. I'm sure she understands.

"No worries," Fawn chirps. I grab the remote controlling the image wall. Fawn is busy with her conversation, so even if she notices me she'll forget that what I'm doing annoys her.

I flick to the next photograph, not willing to take any bigger of a risk. It's a beautiful scene: three mouths of water draping over a murky lake to create a waterfall, framed by trees that look like bluish-green broccoli. A man kayaks in a bright yellow canoe, not knowing how lucky he is to be swallowed up by the beauty of the drooling waterfall mouth.

Mr. Green leans forward in his chair and pushes his fingers together into a tan triangle outline. His eyes flick from Fawn's face to mine. I bristle, adjusting my weight from side to side. "For this mission, I am not able to bring my…*subject* here. It's much too risky and…well, you'll understand soon enough. However, I must know if the girl has ever attempted to Memory Jump into the mind of an unconscious person."

Panic ripples through me. Unconscious? How can that be moral in any way? Also, I don't like how he's refusing to talk to me. *I'm in the room and I can hear everything you're saying.*

Fawn gives me a pointed look. I can almost read her mind. *Don't chicken out. Especially not now.*

I am about to cry, but I answer this question for myself. "I've never tried it."

Mr. Green leans back, disappointed. Fawn leans towards him, eyes wide in desperation. "She'd be willing to try, though."

"I can't have her *trying* during this mission," Mr. Green snaps. "It's very time sensitive. She must be able to Memory Jump, and do it quickly, no ifs, ands, or buts."

"Can we have a trial?" Fawn suggests.

"How?"

"Bring an unconscious person here, and Adelaide will Memory Jump on him."

I make a face, and I'm sure Green is making one too, underneath all that fabric. But he's the one who speaks, because he's not afraid like me. "I can't bring an unconscious person here."

Fawn lifts her chin. It sounds as if they are about to fight.

"Then we will go out and find one ourselves. Adelaide can Memory Jump inside *anyone's* mind."

"That's great." Mr. Green stands up in finality. "But until then, I will not be in contact with you. This mission is to stay top secret. I have a schedule to keep and I cannot wait. I must seek other options."

He stands up from the couch, his stance military-like.

"Please," Fawn pleads. "We can do this."

"I don't have tons of time on my hands. If you are successful, contact me." His eyes rest on Fawn a little longer than necessary. Then he makes his way to our teleporter.

Fawn's head shoots to me as soon as the teleporter doors close. Her eyes are on fire, her glare lasering holes through my head. "You ruined it."

I swallow down a ball of fear.

"You should have said you can do it." Fawn throws her hands in the air. She grabs the nearest object—my vase on the entryway table. It's the second vase I ever made, half muddy-brown, half aqua. If it were up to me, I would go to The Outside every day and fill the vase with fresh flowers.

Now she throws it at a wall. It explodes into sharp pieces. I cringe as if the pieces were slicing through me: my creation is destroyed in an instant.

"I'm going to ask Buddy and Perkins for advice." They love when she uses their Envisioning. They feel like they're helping, but they have a choice. My power is different, made into a curse. Fawn flings a finger at me as I fight back tears, already trying to figure out if my vase is salvageable. "Why don't you go do something useful?"

I take a deep breath and walk away. I force myself to let out the dark feeling in my heart with each step I take.

I go into my pottery room. I toss water on the wheel and throw a chunk of clay on it. I start the wheel spinning, then shove my hands against the shapeless mass. It's stubborn, but I patiently apply more pressure. It feels good to be in control of something, even if it's a slow process.

I smooth out the top, my fingers all gloopy. I throw some more water onto the clay since it's starting to dry out.

I force myself to forget my situation and instead focus on the task in front of me. Make a mug. Pull up the walls. Make them uniformly thick. Pull the top out a bit to create flair.

The door flies open and hits my stool. I jump in the air and hit the pedal a bit too fast, losing my grip on my creation. It slingshots around for a couple of sad seconds, melting right before my eyes. I take my foot off the pedal. Tears well up in my eyes. Angry tears.

I look over at Fawn, too scared to glare outwardly.

She laughs. Not with me: at me. "Oh wow…that sucks."

Yes. Yes, it does.

"But this will make it better." I highly doubt that. "Come on, we're going out right now."

It's like whiplash. The heartless comment, the laughter, and then the promise of my lifelong dream. "We're going…*outside?*"

"Yes. Come on."

"Okay, I'll wash my hands…just a second." She disappears from the doorframe, and it takes me a second to react.

I'm going to go to The Outside. I could cry with excitement. I clean up my area as quickly as I can, then wash my hands with rabid energy. I can't get out of this room fast enough.

I trip over my own two feet in my excitedness, which makes me fall into a sprint of sorts. I launch myself into the hallway to see Fawn leaning against the wall, glancing at her Communicator with zero interest.

"Wait a second," she says, lowering her Communicator

and glancing down at my socks. "I had the boys bring you some shoes. I hope I guessed your size right."

She disappears around the corner. Ooh, I get to wear shoes too! I've never owned a pair. Since I'm inside all the time, I've never needed any.

When Fawn comes back, she holds a pair of persnickety sneakers with a thick bottom part. Silvery studs and sequins decorate the shoes in sparse patches.

"Hope these fit," she says. I put them on, and they're a little too big, but not enough to pose any tripping threat.

Fawn grins, putting on false bravado that makes me laugh. "I'm just *that* good."

I look down at the shoes again. I have a confession to make. "Um…well, I don't actually…I don't know how to tie shoelaces."

Fawn chuckles, not the reaction I'm expecting. "Of course you don't."

And she…gets down on her knees and ties my shoes. Like a mom. I grin, and the shoes don't suddenly look as big or as ugly. Everything looks a whole lot better now, actually.

"Did Buddy and Perkins already come?"

She hesitates. "Yes."

Of course, she won't bother telling me what they Envisioned. I wonder if it has anything to do with going to The Outside.

Fawn ties the second shoelace with finesse, then stands up and assesses her work. "I don't know if I should be seen with you and these ghastly shoes, but whatever. Let's go."

We head to the entryway.

"When we go up there," Fawn begins, "don't speak to anyone. Don't look at anyone, stay close to me, and don't get lost. We're going to find someone for you to Memory Jump on."

Fawn pushes the button next to the doors, and they open with a swish. It's as if Fawn is trying to punish me, but this is the best punishment ever. I'd misbehave more often if I could go...*Outside*. I've heard the sound of the teleporter every afternoon for as long as I can remember, but I never imagined I would actually be going outside.

Outside.

The word thrills my soul. To me, Outside is synonymous with freedom. It's the world I've read about for so long: a world in a mad dash for happiness. Some attempt to find it through gaining power, through building the best machines, through flying to the moon.

Fawn steps into the teleporter and I follow. The walls are all metal and so shiny I can see my reflection, blurred out into purple blobs and bits of blue from my dress.

There is only one button, with a square on it. That must be the teleport button. There's also a keypad. Fawn types in a number, 001, then presses the button with the square. Nothing happens for a moment, and my breath hitches.

USELESS FACT #17
A moment is actually a medieval unit of time that is equal to 1.5 minutes. There are 40 moments in an hour.

Then the teleporter groans as if upset it has to carry me in it. It hums and buzzes with energy. Everything grows shimmery for a second, and a slippery feeling plummets down my spine. I clench my fists and squeeze my thumbs to keep myself from shrieking with excitement.

"Stop fidgeting," Fawn snaps. "You know that makes me nervous."

I don't even really know what I'm doing that bothers her, but I apologize anyway. "I'm sorry."

Blobs of white and gray dance in front of me, growing sharper and sharper. The teleporter halts and judders, powering down as a world is painted in front of my eyes. But it's not the world I expected.

A massive white wall blocks off portions of a city, cold metal towers standing within them. This must be the Kendror, which Fawn has told me we live on the outskirts of. The blue sky, peeking out from above the pristine walls, catches my attention, but my heart plummets. Is this all of the world that is left? Is what I've been seeing in my books, on my screens, a lie?

The glass doors slide open and Fawn moves ahead.

"Addy, let's go!"

"But…but can't people get in here?"

She rolls her eyes as if I've teleported a million times. "*Honey*, that's a communal teleporter for the town. They'd need our zone number to get back to our place, but it's top secret and—well, don't worry your pretty little head about it."

I follow automatically, my hands and legs shaking so badly that every movement is a miracle.

Then…I stumble into the grass, shoes catching on earth, tears bright in my eyes. I turn around and that's when I see what I had been imagining.

I've tried to capture this nature with my songs, with my paints, with my pottery for years, but to do so would have been a crime. Like writing a book after reading half a dictionary. My painting attempts would've been like replacing a stained glass window with plexiglass.

But the world before me right now is all stained glass. The seafoam sky above me billows in shades of the happiest blue I've ever seen, explored by cloud ships nearing whipped cream islands. Whoever draws the sky in the mornings took a snowplow to part of the sky map, doing a halfway decent job of splitting fluff to form an aisle for white cumulus brides.

The ground is a combination of sea and sky: mounds of tufted green land clouds hold their ground, the carpet of some grand *maharaja*. Cumulonimbus mountains leer behind them, shifting into fog as distance pulls them into the faraway places my feet can never touch. Maple lighthouses and fir buoys mark the way, leaves bobbing with the wind, caressed by invisible channels.

I'm in nature, yet nature is in me. Every deep breath invites the soil, the air, the water, the *green* to awaken the heart that's been surrounded by hard walls for all the life she can remember. All the fake and manufactured give way to the organic and inspired.

I swear the earth is grabbing my ankles, shoots digging into my ankles and giving me the nurturing I've never received.

For all the life I can recollect, I've been a flower finding chlorophyll in artificial sunlight. The gardener comes around with a watering can but demands so much of me that my leaves wither. She will scoop me up in the morning and sell me to the highest bidder.

I stand amidst it, aghast. I'm a waif in Dickens' world, just a step away from a loaf of bread.

Everything is so delicious, I need months to take it all in.

"Adelaide," Fawn warns, but the buzz in my head drowns her out.

I can't help myself. I fall to the ground, humbled by the almost religious experience. The grass tickles my hands and pokes at them like bits of plastic streamers. I tear a few pieces off and rub my fingers over it. It's kind of sticky, something I never imagined. Everything smells so clean, so fresh, so *green*. A feeble breeze welcomes me to life and I move with it.

"Addy!" Fawn enunciates both syllables with annoyance. Her hand grabs me.

"It's just so wonderful!"

"Nature is gross," she counters. "It gets everywhere. Ever wonder why you have to sweep the area in front of the teleporter? All those brown things are dirt and leaves. It's *messy*."

Fawn grabs my shoulders and spins me back around towards the cold, harsh city and we march towards it. As we grow closer and closer, my stomach drops at the sound of so many voices. It's like a storm—you can feel it coming.

There's a gap between the walls that gives a peek into the city inside. The people talking grows louder and louder until BAM! There are people everywhere. Fawn and I enter the town and suddenly men, women, and children swarm around me. They're all wearing various shades of blue, gray, and white. I'm afraid they've found out I'm a Memory Jumper and are about to pounce on me and force me to use my powers. I cover my face with my hands as if I'm about to receive a blow.

"Stop it!" Fawn hisses in my ear. "Just act natural, for crying out loud."

A plump woman with a dull blue dress walks by me. She doesn't even look at me as she heads towards her target, a booth selling metal flowers. The booth floats above the ground and stocks glass orbs that hold pairs of shoes so ridiculous you couldn't walk in them. A man bumps my shoulder and a little boy runs in between Fawn and me. He has to duck down to make it through us and underestimates, Fawn's elbow cuffing him across the head as she jostles like Jell-o at a Thanksgiving.

I want to both hug and hide from all these people around me. I want them to tell me their life stories, their favorite desserts, and the color of their living room walls.

A group of girls my age walk by, looking me up and down. I stare too because I've met so few girls my age. And I've never seen so many together. They're tall and willowy and light, totally the opposite of everything I am.

I grab at my own hair, which I didn't even bother to fix before leaving the house. I'm a bit ashamed. Is this what it's like to be around people?

"Stay close," Fawn says. "Don't get lost, do you hear me?"

SIX
ADELAIDE

We dive into the sea of humans. There are so many heads, so many arms, so many smells. I'm drowning, but living at the same time. Really, finally living.

An old woman with milky eyes runs at me with a stack of fans.

"Buy one, get one free!" She croons. She throws one in the air and it stops right above her head and levitates. I shriek and Fawn yanks me away. Another man approaches me. He's speaking so quickly I can't even understand him. He shoves a silver butterfly pin at me. I'm captivated by it. The ridges are so delicate, with dips and rivets and bumps. Tiny gems decorate the borders of the wings, and a pair of antennae curl out from the body. My hands gravitate towards the wings with a mind of their own and, before I know it, it's in my hands. But now Fawn pulls me away, yet I still have the pin.

"Hey, hey, hey!" The guy screams, but over the ruckus he is not heard and I get away with the hair accessory. I'm both ashamed and excited.

Then a boy comes up to me. He wears thick, black geeky glasses and a shirt that's too bright a shade of blue to fit in with his surroundings. His hair is as thick as his glasses, and he blinks way too much. On his hip is a pouch, half-opened with tiny wires and computer chips sticking out.

"Have something broken? Look no further! I'm a tech whiz. I can fix anything and everything for a low fee!" He looks like perhaps he's twenty. His eyes make me stand still. They're a blueish green, so beautiful I've been transported to the Caribbean. I've only ever seen pictures of the water there, but right now I'm closer to those beautiful beaches than ever. I can't stop looking at them.

I've never met a boy my age before.

He's soft in a way I didn't expect, with brighter eyes and less sharp edges. I'm drawn to how much bigger he is than me, how much more confident.

I'm so scared, I can't even speak. I just nod politely and then skirt around him but he inserts himself in my pathway again.

"I'm sure you have something at home that needs fixing!" His quick eyes rest on the butterfly hairpin I grip in my fingers. "Or would you like to trade that for something? I also—"

"No!" I look him straight in the eyes as I shove the pin into my dress for safekeeping. His face drops and I feel bad, but I leave him in the dust and continue following Fawn.

Her shoulders raise like an alerted cat and her hands dive behind her to find me. She stops in her tracks and then turns to me, her eyes wide. "This was a bad idea. We need to go back home…now."

She maneuvers back through the crowd, the same way we came. The people mesh around me and I'm overwhelmed with claustrophobia. Fawn grabs my hand and swings around me, then drags me forward. The world shifts a bit, going from light to a shade darker. I look up and find that a lone cloud has blocked out the sun. The temperature drops a tiny bit, accompanied by a light breeze.

We explode out of the town and my stomach drops as I truly accept that we're going back to our house. What if this was my first and last time being out here? The town bleeds away behind me, giving way to the nature of the forest. It's such an abrupt transition, clearly a work in progress. Exactly what you would expect of a town rebuilt from the ashes of a rebellion.

As Fawn yanks me towards the teleporter, the sky darkens ominously and a loud, low crackle sounds. It's only now that I notice that the teleporter is bolted to the ground, maybe to keep people from stealing it. It seems so ominous, paired with the simmering thunder.

We step into the teleporter, and I stare through the glass, desperate for one last piece of this world I have wanted so much. Fawn types in the code for our home.

"Ah," she yells. Are her hands trembling? "I'm so upset, I can barely even type in our code. Don't want to end up in the king's backyard or something."

"Could we really end up there?"

I wonder where else she's been. I want to shove her hands away from the keypad and commandeer the teleporter, to go somewhere—anywhere—except that box in the ground. My own personal version of *absolutely nowhere*.

"Now is not really the time for stupid questions," Fawn huffs, eyes wild. But then she sees the look in my eyes: really sees. And for just a second, the ice melts. "But yes, the king is the only person who can afford a personal one. He's had them installed around towns for common use otherwise."

Then she pauses. "Um…could you type the code in for me? I just need to breathe for a second."

My fingers hover over the keypad, and they're like magnets. Again, I think about just typing something, anything.

"Type in 3225-YMN*." I obey immediately, leaving no room to think anymore.

3225-YMN*.

Three minus one twice, five, Yes Maybe No asterisk. My brain creates a way for me to remember the zone number.

I repeat it again: Three minus one twice, five, Yes Maybe No asterisk.

What if I *can* remember things? Why should I believe I can't?

The world is blurring and shifting and changing. It drips away from existence, and for a second I think I'm waking up from a dream…but it's only the teleporter, transporting us back home.

The panels change from glass to shiny metal, and a sad, small girl stares back at me in blobs: my reflection.

Now Fawn gives the signal: *thunk, tap-tap, thunk, tap, thunk.* It's strange actually seeing her do it; far less ceremonial than I'd always imagined it to be. The teleporter descends and we stare in front of us.

Buddy and Perkins are just as confused as I am when we climb out of the teleporter. They cast searching looks at my face, as if they can know with one glance what happened.

"How did you guys get in—" I start.

"I thought you were getting—" they start.

"Change of plans," Fawn chirps, a little too brightly. "We'll go back out tomorrow."

She grabs my hands, and I flinch, thinking she's going to pinch me or give me a lecture. She frowns like I hurt her feelings. "Addy, what's wrong?"

I don't speak.

"We'll go out tomorrow, I promise." She moves her hands with gusto, dragging mine with them. "I saw a couple of people in The Switch who are known to be anti-Memory-Jumper, and it just made me a little nervous."

My heart drops. "Really?"

She nods. "Yes, but don't worry. You're safe now. If you don't want to go out tomorrow, I—"

"No, that's okay. I'll be fine."

She drops my hands and dismisses me just like that. She, Buddy, and Perkins move into the kitchen. I know she's telling them something and she won't bother to explain anything to me.

As usual.

The conversations that involve me usually contain a variation of the following:

"No, your opinion, in fact, does not matter."

"You're a ditz."

"You couldn't possibly have a good idea."

Nineteen years of my faults being clearly explained.

I grab a blanket from my room and bury myself underneath it in the living room. I turn the wall on to a scene of some kind of country night scene with rolling hills and a bejeweled sky.

I stare at it for what seems like an eternity and memorize every wisp of grass, every delicious color, every bit of freedom I can remember from my firsthand experience.

"Get up." I bolt up off of the floor at the sound of Fawn's grumpy voice. A headache rips through me, probably since I slept here all night without a proper pillow. "You aren't supposed to sleep out here; you have a room for a reason."

I scurry to my room and throw on some clothes. Then I sit down to start on my itinerary for the day, not even bothering to grab breakfast.

Three minutes later my adopted mother storms into my room like a hurricane at sea, holding my giant, bedazzled sneakers. "What are you doing? Did I say to…" She glances at the task in front of me; it's already been condemned, no matter its description. "Start your itinerary?"

That's just what I do *every single day*…"No, ma'am."

"Get ready, then come to the living room. We're going out." She throws the shoes at my legs, and I drop my butterfly-patterned pencil.

"Seriously?"

She rolls her eyes. "Really, Addy. Also, will you do my hair? It's been atrocious lately."

I was used to telling myself to believe her with my head and not with my heart, always fully aware that she was only baiting me. And now, twice in twenty-four hours, she's actually followed through.

I've never dressed so quickly in my life. I choose to wear my best and favorite dress, the one that's the color of a dewy rainforest and made by Fawn in her sewing days. It even has pockets. I swallow any pride I had left when I put my ugly shoes on again.

I find Fawn in the living room, tying her own newer black sneakers. I French braid Fawn's hair, add a blue headscarf, and then say it's perfect. We go to the entryway and climb into the teleporter.

As we transport, Fawn keeps glancing at me with a searching look.

"What's wrong?" I ask.

She shakes her head. "So...Buddy and Perkins Envisioned something yesterday. I just wanted to—to change it."

She pauses, more information on the tip of her tongue. I will her to speak to me, to trust me.

She opens her mouth and stares at me again with that strange almost pained look. Then she shakes her head. "It's not going to happen. That's all the information I need to burden you with."

If only I could get Buddy and Perkins alone...but Fawn is very careful to never let us have alone time. Our card games are supervised, their visits short. She knows they have a soft spot for me. *And* access to The Outside. A dangerous combination.

Once we get outside, I notice that the day has a different tint than yesterday's: a bit less dangerous, a little brighter. There are no clouds in the sky today, and the sun sends its rays down to prickle my arms. I finally know what toast feels like.

I spot a dandelion and pick it, marveling at the tiny white puffs. I know what to do with it because of all the movies I've watched.

"I wish that, someday, I can come outside every day," I whisper as we walk towards the city. Fawn walks quickly. My attempts at keeping up with her make some of the dandelion fuzz fly away, and I'm left blowing a half-empty dandelion.

Oh well. Even if half my wish comes true, I'll be content.

I shove the dandelion stem into my pocket. I also save a leaf, a stick, and a sad flower petal which is a color more brown than pink and crinkled at the edges. But it's still a real flower. This I stick behind my ear. The rest I stick in my pocket with the dandelion stem.

"Remember, Addy: Don't get lost." Fawn told me the same thing yesterday. She repeats what she says to me often because of my bad memory, a cruel irony.

We dive into the mass of humans. Fawn expertly shoves her way through the braid of people.

I'm flummoxed by all the different outdoor shops. Some of them are booths, some of them are mini tents or even sheds. One woman shows a young mother a small shirt, then pulls it up and down. The material ripples and contorts to grow larger. A boy sells white strawberries, packaged in see-through boxes.

I trip on the giant shoes but regain my balance before hitting the floor—that's all I need. *Yes, hello—I'm a human freak, never worn shoes before.* As usual, I'm ashamed of myself.

I look down and see a robotic dog; it's white and has LED eyes. It doesn't look real at all. It cocks its head at me and lets out a panting sound. I jump over it and look for Fawn, the shoes slapping the pavement like dynamite. She's a few people away from me. I run through the crowd, trying to catch up to her.

"Fawn!" My voice is drowned out amidst all the haggling.

Fawn's head appears less and less until it blends in with all the other heads. My heart rolls in my chest; bile rises in my throat. I want to cry.

I've lost her.

People pulsate around me. I can only imagine what a bird would see if it looked down on us: a squirming toothpaste wad of humans wriggling to their destinations.

"Hey, you're back!" I turn my head, only to see the boy who tried to talk to me yesterday. Great. I ignore him and crane my neck to find Fawn.

"You don't say much," the boy shrieks over the noise of the crowd. I decide to put him to use.

"How do I get out of this crowd?"

"You asked the right person. Make sure you keep up." He grabs my arm—I nearly scream—and then he swerves around people like an agile ferret, yanking me behind him. I crash into a few bodies and immediately jerk away, but most people don't even notice I touched them. Finally, I see an empty space in front of me. I explode out of it, gasping as if there wasn't enough air in the mound of people.

The friendly boy stands in front of me, his glittering seawater eyes staring at me intently from behind those crooked glasses as if trying to figure me out. I gasp a few more times and close my eyes, allowing the fresh air to soak into my lungs and relax me.

When I open my eyes again, the boy watches me. I nod politely. "Thanks."

I walk away but he follows. "You act surprised at this."

"I am." I'm not fast enough to pretend I'm normal. "I, uh, I'm a visitor. To Kendror."

"Oh, neat!" He accepts my lie without blinking. "Well, it's not always like this. It's just the Crowning Season."

"The what?"

"The Crowning Season. Ya know, where the prince chooses a wife so he can become king?"

Oh, so like a Cinderella thing. I couldn't honestly care less at this point. "Yeah, no…I'm *really* not from around here."

USELESS FACT #721

The Cinderella story dates back to the first century.

"Oh, where are you from?"

"I'd rather not say. Sorry." Being rude comes naturally to me. I wish I could be more open. He seems nice. "I just met you."

"Oh, yeah, I totally get it. Well, Crowning Season is *really* fun. We do gift exchanges and make really good ham and collard greens, and it's a great time for business." Wow, how did I not know about this? Fawn must have me reading really old history textbooks. I know so little about Kendror. "Up front, what you just went through, that's what we call The Trading Post, or The Post for short. All the *best* creators and inventors in Kendror get booths up there."

He grins, glancing behind us and scanning the mass of humans and products. "One day I'll be there. I'm an inventor, actually. Do you know about the inventors of Kendror?"

I shake my head.

"The city of Kendror is a collection of the best inventors in Frelsi—our country."

Okay, I'm not *that* unaware. "I *know* what our country is called."

"Okay, okay!" He shakes his head. "Sorry, not sure where you're starting out from. Anyway, the king is always allowing people to show him their inventions and apply to be a Kendrorian. You get to live in the city and sell your inventions at the market.

"People come from all over the country to buy these items, and most of the inventors are part of the richest people in the world. There are also creators, people that paint and make art and stuff like that. Right and left brains come together for a beautiful society."

"Sounds like a dream," I say, but there's not much heart behind my voice. Riches just seem so empty compared to what already this boy has: the ability to go outside every day. To roam free, to fail and to succeed.

"Yeah, I'm working on a robot with Artificial Intelligence right now. My goal is to enable it to scan humans and then conform to their appearance exactly.

I suddenly remember why I'm standing here, chatting it up with a stranger: I lost Fawn. My moment of joy is over, and

I get a sick feeling in my stomach imagining how mad she's going to be.

Should I stay here and wait? Or should I go home? The thing is, she should be able to find me easily.

Fawn will always know where I am. She installed a tracking device in my neck as a child. She told me it was a precaution against someone kidnapping me. If someone stole me for my talent, Fawn would hunt them down and save me.

And right now, I'm *majorly* grateful for it.

But…she's not coming. Panic flies through me: what if she was kidnapped? What if someone recognized her? What if they're holding her hostage, hoping to get to me?

"Did you visit by yourself? That's a shame."

I shake a little. "No, I lost my mo—my—" What is Fawn? Should this boy think she's my mom? "I lost my friend."

"Do you need help finding her?"

"Um…no. I mean, thanks. But no."

"It's okay, you'll find her." The boy laughs. The seriousness on my face melts his mirth like ice cream left out on the kitchen counter.

I tear up; I can't help myself.

"Hey, you're not allowed to cry. I'm not good at situations like that." His voice switches from an obnoxious young salesman to a concerned young man. His honest statement makes me smile a tiny bit, and I'm shocked at myself. I shake my head and crane my neck, searching for Fawn in the slight chance that she's circled back here.

"Why are you so upset?" People file out of the shopping area, calm and normal. They know all about Crowning Season and collard greens. They have no clue I'm such an unsocialized underground dweller.

"You wouldn't understand."

My tone doesn't affect the boy. "Well, come on, let's find

her. We'll just walk through The Switch—that's the different areas of inventions and art. We group them by category. Where were you going?"

I literally just followed my adopted mother out of my house, no questions asked. "Um...we were just taking a stroll around...what did you call it? Switch."

"Don't you have a Communicator?"

I shake my head no, providing no further explanation.

"Weird. I mean, *everyone* has one. I don't know how you live without it."

I give a bitter laugh. "I guess I'm what some people would call a minimalist."

My eyes search the area around me. Fawn had a blue shirt on and a white headscarf tied in her hair...or was it a white shirt and a blue headscarf? Were her pants even blue? It doesn't help that she was dressed in the colors of this town, so she won't exactly stick out.

"Maybe...um...I just..."

He watches me, and I feel as if he's inserting meaning into every quirk of my jaw. "It's okay, we can just walk around for a little bit. Maybe we'll get lucky and bump into her. I can show you my favorite Switches."

I laugh at the idea of luck.

"What's your name?" The boy asks.

Should I give him my real name? I decide against it, Fawn's narrowed, dangerous eyes in my mind. "Alexandra."

"I'm Mason. Nice to meet you." I nod, trying not to be too friendly. Fawn will be so mad if she sees him. I continue on, and Mason follows. My eyes look around frantically. I'm so terrified. I keep thinking I see Fawn, but then the person turns around and has the wrong eyes, or the wrong nose, or the wrong face shape.

My brain throws future scenarios at me and I try not to

sob. Fawn is going to *kill* me. No, correction: she's going to make me wish she killed me.

You're okay, you're okay, you're okay.

She loves me, she loves me, she loves me.

Mason whistles, and it really bugs me, but I'm too scared to say anything.

I'm at the end of my rope. I'm panicking, and hard. My hands are clammy and I want to start crying again. And Mason's humming is like someone drilling a nail into my head.

"I think I'm going to go home, actually," I say.

The zone. I need the zone number.

I panic for a moment before taking a deep breath: how did I remember it?

Three minus one…twice, five…

Yes Maybe No asterisk.

I can't believe it.

3225-YMN*.

I remembered.

We can head back out later or maybe try again tomorrow. Maybe I'll make her favorite meal to soften her up; sometimes that works. I imagine our pantry in my head and try to remember if we have the right ingredients for four-cheese pizza.

"Okay. Well…I guess I'll leave then."

I sigh. "Thanks for calming me down."

"Yeah. No problem."

I walk off in the direction I'm facing…and then realize I have no idea where I'm going.

"Hey, Mason?"

The boy is at my side in an instant. "Yeah?"

"Um…I can't remember where I came from."

"Oh." He looks a bit worried. I can't blame him.

"I mean, I don't live in houses in town like *normal* people. I'm—" I can't believe I'm telling him this. This is so bad. I pause. There's no easy way out of this. "I live in the forest."

Mason's eyes widen. "I do too."

"Wait, seriously?"

"Yeah. What's your zone number?"

I send a shoulder up in a disgruntled gesture. "Why should I tell you?"

"Oh, sorry there." His voice has a tinge of sarcasm which stings a bit too much. He pauses and we stand in silence. "But, I mean, there are two large forest areas. One on the south side of town, and one on the north side."

Panicking. Again.

"I don't know which...I—"

"What shops did you see when you came in here?"

Remembering? Oh crud. "I can't remember...I'm just...I can't..."

But I remembered my zone number. And that was a random grouping of numbers. If I could remember that, maybe...

"Hey!" Mason calms me down with just a look in his eyes. It's like he's putting his hands on my shoulders, reminding me to breathe. "It's gonna be okay. Just relax."

I close my eyes and form an "o" with my mouth, breathing in and out. "Okay...there was a flower booth. And these clothes that get bigger."

He stares at me like I admitted the sky is blue.

"Okay, okay...the booth was the color of the sea on a stormy day. It had those purply flowers, lavender I think, and baby's breath, and colorful roses. And a really...*important* man with a black mustache and judging eyes and a white suit was in charge of it."

"Oh," Mason says. "That's Robin. He sells flowers made

of all types of metals. He's on the south side of town, near the Southerly Forest.

He begins to walk away, and I follow, but then he pauses and glances at me. "That was really insightful of you, by the way."

I've never thought of myself as insightful. "What?"

"Your description of Robin. He really does think he's better than everyone else. It's amazing you picked up on that so quickly."

It took Fawn about ten years to give me a real comment; this guy has known me for barely five minutes and already lavished a compliment on me. I open my mouth to say thank you, but it doesn't come out.

We start walking again and I'm more careful to take in my surroundings. People mill around us, but not in droves like before.

The houses are minuscule and boxy, each painted a different shade of blue, white, or gray. The windows explode with flowers and hovering booths are scattered throughout the white cement streets selling all kinds of creative art pieces and inventions. One booth is full of piles of scarves (which look totally normal from this distance), and a gypsy-looking woman calls to me with glittering eyes. I step a bit closer to Mason and continue on.

An overly short, rotund man with a pristine haircut sells metallic bottles. He holds pills in his hands and passes them out to people as they walk by. The banner over his booth states that they're food pills.

Next to him stands a woman selling various kinds of plastic white jewelry that's painfully geometric. She is a head and a half taller than the man. They stand next to each other, chatting up a storm as the woman runs a machine. She prints necklaces as she talks.

We continue walking. We pass groups of kids wearing goggles, a woman getting her hair braided by an older woman, and a child begging his mother to let him keep a robotic salamander he found on the front doorstep.

"We're almost to the edge of town," Mason says sometime later. I'm so absorbed in the beauty of normalcy; I jump a little bit.

I see the torrent of people ahead of me and my heart skips a beat. I open my mouth to ask Mason if we can go around all the people, but he dives in. We are pushed and smacked and stepped on in a flurry of activity.

Women trade hologram clocks and thick white shoes; people scan their watches against tiny machines; little boys try out hoverboards. It's a mess of activity.

Mason is like a steady needle, penetrating the mass of humans. People crash into him but he stays on course and tugs me behind him.

With a final yank, I find myself outside of the town next to Mason. We look behind us at the gap marking the entrance to the city. In front of us is the teleporter, sitting in front of a semi-thick forest.

I feel like this is a goodbye moment, but it's like I don't want this interaction to be over. I feel so…normal.

My mouth asks a question my brain didn't even process. "Where do you live?"

Mason stops in his tracks.

"You won't tell me where you live, and you expect me to tell you where I live?"

I pause for a second. "Oh…well…"

Mason sighs. "I live with my aunt. Zone 417."

I nod.

Mason stares at me, and I don't like it. I'm afraid if he looks too hard, he'll see right through me. People usually just see me as a means to an end or a villain. They don't look hard enough to see I'm just a shell.

"I've only known you for a short time, but these three things are clear: You have no sense of direction, you're forgetful, and most importantly, you're afraid. Of everything."

ADELAIDE'S USELESS FACT #1029
Boys are know-it-alls.

"How insightful." I huff at Mason's confident judgment. He turns and some kind of computer chip flies out of his pouch and onto the grass. I've watched documentaries on the production of different products; the computer chip was one of my favorites.

"You lost a chip," I say. Mason looks at me as if he thinks that's some kind of code. "Like, a technology chip thing."

He chuckles, then bends over and looks for the chip.

"Do you like marshmallows?" he asks.

I laugh. "Um, that's random."

"There's just something off about you. No offense. But I figured every normal person likes marshmallows."

I squirm a little bit. "Maybe I'm normal and everyone else is insane. Anyways, I love marshmallows, but…Fawn—*Mom* doesn't like me eating sugar."

Mason pockets the chip. "You call your mom by her first name?"

I tear a flower from the ground. The one that had been behind my ear is long-gone now, an unfortunate victim of the crowds. This flower is beautiful, a purple burst of color and fragrance. "It's complicated."

Mason nods. "I guess I don't call my aunt *Mom* either, even though I guess…she technically is my mom? Her name is Pippa."

71

"Cute name! So, why do you live with your aunt?" I smell the flower and make a face. How disappointing…it's bitter and dirty, not perfumey like I always thought it would be.

"Some generic thing like my parents died a long time ago."

"Hey, yeah! That's what Fawn tells me too."

Mason smiles and gives me a look like we share an inside joke. "They don't give you many details, do they?"

"No." I'm glad now that Mason came with me. I don't feel so alone as I did an hour ago. Are all humans this nice? "I've asked so many times. All I get is that I was saved from a near-death experience and I ought to be grateful."

"Ha, lucky," Mason says. "I don't even get that much."

His eyes narrow a bit.

"What?"

"Nothing. You're just…really mysterious."

I'm too stressed to laugh. I'm too stressed to reply, either, so I just shrug.

"What's your favorite thing to do?"

He's seriously going to have a conversation with me? I need to leave. Right now. I don't like the idea of being out here in the open. I feel bare, like everyone sees me and immediately knows I'm a Memory Jumper.

"I don't know…I…I sweep and I—I play guitar. And I make pottery."

"Why would you start that fascinating list with *I sweep?*" Now he's annoying me.

"I don't know—"

"Is there a particular reason you sweep?" My eyes dart behind him, staring at the teleporter that I *should* have been climbing into five minutes ago. "Like are you a superhero and that's your power?"

"No, it was just the first thing that came to mind."

"I changed the world of sweeping forever. I programmed a vacuum cleaner to clean by itself and gave it to my aunt last Crowning Season."

Know-it-all. Proud know-it-all. But, I'm impressed regardless. "You *programmed* a vacuum cleaner?"

"Yeah! But you making pottery is cool too," Mason adds. "Don't discredit yourself because your projects don't whir and blink. Kendror is made up of inventors *and* artists, don't forget that."

This kind of language doesn't compute with me. The building up, the compliments, the attention. "Okay, well, I'm gonna leave now. I really have to get home."

"Oh, which way are you? Maybe we're going in the same direction."

I think about walking with him for one second, but then Fawn's disapproving look sears through my mind. "Well, I think I'm going to take the teleporter."

"Ah, no fun," he says. I stare back at him blankly. "You can laugh sometimes, you know that right? You're making me feel like I have a terrible sense of humor."

I force an uncomfortable chuckle. I'm not used to other people making me laugh. "Well, I really need to go."

He puts his hands up in the air. "Fine, fine! Well, maybe I'll see you around again?"

Most definitely not. But I smile anyway. "Definitely. See ya!"

He heads off into the forest, and I climb into the teleporter and type in 3225-YMN*. The Outside smooshes together, colors turning into simple streaks of light growing brighter and brighter. Then, the cold metal of the teleporter replaces the light.

I hesitate for a second—What if Fawn isn't down there?

What do I do if she actually was captured? I knock out the familiar signal.

It takes a couple of seconds, but soon the teleporter is whirring down. Okay, good: *someone* is here.

The teleporter settles and the doors open gently—

"Addy!"

Fawn stands right in front of the teleporter, eyes smoldering clouds of smoke.

I was right; she's no animal. She's a nuclear weapon.

SEVEN
ADELAIDE

H er hand descends on my shoulder with the force of an eagle catching an innocent fish. My shoulder stings as her nails bury themselves in my flesh. I panic; I want to run. But there's nowhere to run to.

"I'm sorry," I try to say, but she yanks me out of the teleporter. All the while, I wonder: *why didn't she come for me?*

I can't even look into her eyes. I hide from the fear by replaying Mason's words in my head: "You have no sense of direction, you're forgetful, and most importantly you're afraid. Of everything."

Mason was right: I am lost, forgetful, and afraid. Maybe not in the ways he thought. I'm not physically lost.

But mentally? I've been lost for a long time.

I fight the tears. I won't let Fawn have the pleasure of making me cry.

Fawn drags me into the kitchen and then lets go of me for the first time in what seems like forever. She plows through our drawers, her temper absolutely out of control. Apple corers, forks, and chopsticks fall to the ground in a symphony of terrifying clinks.

"Say something," I beg. No reply. I close my eyes. She's a madwoman, and I don't know what she's going to do to me. "I'm sorry. I'm so, so sorry."

Then she pauses. Her face loses its wrath for a moment. She turns to me and looks at me from underneath her lashes, a cool look across her pupils.

Her hands pull out a pair of scissors. My mouth opens and ragged breaths of air escape.

"Don't do this," I plead with her. She comes at me and I yell. The tears I tried so hard to hold in finally fall.

"Don't fight me, Addy," she demands. My muscles won't move. My bones refuse to obey me. I stand there, whimpering, paralyzed in fear. Her nails poke me. "You'll only make it worse for yourself."

She grabs my hair. With a sickening clip, she lops off a chunk.

A cry rips out from my throat and Fawn hits me across the forehead with the scissor handle. "Shut up!"

My arms vibrate now. I'm afraid I might do something. She hacks at my hair again and the curtain of hair hits my arm as it falls. I tremble, grabbing myself like I'm about to shoot into the stratosphere and this is the only way to keep myself rooted to the earth.

Fawn swings me around and pokes the scissors at my face. With the other hand, she squeezes my arm so tightly that I swear I can feel my pulse. "You will never again disobey me. If I say do not get lost, you will do *everything* in your power not to. You were gone for *hours*. That is unacceptable. You will not speak to anyone unless I tell you to, you will not go outside unless I tell you to, and you will not be allowed to grow your hair long again so long as you disobey me."

I sob quietly as her words stab me. The scissors glint, threatening worse things than chopped hair.

"I need you, Adelaide," she says. Her voice breaks and she grabs my wrists gently. "I don't want you to get hurt. This is the best method I can think of to protect you."

Something in me snaps. Something in me breaks into a million pieces, splashes all over the walls.

The word that's been inside of me for so long threatens to come out: an explosive, loud, short *no*. But I'm not brave enough. I can only think it, eyes closed. The word is soundless, sent into the atmosphere with no ripple or sound.

I don't know what it means. No, she doesn't really need me? No, she doesn't really want me to get hurt? No...no what?

Sometimes people cry so hard it hurts. Your heart is in your throat; the tears are in your soul. You drop to your knees and bend over into a ball. The pain seems like it'll never go away. Continued existence seems impossible. I've experienced this in so many memories, not to mention my own life.

I'm on the floor, crying like I've never cried before. The worst kind of crying is the noiseless one, the one where it seems like you aren't even crying, just convulsing. I never thought Fawn would actually do this.

It's a statement. A flaunting of power. A wordless promise of a torturous forever.

Fawn is capable of so many different terrible things.

Footsteps thunk around my face. I can't even open my eyes to see if it's Fawn, ready to give me some other lecture. But she usually wears high heels. Her footsteps are clicks.

Large, thick hands—two sets of them, the twins—grab me and help set me upright. I'm pulled into a sandwich hug that smells of dirt and sunshine.

"What happened?" Perkins asks. "She was absolutely *losing*

it; said there were updates needed on your tracking device, but she'd been putting it off. So when she needed to track you today, it wouldn't work."

"Is she gone?" I sob through water and snot.

"Yes, she stormed out of here. Looked like she was crying."

I laugh, and it hurts. Fawn? Crying? Impossible.

"I got lost," I try to explain. There's no way the two brothers can understand what I'm saying through my tears, but I feel one nod his head. "She was there one minute, and then the crowd was dragging her away."

"And so…Fawn cut your hair?" Buddy asks. "It doesn't sound like it was your fault."

I shake my head. Buddy pulls away from me and I fall a little, like a pathetic underdone ravioli. Buddy holds me up. "You don't know the real Fawn. She puts on an act for you guys, for the clients, for anyone who isn't me. Only I know what she's really like."

"Wait—seriously?" Perkins asks.

I scoff. "Of course you don't believe me."

"Well, actually…that would make a lot of sense. Based on the Envisioning…" Buddy whispers.

"What Envisioning?"

"This calls for gummy bears first," Perkins says, and the pair head to the kitchen. I waddle after them, feeling like a silly little sister.

"Guys, guys, what did you Envision?"

"You know about my secret stash?" Buddy yells at Perkins, completely ignoring me.

"Shushhhhhhhhh," Perkins hisses.

Two minutes later, we sit at the kitchen table with a communal bag of gummy bears, and I get the guys to spill the secrets.

USELESS FACT #163

The biggest gummy bear money can buy is 26 pounds. It contains 32,000 calories.

Perkins grabs a handful and dumps it in front of me. It takes me a while to grab one, but once I do, I'm glad I did. It doesn't make my hair grow back, but for one second I feel cared for.

Perkins doesn't look me in the eyes. "A couple of days ago, Fawn had us Envision for her. But it scared her out of her mind. That's why she took you outside. She thought she could change what she saw."

"What did you Envision?"

The twins look at each other. It's Buddy who speaks. "Something super out of character, for you both."

"Please, can I see?"

"I don't know…" Perkins says.

"*Please,*" I beg. "Please, for once—can I just know what's going on?"

Buddy and Perkins nod. They hold hands and reach out for mine. I hold both their hands. The world flickers for a moment, then goes black. I blink. I've Envisioned with the twins before, so I'm not shocked by the initial experience.

A scene drips into view. There's metal…metal bars. They're lit up by the tiniest hint of light. A hand shoots out, then curls around the bars.

The fingernails are red.

It's Fawn. In a cell.

The scene changes. There's grass and sky and…

The boy from the marketplace. He's walking through a grassy field, looking at something.

Looking at someone.

And that someone is me.

There's a whoosh, a flash, and then the kitchen is back.

I'm gasping. "I know that boy. I've seen him twice in the marketplace. But…what does it mean?"

Buddy and Perkins glance at each other. They say nothing, but I know they're having a conversation. And it doesn't have to do with the whole *twin* thing either. They're just in tune with people like that.

"That's not what Fawn saw," Buddy says slowly.

"The part about the boy wasn't in there," Perkins muses. I can almost see him replaying the memory of the previous Envisioning in his head. "The future deviations must've changed drastically since you went outside. Fawn's plan didn't work."

"What did *she* see?"

Buddy hesitates. Perkins rubs his forehead. "She saw a world where you never leave this house, Adelaide. And the part about her being in a cell. She thought if you could go outside, the cell would disappear."

I shake my head, the lack of weight from my hair a haunting ghost. I feel ill just thinking about it. "What does this all mean?"

"Well…what is Fawn *really* like, Adelaide?"

I hover over the truth. Do they *really* want to know? *Should* they really know?

A memory flickers before me, a warning against oversharing. Because once, a long time ago…I was close.

So close to freedom.

Fawn had left the room for not thirty seconds before our Memory Jumping client, an old man named Wilbur, looked deep into my eyes. "Are you safe? Are you okay down here?"

I was only ten. Fawn was my normal. She was the definition of a mother to me. But there was a tiny sliver of doubt deep inside me, doubt that whispered in my ear that she was more of a jailer than an adopted mother. "Yes, I'm fine."

He shook his head. He told me how he worked with children sold into slavery—trafficking, I knew now—and he recognized a trapped look in my eyes. "Child, tell me the truth: I will not ask again. Does your mother love you? Does she ever hurt you? Does she yell at you a lot?"

He didn't know about Fawn's cameras. He didn't know that she was listening.

Fawn forced me to wipe out his memory and the twins dropped him off where they'd found him. I cried and cried and cried. That's when I realized: there was no hope.

And here is the same situation. I could tell the twins the truth…but if they find out, Fawn will see it on her stupid cameras. She'll be angry and force me to wipe their memories.

I'll lose my friends, my family.

I'll be truly, a hundred percent alone.

So I look Buddy and Perkins in the eyes…

And I lie.

"She's just kinda rude sometimes." I sigh like a melodramatic teenager.

"Her cutting your hair is…really severe," Perkins comments.

I force a chuckle. I am the best actress in the world, *chuckle chuckle*. "I don't think she knows how to parent, that's all. No parent is perfect."

There's no way the twins believe me. But I will not be the one to ruin their lives. If they want to bring this up with Fawn, that must be their choice.

I can't destroy any more people.

EIGHT
COLETTE

My husband and I sit in the Great Room of our castle, and the smartest creators and inventors from all across the country (and even the world) pitch their ideas for a chance to live in Kendror, the city just outside the walls of our castle.

I love when I get to explore Kendror. Divided into eight shopping zones, which we call Switches, you can find the best and most innovative products. Most of the items in our castle are from The Switch.

The inventors and creators, paired with ingenious marketers and salespeople, have rebuilt the economy of our country, Frelsi, from the ground up after America went down in flames. They are the true celebrities, the new and better Hollywood.

This morning, I paid extra attention to my wardrobe and makeup. If Wesley is in a bad mood, he accepts fewer sales pitches. I do my best to look extra nice on these days. My thinking is that, subconsciously, he'll be happier with me, and therefore with the citizens. All the while, my thoughts hover

over the health of my son. I think of him now, lying in bed upstairs. We haven't told him what we really think is wrong with him.

Now I sit in the Great Room, draped in blue silk, silver chains, and glitter. My updo is so intricate that I worry every time I turn my head, which thankfully is not very often.

Through the first three invention pitches, Wesley seems fairly pleasant. He passes on two inventions and accepts one, but he doesn't break into a rant or outburst when the second invention flops.

The fourth person of the morning is a scrawny kid, all angles and bones. His face is so red with pimples that it appears swollen. I worry he hasn't eaten in many days, but I hear Wesley in my head: "That's none of your concern, Colette."

The boy holds a strange, humped, metallic item. Two black knobs are on the front, and a cord drags from the back of the machine like a tail.

"What is your name?" asks our burly head of security, Magnus, who is ninety percent water, ten percent sparkling grape juice (I often see him enjoying cans of it during his breaks).

"Torben, Your Honor—I mean sir, I mean—"

Wesley chuckles, cruelly. "Stop bumbling, boy, or we'll send you out immediately. You know we only want the most intelligent of all people in this room, and right now you sound like a brainless ogre."

The boy blinks as if staring into the sun, holding his invention like an infant. "I'm sorry, Your Majesty."

"What do you have to offer?"

"Sir, I have with me a mind-reading machine."

Wesley leans forward on his throne, a creak erupting throughout the room. "A what?"

"A mind-reading machine." Torben is obviously nervous. His eyes dart back and forth from Wesley to me to Magnus, and he licks his chapped lips repeatedly. I'm worried they'll burst any minute, bleeding over his already-red face.

"We already have mind readers." Everyone freezes— Wesley is referring to Memory Jumpers, a race of people with the ability to read minds. Most of them were killed during The Memory Wipe, but a few stragglers have always remained. Wesley had two executed last year. I tremble at the memory.

"But this is—well, I mean, this would be legal." Torben lets out a nervous chuckle, and I desperately want to rush to him and lead him out of the room. I cannot see this ending well.

Wesley leans back, grunting. "Well, give us a demonstration, boy! I'm going to think of a word, and you tell me what it is."

The boy sets his silver humpbacked invention on the ground, then picks up the black tail and sticks it in his mouth. He closes his eyes, and we all watch.

He sucks on the cord like a pacifier for about ten seconds, then removes it.

"King Wesley, you are thinking of the word...*superimposed*."

We all turn to look at the king for verification. As usual, his face is ambivalent.

"Hmm. Correct. But I'm not convinced." I've been married to the man for twenty years; despite his coldness towards me, I can still read him better than other people. And right now, I'm worried.

There's something simmering beneath the surface, danger broiling and brewing and seething. Wesley is playing the boy. But why?

Torben repeats the strange routine, and we all watch in

fascination. He looks at my husband and grins a boyish grin. "The word is *correction*."

"Once more."

The boy's smile falters, and he again sets the machine on the floor and sticks the tail in his mouth. I adjust in my seat, my dress crunching against me. I suddenly feel exhausted at the idea of another three hours of these demonstrations and explanations.

The boy removes the black tail, then looks confidently at Wesley. "The final word is: *fraudulent*."

Wesley jumps to his feet. His voice is thunder, his rage like burning rain in myths of old. He is a Greek god, a harbinger of destruction. His eyes are darkness and fire and brimstone. With hate piercing from his tongue, two words rip out into the Great Room: "MEMORY JUMPER!"

How my husband hates Memory Jumpers. And yet, he knows just as well as I do, that if we're ever in a corner, we have our ways of contacting a Jumper to erase the mess.

Like once before, when our son learned the truth about who he was. And we erased his memory.

And now, he's dying.

Torben's face turns from red to white in an instant. He drops the machine, which falls on his foot. He screams in pain and drops to the floor, meanwhile yelling, "Please, no! I'm not! I swear it! It's the machine! The machine works! Please!"

Magnus moves swiftly, and six other guards leave their posts on the borders of the room and grab the boy who couldn't even crush a fly.

"Please! My family needs this! I'm all they have! Please!" His pleas might as well have been in another language. Wesley sits on his throne, not a muscle in his face flinching.

I'm dying on the inside. A scream rips through me, but I

know the feeling well enough by now to keep it inside. I know how to scream silently.

My brain asks my feet to leave the scene, to run to my room, to run to the bathroom, to get away. It needs to understand what just happened, to accept that a possibly innocent soul is being detained…and possibly will be killed.

The guards drag Torben away, leaving his machine broken on the floor in front of us. Only two guards have stayed in the room, and Wesley calmly asks for a maid to be sent to clean up the mess.

"You are safe, my love," he says to me without looking into my eyes. "You are safe from the terror of the Memory Jumper."

I stare straight ahead as well, speaking to the walls who actually listen. "Thank you, dearest."

The boy is executed two days later. I am required to watch, but I don't see. I hear the cruel snap of the gun, the scream of boy meeting bullet. Pain has no meaning to me anymore. If I were still human, I would worry about this collapse into ambivalence.

But not even the shadows of worry reach me.

Pain is breathing. Pain is waking up to another twenty-four hours of a ruler that watches my every move, judges my every blink.

Pain is seeing my son turn into the man I don't even have the will to hate.

Now my son, Adam, the one I bandaged and hugged and sang to sleep—my boy is deathly ill. Sometimes I have terrible thoughts, thoughts that perhaps this is for the best.

"Accompany me on a Color Sweep," the king commands.

I nod. We turn away from the mess, from the Memory Jumper's meaningless life.

Why are Memory Jumpers so terrible? I've been told repeatedly that they're terrorists, that their power is too strong and can't be contained, posing a threat to humanity itself. But anything can be used for evil. What if we focus on using their power for good? When the Memory Jumper came to the castle all those years ago…no, I've locked that away.

Wesley and I, accompanied by ten guards in black armor, walk to the Tram. It's a series of white driverless cars that hover above the ground, emitting eerie aqua light. The door of the first car senses our approach and peels itself open, revealing plush gray seats, chilled drinks, and carefully selected snacks (no nuts; Wesley is deathly allergic).

We climb in, both of us on either side of the vehicle. The guards will follow behind us in other snackless trams.

I hate Color Guard. Wesley is ruthlessly logical, no fuss or frills. At the beginning of the regime, in order to *streamline*, he ordered all clothes to be simple and in muted colors: blues, grays, blacks, and whites.

I remember wearing yellow as a girl and feeling like a daffodil.

After we were stabilized, Wesley never removed the order. Now he routinely performs a Color Guard, where we drive around town and pretend to engage with the people, but really Wesley is looking for people breaking code and wearing unapproved colors.

After Adam was born, Wesley and I started sleeping in separate rooms. Sometimes, at night, I wear a red nightgown my sister smuggled to me. She is the only one who ever knew the truth about how Wesley treated me: as a subject to be subjugated.

Red is bold, defiant. Sometimes I hope a fire will start, and

I'll have to race out of the mansion, myself an uncontrollable flame.

The people smile at us, but it's an act. I know a fake smile when I see one. These people know they're being used: used for their brains, for their abilities, for rebuilding a country. And yet, in a way, I have no pity for them. If they wanted freedom, they could get it.

Maybe I shouldn't feel bad for myself either, then. I'm letting myself be bullied. I have momentary blips of insanity where I consider leaving Wesley, but I always shake it off. He's obsessive about everything he does. I've never seen him fail for as long as I've known him. If he wanted to find me to punish me, he could. I have no doubt.

"Color is unnecessary," Wesley muses. He goes on monologues sometimes, and I wonder if having complete control over everything scares him. He doesn't need to ask permission, he has no reason to bounce ideas off of another person. His word is law. I can't imagine the weight of that. So, he resorts to talking *at* me. Talking to himself. Reassuring himself that what he is doing is true, right, and virtuous.

He continues his rant. "It gets people's minds onto things that do not matter. They could be doing much more productive things besides worrying about what shade of red matches their skin tone."

I think again of my red nightgown. Maybe, once, I was the color red. But now, Wesley has turned me into one of his blues.

Maybe even gray. And I can't complain. Because gray has no emotion. And neither do I. It's better that way, after all.

NINE
ADELAIDE

To distract me from the turmoil that just occurred, Perkins goes to get a card game and we play for a while. The twins fight every other play, but it's all in good nature. I laugh, an act that feels hollow and foreign.

But I beat the boys in multiple rounds, my smile growing bigger and more real.

Maybe they just let me win to make me feel better. But I don't care if my victory was real or not, just that it looked like one.

When the signal comes, I guarantee my blood isn't the only blood that turns cold.

"Go to your room," Perkins commands. He sweeps the cards into their box. His arm shakes a little. "If she checks the cameras, you'll be busted. We'll be busted. She'll never leave us alone again."

Buddy grabs his gummy bears and brings them to safety.

"Go, go!" Perkins shrieks. I throw my arms around him in an awkward hug.

"Thanks," I say. Then I sprint to my room.

I wish I could spend every day with the brothers. I would *love* for them to stay down here with me; I could play games and eat gummy bears with them every day. I'm a bit shocked at myself. I've always had this feeling, but always shoved it down. It's like being with Mason today made me realize, and accept, just how long I've been…lonely. I guess I just never allowed myself to acknowledge it.

The signal comes again. I bet Fawn is fuming. I brace myself for the verbal lashing I'm sure to get. All of my bravado drains faster than bathwater. I wonder if I should go say *hi* to her, but decide against it.

I shove my hands in my pockets, a bit desperate; and, yes, I still have it. The leaf is missing a bit of itself, but I have it. My living, breathing token that proves I saw the sun.

I sit on my bed and stare at my wall.

It's more full than my life is. There are pictures of the Acropolis, the Great Wall of China, Niagara Falls, pre-Frelsi New York City, as well as the Statue of Liberty. Only Lady Liberty's torch and the bottom half of her dress exist now.

The only other thing besides photographs is a simple drawing of Fawn and me that I drew when I was six or seven.

We've never taken a picture together.

The emptiness inside me threatens to explode. I sit there on my bed for a solid ten minutes. I'm too afraid to move. When I realize Fawn isn't coming to yell at me again, I sit down and do my schoolwork.

I'm in my room the rest of the day. She never comes to ask for dinner, so I don't bother cooking. 9:00 comes and I shut off my lights and go to bed.

The house is still. I try to breathe while staying completely still. The darkness is a welcome friend, more so than Fawn's presence and the disaster she brings with her.

I lie in bed wide awake all night, trying to delete the memories of Fawn's sizzling anger. But Memory Jumping doesn't work on me.

I will stay here forever, I decide childishly. I will lay here under the covers for the rest of eternity. Maybe if I close my eyes, I'll absorb into the sheets. When I wake up, I'll just be a set of simple sheets.

Fawn would know. She just would. She'd ball me up and throw me into the washer until I drowned. She would never relinquish her control of me, inanimate object or not.

Maybe I could smother myself.

I pull the sheets closer; they smell like nothing. I have no fragrance, no presence. I'm a ghost. The sheets caress my face. They're not as smooth as I would've thought. I press them to my nose but automatically hold my breath.

I let go with a whoosh. Forget this. I'm not even brave enough to give up.

The next morning, no one is here. Fawn is gone; Buddy and Perkins are gone. I'm all alone.

I don't even bother making an itinerary, knowing I'll regret that later. After completing my school for the day, Fawn still isn't back, so I pick up *Jane Eyre*.

Two hours later, I'm beginning to grow anxious.

I might as well make some more mugs to sell. I drag myself to the pottery room, not feeling in a creative mood at all. The lump of clay I grab looks way too big, but I slam it down on the wheel anyway.

I push, I pull, the wheel turning madly. My brain turns off, allowing my hands to work the clay by instinct.

Suddenly, a strange sound hums through our underground home. *It's the teleporter coming down.*

My foot releases from the wheel's pedal. My hands stay on the clay as I try to make sense of the situation, but they want to fly up to my mouth to cover the scream perching on my tongue.

Have they found me?

Are the Memory Jumper haters here to kill me?

Is someone here to kidnap me and use my powers?

This is what Fawn has warned me about, what she has prepared me for my entire life. This is what keeps me underground, this is why the sunlight cannot reach me.

I am paralyzed.

The teleporter doors swish open, and the sound carries down the hallway to me. Then, slow footsteps.

How can I protect myself? What can I do? I look around the room, panicked. I have a mop in the corner that I use to clean the floor; maybe I can knock the person out with the handle.

I climb off of my chair and grab the mop, quiet as death.

The seconds that tick by feel like small hours.

Then, a voice.

"Alexandra?" Wait…my grip on the mop handle loosens. Is that…is that Mason? I'm confused by the name for a second and then remember he still thinks my name is Alexandra.

"Alexandra?"

I lower the mop. How did Mason find me?

What do I say? What do I do? Should I pretend I'm not here?

"Alexandra, ya here?" He's getting closer. I growl under my breath. Fawn is going to find out and blame this on me too. Then I'll surely go mad.

I fly out of the room, mop in my hand like a ninja sword. Mason stands in the hallway gawking, his eyes wide open like a kid in a candy store.

"Alexandra, hey! What's up with the mop?"

"Mason! What are you doing here?"

"Dude, this place is *so cool*," he breathes. I'm sweating like a sinner in church. "Is this one of those safe houses? I heard they built some for Memory Jumpers and Envisioners back in the day—Wait…what happened to your hair?"

My hand flies to my back but feels only the collar of my dress. I pull my hand up to the nape of my neck and finally find where my hair ends. The lack of weight is a ghostly memory of my deadly mistake yesterday.

"It's nothing. I just…I cut it."

"It looks like a hamster was gnawing on the back of your head." I force myself to not give in to the tears. Mason sees my tears and backtracks. "I mean, I'm sorry…I just say stuff. My bad."

I relinquish my mop, setting it against the wall. I need to get him off this topic before I start crying. "How did you get in here?"

"Um…well…I thought you might be in danger." No one has ever worried about my safety. Fawn has made sure of that by expertly schmoozing any client decent enough to ever worry about me. "I didn't go home after I left you; I changed my mind once I passed the city gate, thought I'd go home and grab some lunch.

"When I went back to the teleporter, the zone you typed in was still in there. You forgot to select Incognito Mode."

Fawn would *not* be happy about that. But how was I supposed to know? It was a small miracle I had noticed and remembered what zone she typed in the first place.

"Just, some of the things you said about your mom didn't

sit right with me. I'm sorry, I was going to ignore it but… curiosity got the best of me." My cheeks redden with something, a combination of anger, annoyance, and confusion. "I couldn't sleep last night. So I thought I'd just make sure you got back okay."

I'm speechless. Which is fine, because he's soliloquizing in the hallway like there's no tomorrow. "By the way, I thought you were from a different *country*. Should I call you a liar?"

That word hurts a little more than it should, memories of Fawn using it playing before my eyes.

"Um, haha, sorry," I say. "I was just embarrassed I knew so little."

"Well, it all makes sense now since you're…well, underground. Your zone is different from most zone numbers."

"Yeah, Fawn is…secretive. It's a small miracle I could remember that code; it's kinda long and I have the memory of a diseased goldfish."

"I'm sure that's not true," Mason chuckles.

This boy has lunged into my life and turned over everything I know. He's the complete opposite of Fawn in every way possible. Do I have person whiplash?

"Wait, how did you get the teleporter to come down? Fawn and I have a code."

Mason scrunches his eyes. "A code?"

"Yeah, she gives a little code by hitting the teleporter walls: *thunk, tap-tap, thunk, tap, thunk*, then she stomps."

"Oh, I just—Well, I can't resist a challenge." Of course he can't. Of course he can't leave well enough alone. Of course he can't just walk away and keep himself safe and mind his own business. "There wasn't any button I could see to make the teleporter go down, so I just dug through the teleportation settings. Couldn't find anything, so I tried my Monitor device and, well…I got into the system and just operated the moving mechanisms from my device."

He shrugs. "My aunt says I speak machine."

I shake my head at this brainiac.

"Okay, fascinating. But we should probably stop chittering and start moving," I order, suddenly serious. "Fawn is gonna murder you if she—"

"Why do you say stuff like that? Murdering you?"

I shrug. I don't have to explain myself to him. "I don't know. It's just—it's just a figure of speech."

"I don't know if I believe that…Hey, how do you get light in here? Is it ever hard to breathe? What's the wiring like? Did you—"

I need duct tape, and a lot of it. "Stop. Talking."

Thunk, tap-tap, thunk, tap, thunk, stomp. The sound echoes forebodingly from above me.

"Ohhhh *that's* the signal!" Mason says.

All the breath whooshes out of me. Spikes of terror spread through my face, and I break into a cold sweat. His memory is *actually* in danger now. If Fawn finds him, she'll force me to do a total wipe on him.

His robots. His life. His goal to be an inventor of Kendror.

By knowing me, he could lose all of that.

The world spins.

"That's Fawn, right?" My colorless face is enough of an answer for him.

Mason moves. Boy, does he move. He follows me through the living room, down the hallway, and into my bedroom. I fling my closet open, Fawn's taps reverberating through the whole house and growing louder and more irritated.

"Stay in here," I demand. "Don't breathe. Don't move."

Then I slam the door and sprint back to the teleporter. I

thunk into the wall, but it's worth it because my finger hits the button to send the teleporter down. I force myself to breathe, to calm down, to stop panicking. I'm *so scared* right now. Not only do I have to face Fawn for the first time since I *defied* her, but a souvenir from my trip invited itself into my home.

I place myself in front of the teleporter right before it opens to reveal Fawn.

"You're getting slower and slower," she hisses. "When I give the signal, I want you to immediately stop what you are doing and send the teleporter down."

"I'm sorry." My voice trembles.

She thunders out.

"You're such a ditz, you know?" The words scorch me unlike any physical pain. She spins on me. "Yesterday when you got lost, you were absolutely pathetic. Where did I tell you to go if you got lost?"

You didn't tell me that. My brain commands my mouth to say the words, but nothing happens. "Oh…um, did you tell me that?"

"Yes, I did." Fawn huffs and throws her hands in the air. "You have such a terrible memory. It's ironic. It should be funny. But it's ridiculous."

I judder.

"Now, come to the living room. I need to make some updates to your tracking device." *She's not going to tell me that's the reason she couldn't find me. She's not going to take the blame as she should.* We go to the living room, even though all I want to do is run to my bedroom and lock the door permanently.

She pulls her Communicator out of her pants pocket and opens it. I sit down on the couch, the silence searing through us both. She presses buttons; the tracker on my neck beeps every now and then.

Fawn finally speaks. "Okay, good. Updates are done. Now,

I'm going to rest, and then I'm going back outside. I'm finding you a person, and you are going to Memory Jump on their unconscious brain or so help me—"

She doesn't finish her sentence, just glares at me.

"You aren't joining me, either. You've proven you can't go outside."

That really breaks me. My face manages to stay composed, but a few telltale tears fall.

I am shut back up in this box for the rest of my life.

My hand shakes a tiny bit and I fight to keep it under control. Fawn storms to her room and I just sit in the living room, rooted to the couch.

For a second, I have a crazy thought. What would happen if I just…left? I stare in the direction of the teleporter.

No. One moment at a time. One problem at a time.

I walk back to my room, my hands on the walls around me to support myself. My bones are as limp as Fawn's one-time attempt at spaghetti.

Spaghetti.

I have to make dinner for Fawn.

And Mason is still in my room.

I dive back into the hallway and to the kitchen, then scrounge up a quick meal of salmon doused in olive oil, topped with a seasoning mix of paprika, cumin, and basil. I also make a salad with a balsamic vinaigrette, cranberries, and walnuts.

I keep a careful eye on the time and deliver the meal at exactly 6:00, along with a glass of water. Fawn doesn't answer my knocks on her door so I leave it outside and escape to my room.

I enter the room, head spinning from my strange day.

"Alexandra?" The voice scares the sparkles out of me, and

I jump sky-high. The voice is Mason. I realize this a second too late, and tears finally fall from my eyes.

USELESS FACT #732

When a person cries and the first drop of tears comes from the right eye, it's happiness. If it is from the left, it's pain.

Mason's peeking out from the closet. "I heard some of your conversation. I'm sorry, I didn't mean to eavesdrop. I…I really shouldn't be here."

His tone is no longer blithe. He's lost his goofiness. He steps out from the closet, and I'm hit with the realization that he's so much taller than me. So much bigger, even. My five foot four is minuscule compared to his six feet.

All I want is to be safe right now. And he looks like the safest thing I've got. I have a terrible desire to hug him like they do in the movies I watch. In the music I hear. In the versions of normal life I absorb myself in to forget my reality.

I force myself to stay glued to my place on the ground.

"You need to go," I whisper. "Fawn has a camera in some of the rooms here. She's going to see you were here."

He rolls his eyes. "You forget I'm a tech wizard. Listen, I have a few tricks up my sleeves. You'll be fine. Just show me the camera."

"But she's going to find out and think I—"

"Do you trust me?"

Is he crazy? I met him yesterday.

But the Envisioning comes back to me again, and the world pauses for a second.

I see those red fingernails again, behind bars. I hear Buddy and Perkins asking me how Fawn really is. And I see him, somehow a part of my story. I figure, if I keep doing what I'm doing right now, nothing is ever going to change.

I close my eyes. "Yes."

He pulls out a small device from his ever-present fanny pack, a squarish white object. "I'm going to use this to hack into your cameras. I think they're controlled by…" he starts throwing out techy terms and I lose him. "You do the same thing every day pretty much…right?"

"Yeah. But she doesn't sit there and watch everything."

"Okay…I'm going to upload all the previous footage and then weave it together. I can program it so it creates a day's worth of footage out of previous footage, compositing new images of you."

I lean against the wall, observing and nodding like I understand what he's saying.

"Is there a pattern of outfits we can have you wearing? So she doesn't figure it out?"

"Um, not really. But I don't have many clothes anyway. I'll write a list out." I grab one of my favorite notebooks, which I painted by hand with various stylized leaves, and write the list.

"It'll take a few days," Mason says, eyes glued to his device. "But for now, I'm deleting the footage with me in it and deleting the timestamp." He casts a gaze my way.

"She's terrible," he comments. My pen stills, hovering over describing outfit number four.

"Well, I mean, she was right about *one* thing…I'm a Memory Jumper and I can't even—"

Mason's eyebrows shoot together in confusion and he shakes his head. "Wait—you're a Memory Jumper?"

My pen slips. "Um…no. I mean—I—"

I'm too tired to even come up with a lie.

"Is that why she keeps you here? She uses your powers?"

"She doesn't use me." I can't believe I'm covering for Fawn. Nausea overwhelms me.

"You know, there's something off with everything you say."

His hands leave the camera, and I have his full attention. "It's like you're saying two things at once. It's *not* nothing."

I push my hair back, away from my forehead. I'm still getting used to how little of it there is. I put the butterfly pin I *stole* in my hair this morning. It's like a silent form of rebellion, and I love that.

Mason's insightfulness scares me.

"You need to leave," I tell him. "After Fawn takes her nap and goes back to The Outside, I'm sending you back up."

"You need to leave too," Mason says.

"I can't."

"Why not? You let her get away with this, treat you like this?"

"She's raised me," I argue. "We're a team. And anyway, it's not like I'm accepted out there anyway. It's always dangerous…I'm illegal."

There's another piece to this, but I won't tell Mason. I can't. I'm embarrassed that the truth will launch him into an even longer soliloquy about me leaving…and I'm afraid he'll plant a seed inside of me that cannot be watered.

Fawn will always know where I am: my tracking device will betray me.

Mason's frown deepens. "I really don't like this situation."

"It's not your problem."

"I know about it now, though."

"Listen," I say, taking a step towards him. "I'm okay. Really, I am. I'm used to this. I know how to survive."

"Surviving isn't necessarily living."

I can't believe I'm arguing with this boy who's practically a stranger. "All I'm focused on right now is figuring out how to get *you* out of here."

We're silent for a moment. It hits me that I'm having an

argument. An argument with a boy. I have terrible points, but we're arguing nonetheless.

He breaks through the silence.

"Could you...would you be able to find out what happened to my parents?"

TEN
ADELAIDE

I look him in the eyes. They're so different from Fawn's. There's no accusation.

"N-no. That would be bad. I can't." I rub my fingers over the pin, cold and dainty.

"You can't? Or you won't?"

"Do you not understand what *no* means?" My laugh is bitter.

"I just…" Mason shuffles in place. Then he looks up at me, his softness hardening. "Hey, you're obviously not telling me everything about yourself."

I bristle. "You have no right to know everything about me."

The sentence is harsher than it should be. I'm sure I hurt his feelings. I keep my eyes on the floor, refusing to look at him.

"I'm sorry. I just…I've just felt lost for a long time and I thought maybe you were my answer," he says. I still don't bring my eyes to meet his, afraid I'll crack if I do. "I've given myself goals and I try to work hard every day, but…there's a part of me that just feels empty. I need to know where I came from, who my parents are. It would give me so much peace."

He gives me a little grin. I look down; he does something to me when I'm around him. I guess…I guess he makes me feel like I'm a human.

"You won't tell anyone about my…um, Memory Jumping. Right?"

I feel like a priest caught drinking the communion wine. I was so close to getting out of this predicament with minor implications. Sure, Fawn yelled at me for getting lost, but she hadn't discovered I had talked to someone.

And it was a boy.

And he was in my house.

And he knew about Memory Jumping.

I start sweating like a sailor crossing the bar. And Mason is loving every second of it, judging by the size of his smirk.

"Now, why would I go and do a thing like that?"

"Listen—I'm illegal," I say, knowing full well the jig is up. "You knowing this now, I could be in a lot of danger. And so could you."

"Don't worry, I'm not going to tell anyone about the underground girl who Memory Jumps."

His eyes scan the walls of my room. The tower of Pisa in Italy, the Eiffel tower in Paris, and the pyramids in Egypt. "Is this what you'd do if you could leave this place? Travel?"

"Absolutely," I say. "It's a shame that there's a whole world out there, but some people live their whole lives behind their front door. I think everyone should travel—if they can."

Mason is lost in thought; Fawn gets that look on her face all the time too. But somehow I can tell that if I were to start talking now, he'd listen. "Agreed. So…Memory Jumping. Not mind reading?"

"I mean…it's *kind of* like mind reading." I've never had to explain it to anyone. Fawn always does all the explaining before our client even gets here. "As in, I can get into people's memories and read them. But it's a much more involved process than being a psychic."

"So…"

I sigh. "I can edit old memories and create new ones."

He rattles that around his brain for a few minutes. I can just see the question marks adding up. This conversation is never going to end. "But how?"

If I had a dime for every time someone's asked me that… "I don't know. I just do."

Mason chews my revelation over. "Tell you what: if you Memory Jump on me, I'll bring the world to you."

"What does that mean?"

"Well, you dream of traveling, right? But you can't—*won't*—leave." I scrunch my eyes and shake my head in confusion. "Typical girl-stuck-in-a-metal-box syndrome."

I don't say a word. He continues. "Ever heard of Rapunzel?"

"Of course." I've had plenty of time to read all the old fairy tales, fables, and myths.

"You remind me of her. You even…had the long hair."

I shrug.

He walks closer to me, eyes big and innocent. "Memory Jump on me."

I stare at him, locked in his gaze.

Mason's confidence drops. "Wait…Memory Jumping doesn't…hurt, does it?"

I glance at the doorway, expecting Fawn to burst in. "No, of course not."

He tilts his head, grins, and raises his eyebrows. I can almost hear his thoughts: *Well then, why not?*

My eyes slide to the Eiffel tower, standing stalwartly

against the white wall. All my life I've stared at that wall and pretended I was actually in other countries, surrounded by real people, breathing real air, feeling real freedom.

Every strand of my being is telling me yes. It's Fawn's voice in my head, her dark eyes watching me that scares me.

"Tell you what," Mason starts. "I'll bring you your first country tomorrow and then you can decide if it's worth Memory Jumping on me."

For a second, a summer breeze whispers across my shoulders. The smell of rain dances near my nostrils.

"All right."

"Really?" His eyebrows soar up as if doing a victory dance.

"Yeah," I say.

"Great! *Thunk, tap-tap, thunk, tap, thunk, stomp*, right?"

"Yup. Fawn usually leaves at two to go to town. She finds and meets clients."

We pause.

"Now what?" Mason asks.

"We wait until Fawn wakes up."

"How long will that be?"

"Half an hour. She believes in cat naps."

"Would it be a bad time to tell you I have to go to the bathroom?"

I snort. "Are you kidding me?"

"Wait—you don't have your own bathroom, do you?"

"No, it's at the end of the hall. There are other cameras—"

"I already fixed all of those from the one in your room, no problem. It was too easy not to."

I'm pretty sure this is a dream. I'm going to wake up, hop out of bed, and realize that my friend doesn't even exist. "We just have to hope that Fawn doesn't come out of her room. You can't hold it?"

Mason only needs to dip his chin slightly for me to know that's a dumb question. I tiptoe over to the door.

"What, does she have super-hearing too?" Mason whispers, and I burn a hole through his face with my fiery, hushing gaze.

I return to my work, turning the doorknob in slow-motion. I know just how to pull the door so that it doesn't squeak; it's good for the first couple of inches but there's this awful spot in the middle where it calls me out sometimes. I fling it open at that part and the door is silent as an assassin.

I stick my head out in the hallway like a periscope. There's no sound. I head into the hallway and Mason follows.

We shuffle like spies and I hear a conversation going on somewhere. Fawn usually falls asleep watching a home renovation show or listening to a podcast about gardening even though we don't have a garden. I think she likes ripping on all the dumb questions and calling people *hillbillies* for caring what kind of fertilizer they should use.

Mason and I take a right and I point at the door to the bathroom, which is right across from Fawn's bedroom.

I point towards her room, and he gets my message: *I'm guarding in case she comes out.* He darts into the bathroom and closes the door a bit too fast. I jump like I'm doing something awful like, I don't know, stealing the *Mona Lisa*.

In my nervousness, I rock back and forth. *It's okay, it's okay, it's okay. Fawn would forgive me.* I make up an excuse for standing out here and getting Fawn to leave if she happens to appear.

I'm just taking a break from my room.

I'm contemplating a book I just read.

I'm trying to get up the courage to ask her about something.

I beg life to give me a break. I just need a minute. Maybe two. Then it'll all be okay.

A door clicks, and I'm so scared that I nearly slap myself in the face; it's just Mason, though. He tiptoes (rather poorly) back to me, and we head back to my room. He starts whisper-laughing, which makes me start giggling. We hurry-scurry even faster, shuffling more loudly than we should.

Then another door slams. It's like someone smacked me in the stomach; all the breath rushes out of my lungs.

I shove Mason toward my room.

As he flees for shelter, I can't decide what to do. Fawn will need a reason for the noises she heard. Maybe I can hang out in the hallway? Run to the bathroom? I dart towards the bathroom, then change direction and go to my room, but my body propels forward and somehow I end up on the floor…not one of my options.

"What are you doing?" Fawn shrieks.

"Sorry, I fell." At least that's the truth.

Fawn stares at me like I'm insane as I pull myself up. And maybe I am insane because, again, my dumb body wants to laugh. Why do I find moments like these hilarious? "You really are a ditz."

Her words don't sting for once. I just think about the boy in my room. I stand a little bit taller as she swivels around and stomps off.

Back in my room, I dig around for a recipe for tomorrow. I'm going Thai; I make a mean pad thai. Mason asks me to play a card game, and I promise to just as I find the recipe. He has Skip-Bo in his fanny pack, so I join him in the closet and we begin a round. I forget about Fawn for a blissful ten minutes.

Mason is unceremoniously beating me when the room door bangs open. I drop all the cards in my hands.

"Adelaide?" Again? What even.

I seize the door to the closet and twist it, then promptly fall out.

"What are you doing in the closet?" Fawn stands in the doorway. Her face no longer shows any trace of anger.

"Organizing." I don't miss a beat. She lies to me well; I can lie to her too.

"There's a lump of dried-out clay on your wheel. Wanna explain that to me?"

My eyes widen. Oops. I got distracted by…a boy. "Um…I guess I just forgot."

Fawn's always saying I'm forgetful. I might as well play that card. But there's something in her eyes…she knows what game she's playing. And she doesn't like when I start figuring out how to sort cards to my advantage.

She beams at me and throws her arms out in front of her. I let her hug me.

"Just thought I'd let you know I'm going out," she coos. "I'll be back tomorrow morning." *Where are you going? What are you doing? Can I come?* So many questions, and none of them leave my mouth.

"Okay."

"I love you." The words are empty. Useless. *She loves me, she loves me, she loves me.* She leaves the room and I return to my friend.

He sits on the ground, shuffling cards.

"Adelaide?"

"Oh, yeah…I'm sorry." I sit on the ground, crossing my legs. "I didn't think it would be safe to tell you my real name."

He picks at some gunk on one of his cards. "Understandable. I like Adelaide anyway. Can I call you Addy?"

My heart jumps. "No. That's what Fawn calls me when she—when she's mad at me."

He stares at me as if asking for more information, but I just readjust how I'm sitting. He starts shuffling cards again. They make this really thick, satisfying sound.

"She plays games with me," I confide. "*Mind* games."

I can't help myself; the words keep coming. I never complain about Fawn, largely because I have no one to complain to.

Instead, I complain to my bookshelf.

My skillet.

The occasional animal that appears on the wall scenery.

Once I've started, I can't stop.

"She tells me she loves me; she pretends like nothing ever happened. Like my hair isn't barely below my ears because she overreacted."

Mason just sits there. Maybe he's chewing over my words. Maybe he zoned out. Boys don't seem too good at being consoling. "One minute, she's screaming at me. The next, she's hugging me."

"She's narcissistic. And nuts," he finally says. "But I was right. She did cut your hair."

I bite my lip. I can't comment on that, or else it'll open doors which should stay shut. "Mason…what makes a Mom to you?"

"Fawn isn't your real mom. She's not even a fake mom."

Part of me wants to stand up to Fawn, but the other part is broken. "She takes care of me; she houses me; she feeds me and clothes me."

"That's not a mom," Mason says. He adjusts himself on the floor and rolls his shoulders out. "A mom loves self-sacrificially. She's supposed to be your number one cheerleader, your number one advice-giver. Yeah, she's a promoter of tough love, but—"

"Fawn is the definition of tough love."

"Tough, yeah. But…love?"

"Well, then what is she?"

I never wanted to ask that question. I'm convinced Fawn knows of my betrayal at this moment.

Mason is thoughtful. "A jailer."

I don't say anything.

"I'm going to write up that program," Mason promises. "I'll show you how to delete the footage and change the timestamp."

He sets his cards down and pulls out his device. He swipes across and a screen appears. It's about the span of my arms, all pixelated and see-through. Mason clicks on the *Footage* tab and finds a spot with him in it.

"I've assigned any face that looks like mine the title *X7* and hidden it so Fawn won't see I created a face file. Now I just type *X7* in here and it'll delete any footage with me in it." He types the letter and number into a box on the top right of the screen and then hits enter.

"Now you'll have to go up here—see this tab?—and click *Edit timestamp*. Switch it to *consecutive* and it'll make the time consistent so there are no missing minutes."

I watch him carefully. "Can you write this down?"

Mason shakes his head no. "I don't believe Fawn. I think she's told you lies for so long, you just accept them without question. You're smart. Don't ever forget that. I told you you're forgetful when I first met you, and I'm sorry. I misjudged you."

I don't believe him. I'd like to, but I can't. "Please write it down."

"That you're smart?"

I giggle. The sound is foreign. "No. The instructions for the security camera." His ocean eyes look into mine. I wonder if other human eyes are this beautiful.

He sighs and nods. "Okay. Yeah, I'll do it. And here, you can have this." He hands me his device. "It's called a Communicator; I can get another one *a lot* more easily than you could."

"Wait—seriously?" I take the Communicator, gratefulness swelling up inside of me.

"Yeah, everyone should have one." I think about refusing to keep it for a second...but then a dangerous part of me surfaces, a part that has no second thoughts and absolutely no remorse.

Do something Fawn wouldn't like, for once in your life. I clutch the Communicator, wondering who I'm becoming...and if it's a good thing.

"I'll just write the instructions down on old-fashioned paper. Have a pen?"

I nod and walk over to my desk. There's a huge flamingo-shaped cup and a plastic case, both full of writing things, on my desk. I grab a black marker and then give it to Mason. He stands there and scribbles out the instructions.

Once he's done, he slides the last of his cards into the box.

"This—the security camera thing—that's not the only thing I can do. But I want to ask for your permission."

Okay, he's got my curiosity up 1000%. "What is it?"

"If—*when* I finish my robot—I'm going to have you test it out first. We can make Fawn think it's you and then you can leave this place forever."

My mouth opens and I just sit there shaking my head. "Why would you use it for me?"

"Well...in order to be a Kendrorian inventor, you have to prove that your invention works." I love watching him talk about something he's so passionate about. Every facial movement is more pronounced, and his smile widens to such a distance I fear it'll ping right off of his face. "The more hard evidence you have, the better. If I can prove that my robot is *so good* that a—a, um, *woman* like your mother wouldn't notice we've replaced you with it, they would *have* to let me into Kendror."

I hope for his sake that it works. But the hope doesn't quite reach my heart.

So Mason's promise of freedom was only a beautiful lie to me. And I would lock it away in my heart.

But I tell Mason what he wants to hear: "*When* you build your robot, let's come back to this conversation. I need to think about it. I'm not against you using my story for evidence, but…I just…leaving is a big deal."

Fawn would find me so quickly. And I don't know what she'd be capable of if my escape were unsuccessful.

Her anger is volcanic, her forgiveness petty and fleeting.

How miserable could she make my life? How far would we have to run in order for her to not be able to catch up with us?

These questions are foolish to ask.

"I get it," he says. "Take your time. No rush."

Mason and I chat a little bit longer before he says goodbye and that he'll come back tomorrow.

Beautiful promises. That's what my life is made up of.

And, as usual, I let my head believe it even though my heart doesn't.

I escort him to the teleporter and he leaves. All I can do is stand rooted to my place as I hear the teleporter power up and whir far away from me.

ELEVEN
ADELAIDE

USELESS FACT #203

Daydreaming is linked to solving difficult problems; the more you daydream, the better you are at dealing with complex situations.

I lay on my bed. Mason's promise yesterday to bring the world to me has caused my creative mind to explode with daydreams.

I'm paddling down a canal in Venice, wearing a flowing red dress and holding a parasol. Someone plays a melancholy violin, and I lean over to request he switch to a more uplifting song when I'm interrupted by the signal.

Thunk, tap-tap, thunk, tap, thunk, stomp.

I leave Venice and reenter the real world. I get to the teleporter as quickly as humanly possible. I push the button to let Fawn enter and lean against the wall to wait for her.

But, when the door opens, what I see makes my stomach drop like an overweight mosquito. Fawn drags a body through the doors like it's totally normal.

"Who is this?"

Fawn doesn't answer me. She simply barks, "He fainted from fear, I think. Help me with him."

I grab the body's legs. I can see now that it's a boy, perhaps late teens, but very small and ill-proportioned.

Fawn is breaking all her own rules. First, she took me outside. Now, we're Memory Jumping on someone who's barely not a child. We've never Memory Jumped on someone my age. The youngest might've been twenty-five or twenty-seven.

Another realization hits me: Fawn has brought him for me to...I feel like throwing up. She's going to make me *experiment* on him for Mr. Green.

I want to go back to yesterday when Mason was playing cards with me in my closet. It's like I have to start living my nightmare again.

Fawn and I drag the man into the living room and dump him onto the couch. Well, *she* dumps him. I remember he's a human and ensure all his appendages are in non-awkward positions.

"Try to Memory Jump on him. Now listen: being unconscious inhibits the firing of neurons." Fawn thinks she's speaking above my level of knowledge. "When you go in there, try to find where these neurons are firing. Watch the pattern. If he begins to come into consciousness, you need to shut it down and send him back to unconsciousness."

Her eyes soften a bit, and she throws me a grin. "I'll make you some hot chocolate with whipped cream when you get back."

Does she really think whipped cream can convince me to obey her?

Fawn's eyes glint, and I know it's either whipped cream or a completely emptied room. She'll take away all my hobbies, all the things that sidetrack me. And what will I be left with then?

My eyes sweep over the body. I take a seat on the table behind me. "Do you have any of that dark chocolate mix left?"

"Atta girl. I'll be right back. Go ahead." I turn my conscience off.

Stop, it says. *Stand up against her!*

My conscience gives up almost as soon as I tell it to but leaves a trail of tears in its wake. My hand brushes against the man's forehead before I remember how I Memory Jumped without any skin contact the other day. I wonder if I can do that again. I'll try later, when I'm less flustered.

I've shot myself into the boy's memory. It's so very cold and dark. But it *is* possible for me to enter an unconscious person's mind. *Good job, Adelaide.*

Everything is black, unlike anything I've ever felt before. It's the feeling of being home by yourself at night, not knowing when companionship will return.

But how do I turn his brain on without turning *him* on?

Occasionally, little glints of color pulsate around me like brainwaves attempting to send. They're like lightning in the midst of a great, puffy black cloud. One comes from behind me, and by the time I whirl around, it's gone. Then one brightens up the area to my right. It's brighter than the previous one. And yet another one, this a light blue and barely even there, coming from my left.

I hunch down the tiniest bit, preparing myself to spring at the next blob of color. It flashes in front of me, and I lunge, totally missing. But it's a good idea, and I try again. And again. And again.

One time I'm so close, the heat emanating from the color warms my hand. Finally, I time my jump right and touch the color. It stays in my hands, not disappearing like its brothers. It's crazy hot at first, but then the warmth floods out, and ice replaces it. I squeeze it a bit, and the black surrounding me flashes red. I'm afraid I'm hurting the man, and I almost drop the color.

I pull at the color and it stretches like one of Fawn's resistance bands. Another flash comes from my right, and I grab it and smash it together with the one I already have. The black flashes white, and a bit of color appears before melting back into black. I must be gathering his conscience.

More colors shoot across from me and I collect them like one collects apples or blueberries, smashing them together with the other ones like mental Playdough. Every time, the white stays a bit longer and the colors solidify into more solid objects. I think they're doors.

Suddenly, the blackness seemed to shift. I tilt a bit, which makes no sense since I am suspended in space without any floor for gravity to hold me to. Then it happens again, stronger. Soon, I am bobbing up and down. I drop the consciousness and whimper.

I was so close.

Something is wrong. I shoot myself out of the boy's head and find myself lying across the living room table. My heart beats and a migraine eats away at my brain. I scrunch my eyes together to deal with the pain.

"Addy, what happened?" Fawn asks. Before I can answer, the boy shrieks and I shoot straight upwards.

"Who are you? What...I'm..." The boy has woken up. Fawn takes one quick look at the boy and then glares at me. Obviously, this is all *my* fault.

My temple throbs. I give him my best smile, my brain crying out against me; it isn't the warm one Mason always provokes. My brain begins to replay the moments I've smiled at his humor, but I then freeze: Why did I think of Mason so quickly? How is he so effortlessly becoming a part of my life? I note the warm undertone of the memory.

"It's okay," I tell the boy, even though it isn't. "We're not going to hurt you."

"Can you not do *anything*?" Fawn thunders, not worrying about scaring the boy. "I told you exactly what to do."

The boy's hair flops everywhere. The couch has smooshed it, so while one side puffs out, the other is glued to his head.

"Memory Jump on him so he thinks we're his aunt and cousin," Fawn demands. The boy stares at me with big, scared eyes that beg me to have some decency.

But I'm not even free enough to be kind.

I obey Fawn and Memory Jump while he's still awake. I manipulate a new memory, one where he's visiting his aunt and cousin for a few days. When I get back into the dining room, he's smiling at Fawn with warm recollection.

"Would you like some hot chocolate, dear?" Fawn asks with her heart-stopping smile.

"Yes ma'am," the boy answers.

The hot chocolate will be drugged.

When Fawn brings back three hot chocolates, I'm too scared to even drink mine. She's careful to give him a blue mug, but I don't trust the mug she gives me. And the idea of enjoying a hot chocolate makes my stomach turn.

Once the boy is unconscious, Fawn slams her mug down on the table and demands an explanation as to why I failed the first time.

"It was like...playdough and stars and colors." I can hardly describe it to her. "I don't understand it though, and I don't want to—"

"You're going to do this," Fawn hisses.

I can't help myself; my lips pucker and my cheeks tighten.

A fat tear slips out of my eyes, holds onto my eyelashes for a second, and then streams down my cheek.

Her face melts and she tosses her hand down my cheek lovingly, catching the tear trekking down my face. "Listen, you can do this. I know you can."

"I'm sorry," I manage to choke. Forcing the words out somehow makes more tears fall. "I just..."

"Listen, this job is extremely important to me. To us! We won't have to hide down here anymore." She flicks her eyes up and they look at my hair. She runs her fingers through a bit of it with a smile. "You will get what you want. We'll be able to go outside."

"What if I can't do it?"

Her smile loses its genuineness but grows anyway. "You can. You must. And you will."

She shoves me gently towards the boy. His chest balloons in and out, slowly, peacefully. He's okay. Scared, maybe. But we aren't hurting him. For a moment, I wonder what Fawn will do with him after the experiment.

Experiment.

I shiver. What am I doing? I throw all my feelings away and focus only on the task at hand.

Fawn will have her way, one way or the other. And I'd rather it not be the other.

I take a break from Memory Jumping after nearly five hours of attempts. I mention my migraine and she turns ashen, practically dragging me away from the boy. She says she's going to get Mr. Green and will be back in a few minutes.

"Go, reset," she demands. "Do your pottery or something. You need to take a break."

I hide away in my pottery room, my migraine lessening as I get into the rhythm of molding the clay. I pack pottery orders while Fawn is gone and set the orders by the teleporter for her to bring to Kendror later. I start on more pottery orders. People are ordering mugs like crazy, which are my favorite thing to make anyway. I finish two more mugs before Fawn comes back.

I let the teleporter come down. When the teleporter doors open, I'm surprised to see that Green's lost the bandana. He looks like he's in his late forties, with a rugged nose and a gray beard streaked with black.

The two are deep in conversation and don't bother greeting me, so I just escort them to the living room where they take a seat on the small couch, leaving no room for me. Forever a parenthetical statement, I sit on the living room table.

One of my notebooks and a lone marker lie on the table, so I pick them up and doodle. I'm part of Fawn and Green's conversation but only by default. No one ever asks for my opinion.

I feel like a child, coloring and listening to the big people making plans without me.

"It's going well," Fawn lies. "We're making progress."

"Making progress?" He knows I'm failing, I'm sure of it. I look up from my drawing, and Green's eyes stare at me, dark and accusatory. I shrink back. His irritation is completely pointed at me, whereas Fawn's dark beauty and constantly unimpressed personality has captivated him. I can feel the imprint she's left on his mind, how he holds memories of her close at hand. And yet…they're filled more with admiration than romantic feelings.

Someone else holds his heart.

"Can the girl Memory Jump on an unconscious human or

not?" Oh good. I don't have a name.

She can't, I answer mentally.

"She can. All good things take time."

"I'd rather it not take all the time we have."

But Fawn is as put-together as a politician. She gives her sparkly smile, and Mr. Green relaxes the tiniest bit. "Mr. Green, I also have consulted some top Envisioners on this project. Have you had any dealings with Envisioners?"

"I know what they are, yes. Never done it myself."

Fawn's grin is double-sided, beautiful on the outside but actually quite fangy. "You *have* to meet them and see the Envisioning for yourself. It was…stunningly positive, to say the least."

Green looks anything but impressed. In fact, he looks bored.

"Yes, I'd like to see that. All right, you can have another week."

"Lovely." They both rise at exactly the same time. Fawn extends her hand and gives Mr. Green a solid handshake. Mr. Green glances at me and I pop up and shake his hand as well.

"I'll be back in a week," the man says.

"Perfect. We look forward to your visit." She escorts him to the teleporter, says a few other sickeningly sweet things, and waves as the teleporter doors close. She stands silently until we hear the teleporter stop at the top and whir to teleport him. Then she grits her teeth and throws her hands in the air.

"What an absolute idiot," she vents. I throw myself onto the couch in the living room and run my hands down my face. "Stop that, Addy, you'll get acne and *that's* a memory I won't be able to wipe from my brain."

She chuckles at her brilliant joke. I immediately remove my hands from my face.

"We're going to have to figure this out. You need to practice every minute of the day, with minimal breaks. I'm also going to look at my book." By *my book*, she means a rather thick psychology textbook she purchased in The Outside a long time ago. Although I do almost all of the actual work, it sometimes helps when Fawn can explain to me the inner workings of the human brain.

"Okay." I don't complain. I don't dare to.

"Let's go get the boy," Fawn says. She doesn't know I've named him Tommy. Makes him less of a guinea pig.

We—well, *she*—stuck him in my bedroom closet before Mr. Green visited (the closet is starting to become a hot spot for teen guys, apparently). Green knew we were working on Memory Jumping on unconscious humans, but he didn't need to see our methods.

Fawn likes to act as if doing things like that makes our clients innocent, but in my mind they are equally as guilty. Mr. Green gave us permission to practice on unconscious humans, and he doesn't care how we got that done. I know it isn't right to mess with other peoples' memories, especially without their consent…and maybe, sometimes, even with.

TWELVE
ADELAIDE

We get Tommy, and I make him comfortable on the couch as Fawn goes to get her shoes so she can head into town. He's out like a home run. I take my seat on the table and cross my legs, crunching my eyes in concentration. What am I missing?

Fawn leaves. I know Mason is coming and I desperately want to just wait for him, but I know I need to use this time to practice on Tommy.

I told Mason that Fawn leaves at 2:00. I check the time. It's 1:00. I fidget. What if he doesn't come?

No! I tell myself to get rid of that thought. I Memory Jump on Tommy for a good half hour, but I'm so antsy about my visitor that I can't focus. I don't catch a single glowing color, and my hands wobble.

I decide that Fawn won't mind if I pause just for a little bit. I go to the kitchen and look for something to do: dishes to clean, groceries to stock. There are dishes, and it looks like the twins dropped off our groceries this morning before I woke up. I wash the measly four plates and six utensils.

Then I put all the groceries away and tell myself to move slowly.

At 2:10, I am slowly, but regally, dying. I play a mind game with myself. I'm refusing to admit I'm scared Mason isn't going to come, but I pretend I never thought that.

It's not even on my mind. I don't care if Mason comes or not.

At 2:36, the signal comes from above. For reasons I can't explain, my heart bangs against my chest like a bird trying to escape. I press the button on the teleporter and smooth my hair down at the same time.

The teleporter takes too long to slide down, and then even longer for the doors to whoosh open. Mason stands there, at first just a little sliver of dirty blonde hair, a light gray shirt, and jeans. Then the doors open all the way. His presence smacks me in the face like an elephant. I figure I'm just amazed because he's the first person besides Fawn, Buddy, and Perkins I've ever talked to more than a few times.

"Hi," I say, almost shy.

"Hey," he replies. He has a bundle in his right arm, wrapped in brown paper and twine. He catches me looking at it hungrily. "I've got your Piece of the World. *And* I brought you a Communicator."

My hands grip each other and fly up to my face. I feel dangerous, wild. I never do things I'm not supposed to do, and here I am breaking all the rules.

Mason walks out of the teleporter and follows me toward the living room when—oh, crap, Tommy is still in there. I stop abruptly, and Mason almost bumps into me. The space between us grows smaller, and I smell him. It's something clean and fresh—like the color white, like something fluffy I want to bury my face in.

"We can stay in here," I say.

"Why, is Fawn in the living room?" He laughs but I just chuckle.

"It's a long story. Let's just stay here." He accepts my answer. It's weird to be in charge for once. I take a seat right there in the entryway, and he copies me.

"Okay," he says, pulling the bundle out from under his arm. "Today's country: France."

My fingers flex, eager to dig into the package.

"I figured we would start with the countries on your walls," he explains. I nod, not really caring what he has to say.

He thrusts the package at me, and I tear into it like a madman. "You even wrapped it?"

"My aunt did." The paper flies everywhere and reveals a miniature Eiffel tower made of metal stencils, a print of the *Mona Lisa*, and paintbrushes.

"Where did you find these?" I breathe.

"I trade stuff for fun when I'm not doing techy stuff. I've had the Eiffel tower for a while; I gave it to Pippa but she didn't want it. She pretended she did, but she's awful at pretending." I love the way his eyes soften when he talks about Pippa. "And these paintbrushes are actually from Paris. Got them last week from a man carrying a monkey."

I explode into laughter. "A monkey?"

"No joke," Mason says, chuckling as well. "The monkey was wearing a red vest."

I smile. I laugh too. "These are beautiful!"

I run my fingers across the *Mona Lisa*. It's a small print, just a little bigger than my hand. I look deep into Mona's eyes. Does she want freedom, like me?

Mason starts humming again.

"What's that song you're always singing?"

He looks confused for a second, as if he doesn't realize he was humming. "I don't know the title, but I think it's an old folk song. It's *so* catchy—learned it from one of the shop-keepers in town."

"Pretty." He begins humming again and I just listen. It sounds, if I can even say this, hopeful with a bittersweet tinge.

"Does it have words?"

"Yeah," he says, "but I'm bad at singing."

"Well then, could you look it up? You hum, and I'll sing it." He pulls out his Communicator and finds the words.

> *My father was a sparrow,*
> *My mother was a dove.*
> *The only thing they ever taught*
> *Was how to spoil love.*
> *Call me jaded, call me sad.*
> *You don't have it half as bad.*
> *And the only thing to do*
> *Was make sure I never flew:*
> *Clipped my wings,*
> *Clipped my wings,*
> *"You don't need those silly things.*
> *All that flying does is show you*
> *All the wealth of foolish kings.*
> *You may soar beside the clouds*
> *But all this foolishness allows*
> *Is a higher view*
> *Of this cruel world*
> *That we blindly call our home."*

"Jeez," Mason chuckles, almost like he's uncomfortable. "I actually never heard that first stanza before. What a downer! I know the second stanza better."

So I took all of my treasures
And sold them at the fair
And with all of what I had left
I bought something quite rare
Call me naïve, call me fool,
I've been called names way more cruel.
With my boat and oars, I fled
To the sea, and then I said,
"Got my wings, Got my wings,
How I love these silly things!
Even though I see the pain in life
I accept the joy it brings.
As I row like I can fly
I now know the answer why
All the bitter folk
End up sad and broke:
They just focus on the dark."

Mason joins me in singing this stanza. His voice isn't crazy beautiful, but it's deep and real. To me, that's a type of beauty I can appreciate.

"Your voice is really nice," Mason says. I grin.

"Thanks. I love singing."

"You should make a recording. I hereby name this song…*Her Wings.*"

"Maybe that'll be my next music project!"

"Do it!" Mason agrees. Then, he almost shyly says, "So…"

I remember why he brought me the knick-knacks: to convince me to Memory Jump. Why am I so afraid, honestly? I close my eyes and tell myself everything will be okay.

"How does this work?" Mason asks. "Are you just gonna sit there and meditate?"

I laugh and my eyes pop back open. "Not exactly."

"So, run me through your process. Like, when I have a new invention idea, I have a process I follow to make it a reality. What's your Memory Jumping process?"

I cross my legs and place my hands in my lap. "I just kind of…do it. I focus all my energy on my goal and then I just… transmit myself into your memory."

"What does it look like in there?"

I lean back and imagine it inside my own mind. "There are doors. Lots of doors. Each brain is different, though. Some are dark, some are bright. Some have colors, some don't. Just really depends."

"I wonder what my brain will look like."

"Guess I'm gonna find out." I scratch at a burn I got on my finger from making dinner last night. I was so dumb; I stuck my hand in the oven to flip the chicken and raised my hand a bit too much. It stung so bad.

"Okay! I'm ready." I move to put my hand on his forehead. I know I don't technically have to, but I'm so dizzied by his presence that I don't know if I can do it otherwise.

"Whoa, high tech," Mason laughs.

"Sorry."

"Don't apologize. You don't have to apologize to me." His forehead is so warm and so real. I have a theory that Fawn's forehead is cold and lifeless; I bet you couldn't even feel her pulse.

I close my eyes, feel my target, and Memory Jump.

His mind is heavy with intelligence. All the doors are individual memories arranged in precise alphabetical *and* chronological order. I'm sure not a speck of dust can be found on each doorframe, and the knobs themselves shine brilliantly.

I walk down the hallway and search for the earliest memory Mason has. That's always a good place to start piecing peoples' pasts together. I read some of the labels on the doors.

"Fixing Mrs. Pressley's Communicator."

"Hacking Norman's security system."

"Monkey with a vest." I smile at that one.

I swipe my hand and the doors shoot past me. I swipe again, more doors flying past. Finally, my hand hits an invisible wall, and I pause.

The last door looks just like all the other doors. I rotate the handle and open the door. Inside is a small boy with a slightly dirtied blue shirt and giant, glittering blue eyes, such a familiar color. I feel myself gasp a little. I know without a doubt that he's Mason.

The little boy throws a ball in the air. It looks to be some kind of game; sometimes it floats midair, sometimes it comes back down, sometimes it flickers green. Little Mason cheers when he catches the ball. I half expect him to be surrounded by other children, but then I remember that he was raised as an only child just like me.

There's another door where the little boy is all alone in a room, crying. No one comes to his rescue. No father rushes into the room to console him; no mother picks him up and plants loving kisses on his forehead.

This memory is so…hollow.

I frown a bit. These are the earliest memories he has, and he must've been at least four. These are memories that, although not always easily recovered, are still remembered. I'll have to go down to his subconscious and check there for earlier memories.

I leave the room. I wonder if Mason had a good childhood. I wish I could give his smaller self a hug and tell him everything is gonna be okay, but these are just his interpretations of events.

No matter what, I can never change reality, only the way it was perceived. But I've learned that often, memories are even stronger than reality.

Getting to the subconscious is kind of tricky. There's always a hidden staircase. Usually, it's by the last memory in the person's mind. I kick around the area but don't feel anything. I walk a bit further away from the last memory. My foot catches on something and the black ground starts coming toward my face as I fall. I hit the ground; it's the strangest feeling, like a fuzzy mattress that is falling apart. Bits of the floor form a gradient to the sky, little chunks of blackness floating around like spotty bits of a cloud.

Found it.

I bring myself back up to my feet and kick around carefully. I locate where the staircase begins. Once I grip the handrail, the stairs melt into existence and I climb down. This one is a spiral staircase, black and pointed and ominous. Every subconscious I've been in has been a bit foreboding. Guess it's just part of the territory.

I climb into blackness. The first few times I did this, it really freaked me out, but now I feel more in control. The darkness goes on for a while and I continue climbing down, down, down.

The area around me begins glowing, which means I've almost reached the subconscious. A sudden rush of cold envelopes me, which is basically the welcome mat.

"Let's see what we have here," I say out loud. The glowing grows stronger, like I'm a human flashlight. Rows and rows of dark shelves spread around me, crammed to the brim with objects, memories, feelings, and desires.

Coming down here always feels wrong to me. The subconscious is almost the deepest part of a human, second only to the soul. I try to avert my eyes and not look too hard, but I still have to be looking. It's not usually organized down here. Hatred for a certain person sits right next to a memory long ago repressed; the desire to find a family is right above the need for independence.

My eyes sweep over everything, not totally processing everything I see. Memories hide in black boxes. The really deep ones are locked.

The memories aren't labeled. I feel weird opening them. I pause for a second. I have just enough doubt that I send myself out of Mason's mind. I'm moving a thousand miles an hour, shooting backward.

"Oh my gosh!"

I'm lying flat on the ground.

"Are you okay?"

I laugh, out of breath. "Yeah, that happens a lot actually."

I pull myself up, a bit dizzy from the feeling of leaving Mason's brain. "One second, you were just standing there and the next you, like, shot back and hit the ground!"

"Yeah, time stops when I Memory Jump."

"That's handy."

"Not when you charge by the minute." The humor falls out of my mouth, and I almost jump when Mason laughs. I've never thought of myself as funny. It's hard to when you live with someone who pretty much never laughs unless she's watching a rom-com. Or reruns of bad reality TV.

"So, did you find anything?"

I fall onto the couch, a respectful distance away from Mason. "No."

"Well then why'd you come back?"

I rub at the side of my head, a headache shaking my own brain. "It didn't feel right." The fog clears, and I look him in the eyes. "I was going to have to sift through a lot of your subconscious."

"That's okay with me," he says. "I don't mind."

"But all of your deepest, darkest secrets and desires are down there."

"Eh…well. I trust you. You're not going to judge or rifle around. It needs to be done."

He pulls a smile from me, but the seriousness of the situation subdues the happiness again.

"Please do it," he begs. "I want to know who my parents are."

I refuse to meet his gaze. It's easier for me to deny people if I'm not looking into their souls.

"Don't you want to know who your parents are, too?" Mason asks, his question chilling me. I bite the flesh of my lip, not hard enough to draw blood. "Can you go in your own memory? Find out who *your* real parents are?"

I laugh at Mason's ridiculous idea. "How does that even make sense?"

"How does you having the ability to transmit yourself into people's minds make any sense?"

I shrug. "You have a point."

"So, can you?"

"I've never tried. Maybe I'm a bit afraid to know."

"I'm scared too," he admits.

I pull my knees up to my chest. "I'm kind of tired."

Mason stands. I'm afraid he's going to leave. "No worries, I'm sure Memory Jumping is tiring. I think that's enough for one day."

My cheeks warm. He can't know I want him to stay.

"Okay. Sorry."

"No, I understand. Seriously, you shouldn't have to apologize all the time."

I don't look at him. I can feel his eyes watching me, and I hear him sigh.

"I guess you have to come back," I tell him.

"Well, yeah. Your end of the bargain isn't complete."

"Yeah."

Lucky me.

He presses the *up* button for the teleporter and says good-bye. He steps in, and the machine whirs as the doors close, carrying him to freedom, then only holding nothingness.

Empty as my heart.

Empty as my future.

USELESS FACT #3094

Spending a large amount of time with someone causes you to pick up their habits.

THIRTEEN
ADELAIDE

I hold the glowing orbs together. I am relaxed, but my hands are unyielding. I smoosh them and will them to unlock Tommy's mind.

The whole area around me pulsates and the glowing colors in my hands throb with heat. A few more fireworks of color explode around me and then...doors melt into existence. I whoop, dropping the lights. Nothing happens, and I leave them sitting there on the ground. I transmit myself out of Tommy's mind.

"I did it!" I sprint out of the living room and through the house. Fawn comes running out of her bedroom, wielding a half-closed bottle of red nail polish. "Fawn, I did it! I unlocked his mind!"

Her arms fall as a smile rises on her face. "That's my girl! I knew you could do it, Adelaide!"

I shriek and throw my hands in the air. *Finally.* I was so terrified of what would happen if I didn't pull this off.

"How did you do it?"

"He sensed my fear," I explained. "I had to be absolutely

calm. I also had to get one of each color within a sixty-second period or the brain would reset. I tried so many different combinations."

"So smart." Fawn pinches my cheek in a confusing gesture, then turns to go back to her room.

"So, can we let Tommy go now?" I laugh. "He sounds like some kind of animal. 'Can we let Tommy go…'"

Fawn stops walking, but it takes her a while to turn and face me. "Um…yeah. Yeah. We'll let him go."

I grin. "Great! Can we wake him up now?"

"No, he might try to get away. You have to go into his memory still and delete everything involving us."

"Right…sorry, I totally forgot." Fawn nods her forgiveness and I go back to the living room.

After I'm done, Fawn tells me to go into my room and do a few math lessons.

"How many have you done in the past few days?"

"I've gotten behind, sure, but I thought if anything we would celebrate—"

"Don't you want to finish school on time?" She's trying not to lose her temper. "There will be time for celebration once our deal with Mr. Green is done. Adelaide, with the money he's paying us, we could *move*."

My heart wants to believe her, but my head says *no*.

"Like maybe even to a different country. Where Memory Jumpers are *allowed*."

That does get my attention. "Wait, really?"

Fawn nods. "See what I said about this being life-changing? Just trust me."

Trust. What a silly concept for her to mention. I don't have the mental energy to believe or care about this offer, so I just nod.

Then I turn around and tell my feet to carry me forward

to my bedroom.

When I come back out to the living room later, Tommy is gone.

Fawn won't tell me what happened to him exactly. She said she let him go and then laughed like it was our cutesy inside joke or something.

"I wanted to tell him *bye* and thank him."

"You know we can't do that," Fawn scolds. "We have to protect ourselves—to protect you."

I start walking away, but Fawn calls me back.

"There's another part of this mission I need to discuss with you." She places a hand on my shoulder. Her eyes look straight into mine. I'm afraid she can read everything in my mind—that she knows about Mason and the Piece of the World he brought me yesterday.

I swear my face is dripping off of my skull; spikes of heat spread all throughout my body.

"I need you to take someone into the target's mind."

Did she really just say that? Nothing I do is ever good enough for her. I've barely even started celebrating being able to unlock an unconscious mind, then she demands this next impossibility of me.

Fawn's face melts into something that looks suspiciously like reassurance. "Don't freak out, Addy, I know it sounds crazy—"

"Impossible!" I'm really freaking out. I may actually lose it this time. "Fawn, I can't!"

"You can, and you will." Fawn's smile tightens and almost slingshots off her face. "You just haven't made up your mind to do it."

I stall for time. She can't actually think I'm going to go through with this.

"Would a girls' night tonight help convince you? We can… we can paint our nails and make brownies and watch a movie."

I raise my head, slightly convinced. "*To Catch a Thief?*"

"Whatever you want."

"Okay."

"That's my girl. That'll give you the energy and motivation to start this next step in Memory Jumping, right?"

Do I have a choice? "Yes, ma'am."

"*Perfect.* I'm going to go out and get our clients for the day. We can practice on them." *Without their permission.* Fawn doesn't say it, but I know it. I'm going to have to take Fawn into some poor stranger's mind. "I've left the pottery orders for today on the stool in the pottery room; oh, and your wire and things for the jewelry are in there somewhere too."

Fawn leaves, and I seek solace in the pottery room. I check the orders: another set of mugs, a pair of earrings, and a bowl. Plus, I need to make a *prototype* for my solar system earrings. Suddenly the pottery seems more like a chore than a stress reliever.

Mason is coming. My heart gets this weird flappy feeling. I force myself to settle down. My hands are steady as I drip water onto the clay and start the wheel spinning. I shove it towards the center and carve it with my hands. This is one thing that listens to me; when Fawn is around, I feel a lot like this clay. Being uncomfortably shoved around.

But now I'm the master. I pull up a wall, careful to keep my fingers an equal distance apart so the walls are equal. My hands are steady and focused. They know what they're doing; after all, I've been making pottery since I was ten. I finish the base and set it aside.

As I'm washing the clay off of my hands, the signal comes from above me. It hardly takes me a second to collect myself. I wipe my hands off on a towel and sprint to the teleporter. I press the button letting the teleporter come down.

The doors slide open and Mason's grin makes my world tilt and shine.

I accost him with joy. "What did you bring me today?"

"Whoa, whoa, whoa," Mason chuckles. He steps out of the teleporter, and it shifts. "Hello to you too."

"I'm sorry," I apologize, honestly worried I hurt his feelings.

He makes a face, and I remember our conversation from yesterday. "Ooh, I'm not supposed to do that. Right. I'm not sorry."

He laughs. I love making people laugh. He doesn't have his glasses on today. His eyes look even bigger than before and, without the glass to lessen their effect, they shine. "How are you doing?"

What a weird question to ask. I've never liked that greeting; so hollow. Because no one ever really can handle the truth. "I'm fine. You?"

"Great! Um, and at risk of being rude, I was wondering if...you could Mind Jump on me or whatever first?"

"Memory Jump," I correct. "And...I guess. Let's go to the living room."

I can't lie—I'm nervous, again. I have his permission to dig around, but I always feel like people don't understand how precious their brains are.

There's a reason we can survive solely on the money I make from my Memory Jumping. The things I've seen, the memories I've changed and deleted and added...Memories are powerful.

FOURTEEN
ADELAIDE

The last thing I see before I diffuse into Mason's mind is his eyes staring trustingly into mine. Then I'm back in his memory.

I find the staircase and climb down to his subconscious.

Everyone's subconscious smells different. The smells never mean anything to me, but I know that they would mean something to the person whose mind I'm in. Mason's subconscious smells like a Christmas tree. Fawn has never gotten us a Christmas tree; it's never really mattered to me whether it was Christmas or not, to be honest, so I haven't made a big deal about it. But, for a while, she was really into Christmas tree candles. I make a mental note to ask Mason about that later.

I rifle through the shelves. It's weird to be looking, but not really looking. Mason is right. There aren't any skeletons, at least that I can see.

Then...there's a golden sphere next to our country's flag. I pick it up and it feels like a memory: just a whisper of emotion, a tinge of reality, and a lot of warmth. I swipe my hand across it and it opens, displaying itself in the air like a hologram.

The memory is hazy and in black and white, slightly blurred, with a stain of confusion. Ah…this is a memory from when he was a baby.

Baby Mason focuses on a woman. Her eyes are adoring and she picks him up and holds him tight to her. Her hair is a mess, her eyes tired. The hug tightens and a man's face appears over her shoulder. He rubs a hand over baby Mason.

I memorize the faces. These must have been his parents. It'll be especially hard going off this since I don't even have the color of their hair or eyes. But from what I can tell, his mother has whitish blonde hair and his dad has hair anywhere on the scale of dark brown to black. One of them must have shocking blue eyes.

The memory fades out, and I release myself from Mason's brain.

"Nice landing," he says as soon as I open my eyes. "You aren't on the ground."

"Gee, thanks for reminding me about last time."

Mason sits there expectantly. I pause for a moment. "So?"

"Memories have smells sometimes, and yours smells like a Christmas tree. Why?"

He throws his hands in the air. "That's seriously what you have to report back?"

I shrink back. "I'm sorry."

"No, no—I'm joking," he says quickly. "I'm not actually mad."

"Oh." I sigh. "Okay. Um, but no, I'm really curious."

"I mean, I guess I do love Christmas," he says. "I've had a lot of great Christmases with Pippa. She gave me a lot of gifts that got me to where I am now, being an inventor and all that."

"That's a lame reason," I comment.

He puts his hands on his heart. "Well, I *am* sorry. Now, onto the *real* question: Did you find them?"

I pause for dramatic effect, then: "I saw them."

"Yes! You're the best!" He jumps off the couch and fires his questions. "How old was I? What did they look like? Who are they? Where were they?"

I throw my arms in front of me to shield myself from the bullet-like questions. "Mason, stop! I'll tell you everything, just be patient. You were less than six months old, so the memory was in black-and-white. You look more like your mother, even though she had lighter hair than you."

"And my dad?"

I smile. "He's very handsome. Kinda austere."

"So…where were they?"

"Mason…the thing about baby memories is that they are very, very murky." His smile drops. I feel like I had a present to give him but I unwrapped it first…and the present was awful. Now I'm scrambling to pick up the pieces of wrapping paper to paste them back on. "Babies don't know words, so they interpret things differently, sometimes not at all. They're confused and disoriented. Unfortunately, that's all the information I have."

"Oh." His head lowers, and he doesn't move.

"I'm sorry." So, so sorry. "But I know what they look like! Maybe…"

That won't help him. I can never go back to The Outside. I can't help him find his parents. And he's been so kind to me. What have I done for him? Taken away any hope he had, that's what.

"If you don't want to come back tomorrow, I understand."

I try to think of something inspiring to say, but all I can

think of are facts from the most recent biography I've been reading. And it's about Benedict Arnold.

USELESS FACT #293

When Benedict Arnold made his escape, George Washington was on his way to breakfast. Note: This is exceedingly unhelpful information.

"I really did try; I promise I did."

"I'm not mad at you," Mason says, laughing. "I'm just disappointed in myself, more than anything. I really thought this was gonna work."

I brush over his comment.

"You'll find your parents." There's that stupid, inspiring doodad I was looking for. "You're a smart guy. You'll figure it out."

"I guess." Yes, inspiring indeed.

"Hey, how's your robot coming? I really want to see it in action."

"I'm really close to finishing!" He leans into me. He has a very small personal bubble, which I'm not used to. Even now, it's like the space between us is buzzing, magnetic. He doesn't seem fazed, but he's so close that I can see the freckle dust resting on his cheekbones.

"How close are you?" I ask.

"Well, I'm working with this manufacturer of a new kind of material. They made this face that is so lifelike, it's almost scary. Skin is difficult to copy, in a lot of different ways. The look, the elasticity, the feel..."

"I won't pretend I know what you're talking about." I imagine Fawn walking in, and I actually don't get scared. Right now, I think I could tackle her to the ground. "I know you'll figure it out though."

AMANDA MICHELLE BROWN

He grins. "Yeah. I could be famous!"

Mason sits on the couch, and the warmth inside me instantly leaves. It's like when I was in Tommy's brain and I was deliciously warm for a second before the colors changed. "So, you ready for your Piece of the World?"

I grin, which is as much of a yes as he's going to get out of me since I'm so excited. He hands me a box, wrapped again. I tear it open and find three jars: one with seashells, one with sand, and one with water.

"It's the Atlantic Ocean," Mason says. I open the first jar and run my fingers over each seashell. They still have bits of gritty sand on them, but they're scalloped and beautiful. I especially love the cracked ones. I dig my finger through the beach sand and even dare to smell it. Mason laughs like I'm weird, which I am, but I don't care.

I love how the tiny grains of sand feel on my skin, a symphony of tickles marching across my fingers. My heart yearns for this world.

The last jar is seawater.

"There's an ocean just an hour from here," Mason tells me. "You would *really* love it."

I hold the water up to the light and it sparkles.

"You'll go there someday," Mason says.

With me. I want him to say that. I want him to promise. I want to hold onto that.

"This is *amazing*, Mason. Thank you." I pick up the seashells again and study each one. There's a gray one, a pinky cream one, and an off-white one. A few are absolutely smooth, while others are corrugated.

"I've never met anyone so enthused by seashells."

I laugh. "I'm pretty sure you've never met anyone like me, period."

Mason watches the seashell with eyes that have seen the beach. The real beach. Eyes that can't understand the darkness of the underground. "Touché."

FIFTEEN
ADELAIDE

"That's it," Fawn thunders as she stomps out of the teleporter. Mason left two hours ago and I did a math lesson, then curled up on the couch to read. I slip my bookmark into *Les Mis* and mentally remember the page number 412. Twelve is a multiple of four. I can remember that.

I think.

"What?"

"I'm installing more cameras in here."

A flutter of shock pulsates through my face, down my neck, and all over my body. I try desperately not to show my panic. "Okay...But why?"

"Someone hacked into the teleporter database and found our zone number." I freeze. Oh, Mason...why are you so foolishly brave? "I don't know what they wanted, but they haven't tried anything yet. Buddy and Perkins are coming over tomorrow to install them."

I mentally cross my fingers. "What time?"

"Why, do you have a date?"

USELESS FACT #4920
When lying, people use smaller and/or fewer words.

"No." My statement is confident, but a hair too quick.

ADELAIDE'S USELESS FACT #1
Adelaide is a terrible liar.

Lucky for me, Fawn seems to be bad at spotting lies.

"I'm installing one facing the teleporter and one in the kitchen." So basically everywhere except our rooms and the bathrooms.

Lovely.

I feel like crying. Why, I don't know. Mason figured out how to delete himself from the cameras already in place, but this is getting far too complicated. Maybe this is fate's way of forcing me to…

Let him go.

The Envisioning taps on the fringe of my memory, but I refuse to replay it. That'll just make this whole thing harder.

"These are newer cameras; I can access them at any time on my Monitor too." At any time? My breath hitches. Fawn is relentless. She wants her fingers in every single part of my life; every breath I draw must first be okay-ed by her.

After feeling alive I don't want to be buried again. I've seen the light, and it's intoxicating. I never want to smell incarceration again.

I hope with every bit of strength inside of me that Buddy and Perkins won't come until after Mason has stopped by, and I can see him one last time.

But only the free are allowed to hope.

He will have to find another way to become an inventor of

Kendror, but I'm sure it won't be that hard—he has a world of possibilities.

I go to my room and find the forbidden Communicator device. With watery eyes, I write, *Fawn installed more cameras. This is getting too complicated. Please don't come.*

I almost write, *I'll miss you,* but I don't. Instead, I add, *ever again.* It's harsh, but it gets the point across.

I can only hope Mason will listen to my note; leave and never come back. *Don't endanger yourself. Fawn is not to be messed with.*

That night, Fawn upholds her promise of a girls' night (which I'm not exactly in the mood for). I make popcorn while she sets up the living room screen to show one of our favorite movies, *To Catch a Thief.* She also sets out her nail supplies.

"I'd take a Cary Grant," Fawn comments. I glance over at her. She looks so normal: makeup off, mouse-pattern pajamas on. She hunches down on the couch, sitting on a fuzzy gray blanket, painting her toes that flaming red color.

"Fawn...do you ever think you'll date?" I rifle through her other nail color options: a simple white and a bright plasticky blue. I pick up the blue and try to open the lid, but it's so old that the lid won't budge.

Her gaze doesn't leave her painting. "No. You are my first priority. Any kind of a relationship would only endanger us."

She puts the lid back on her nail polish and looks over at me. There's so much in her eyes, but nothing I can read. Is her smile...sad? "I didn't choose this life, but that's okay. You were given to me as a responsibility, and I've done my best to live up to that task."

Guilt grips me, her words sinking into my soul. "That means giving up a lot of things," she adds. "But I've stayed with you, right? I didn't leave you to flounder down here."

She looks back to the movie. Grace Kelly and Cary Grant

sit in a car, overlooking a beautiful beach city landscape. Grace Kelly adjusts her white gloves, elegance flowing through her every movement.

"You *are* Grace Kelly," I say.

Fawn grins sadly. "I'd like to believe that."

But she isn't. We both know she isn't.

She is darkness. She is the thief in *To Catch a Thief*, pretending she is John Robie, the retired cat burglar.

Alfred Hitchcock would've had a heyday with our life story.

The next morning, the brothers burst into our house at eight. Fawn makes a fuss, running out of her bedroom with her hair all frizzy and her system without coffee. Buddy and Perkins remind her that they're leaving for a few days and wouldn't have been able to do it any other time. Fawn commands me to fix a cup of coffee and retreats to her room, frilly bathrobe fluttering behind her.

I start the coffee pot and scribble out my plan for the day in bright purple ink. I leave the room, but then circle back and put the butterfly pin in my hair. I head back into the kitchen, pour Fawn a cup of coffee, and bring it to her room.

"Hey, Fawn?" She throws the door open, hair half-combed.

"Here's your coffee and my schedule for the day." She takes both wordlessly. I decide I could some brownie points. "Want me to fix your hair?"

The corners of her mouth pull up in a lemony smile. "I know it looks like trash, thanks for reminding me."

She slams the door closed, and angry tears well up in my

eyes. Gone is any goodwill we kindled last night: she's back to being a dinosaur.

I'm already upset enough about the cameras, about Mason…now she has to go and turn my offer of kindness into an insult.

I run to my room and hide. I grab *Les Mis*. I don't want to think about the lack of privacy being installed just steps away from me, so I don't. I lose myself in a world that is unfree and cruel, parallel to mine.

Except my battle isn't fought with a sword. And my Marius can't come back.

What was the page number? I can't remember. That makes me really disappointed in myself, and I almost cry.

I don't even want to look at the cameras once they're up, but Fawn totes me around and shows them off like a proud mother displaying her children. I nod and smile and say *cool* with a very uncool tone of voice.

Once Fawn climbs in the teleporter and leaves me standing in the entryway, I'm terrified to speak. To breathe. I know she can see me now.

Part of me wants Mason to disregard my message, to come down anyway. But the signal never comes.

I'm fighting a losing battle.

But this is what I wanted, right? Mason out of harm's way. It would be selfish of me to keep letting him come over.

It's then that I crack a bit. I run to my room for solace and fall on my bed, just as the tears break through, and I'm sobbing.

I'm so tired of being suppressed. If I'd never met Mason, I never would've come to this point. Maybe I wish I hadn't ever met him…

Do I?

Is it better to know what I'm missing out on?

Is it better to have tasted something beautiful and have that memory to look back on even in the darkness?

When the tears finally subside, my nose is clogged. I can hardly breathe. I hope I get my act together before Fawn comes back.

I find my Communicator. Mason has left a couple of video messages and called three times since I sent him my message.

I press the circle. Mason appears before me, kind of pixelated and see-through, but it's still him.

"What was that message about?"

"This is such a bad idea," I whisper. "You coming over, me having this Communicator…Fawn is going to find out."

"You can't live in fear your whole life," Mason whispers back, but loudly. I hold a finger up to my mouth and give him a warning look. "I can help you."

"Why are you doing this?" I ask him.

"I can't stand watching people hurt."

"But I don't want you to have to fix more cameras. And I can't help you remember your parents. You don't understand the risk you're taking."

Mason takes a seat on his floor, but it looks like he's hovering in the air. It makes me want to laugh, but my face is stone.

"That's no big deal. I'll just reprogram those cameras too."

I shake my head. "It's just too risky."

"Listen—" His voice is harder than it ever has been. "I know about your situation now, and I have a responsibility to make sure you're okay. I can't make you choose what I want you to choose. But I can be a partner in this. Will you let me do this, or will this memory haunt me for the rest of my life? The memory that I left someone behind?"

I lower my eyes. "So…you just don't want to feel guilty for the rest of your life? That's it?"

"No, no, don't be like that. That's not it."

I shut my eyes. I don't want to be alone. I do want a partner, someone to share in this. I feel it's not fair to share my burden with someone else, but it's crushing me. I can't be human anymore.

"Okay."

"It's going to be okay, Adelaide," Mason promises. "Now, send me a 360 image of you and I can fix the cameras remotely."

None of those words make sense.

I clear my throat, trying to put my emotions away and get into action mode. "How do I do that? The picture, I mean."

"The Communicator." He says it like it's obvious. "Press the star and just stand in front of it. Then send it to me."

"Oh, and hey, could you do something for me? Make sure the other cameras are the same brand as the one in your room. That one's Visuli. I also need the number imprinted on the dome of each camera."

"How am I supposed to find that stuff?"

"It's on the camera," he replies. "You're smart. And if all else fails, we still have this Communicator."

"Are you serious? You think Fawn won't find it suspicious that I hide in my closet for an hour every day?"

Mason grins. "Wow, a whole hour?"

Hopefully holographs don't show blushing. I break out into a sweat again. I'm glad he can't see that either. "Okay, I'll do all this. But I really need to go now."

"Okay, okay. But I'm coming tomorrow. So there's your incentive to get the address and the image."

"You can figure all the techy stuff out that fast?"

"Gee whiz, Adelaide, you really don't believe me, do you?"

I hear a thunk, and I gasp. "I gotta go."

"Okay, tap it twice on the bottom to make it shrink so you can put it in your pocket. Just don't wash it." I grin. *I am a ditz after all.* I press the circle again and Mason disappears. I throw the closet door open and throw the Communicator under a pile of dirty clothes.

"Fawn? Are you back?"

No one answers. Then I see that my faux cactus plant fell over, all the pebbles and dirt on the floor; I'm really losing it. *That's* what scared me?

"Poor cactus," I say. If Fawn were watching me right now, maybe she'd think I'm crazy and send me away. I wonder if the asylums nowadays are any better than the ones I read about in the nineteenth century.

I take a leisurely stroll around the house. Not suspicious at all. I take a look at the camera in the living room. I get a good angle by leaning my head against the wall; the brand is Visuli. The number is 280.

I go back to my room and write that number down. Then, a few hours later, I check the camera facing the teleporter and keep track of the number. Then I do the same thing with the kitchen camera.

That night when Fawn is home, I pray she won't be watching me and I sneak into my closet again. I send Mason the name of the camera brand, the three numbers, and then take the 360 picture. Before I duck back out, he sends a message.

"Great. See ya tomorrow."

I'm overwhelmed by everything all of a sudden. I make it out of my closet but have to sit on my bed and collect myself.

What am I doing? Do I seriously think I can pull this off? I'm going to get in *so* much trouble…

SIXTEEN
COLETTE

Things that make me feel better:
* *Rationalizing my inner battle by studying psychology*
* *Working on my inventions*

If I hadn't married Wesley, I like to think I could've pitched my robotic butterflies and lived as an inventor extraordinaire in Kendror. I have a whole other life mapped out.

My butterflies aren't practical, but maybe that's why I like them. Wesley is all logic. If something isn't made of matter, it isn't important to him. *Point A* always goes to *Point B*, even if *Point B* is too painful to head towards.

I'll forever be grateful that he allows me this one thing, this one bit of superfluity in my life. My dresses make sense, my schedule makes sense, my life makes sense. But my butterflies and I don't make sense at our core.

I also feel better when I'm fixing something. Or cleaning something. I can't fix myself or clean myself, but I can fix a loose screw or clean a rusting metal plate.

Time alone is precious to me. It is in this room where I can truly be myself...although every day that person disappears more and more.

I could cross this room in five steps, but I don't need anything majestic. Three walls are unpainted, a mere unconversational beige. The other wall is made of white paneled glass, which peers out into the kingdom. Mine by marriage, mine by association. But nothing in this life is truly mine.

I am not careful enough with the metal wing; it's so fine that it slices my thumb. I wince as red bubbles up, then flows down my finger. I grab a nearby cloth, one I use to polish the metal. I apply pressure and a steady sting ensues.

But the sting is good.

My hobbies lessen the sting that comes from each breath I take.

I welcome the pain; after all, I don't have many friends. If pain can be my friend, who am I to deny him a seat at my table?

SEVENTEEN
ADELAIDE

USELESS FACT #72

Chocolate chip cookies were made by accident. Adelaide's note: Accidents aren't always bad.

"She did it?" Mr. Green still scares me. He came over today to assess our level of readiness, iron out The Plan, and apparently eat all our cookies too. I glare at him over the empty plate of double chocolate chips.

"Yes," Fawn answers. I swipe at a crumb on the plate and Mr. Green gives me a look. What a grump.

His eyes return to Fawn. "And she's actually been able to...*whatever* jump on an unconscious person and bring someone with her?"

"Yes, sir!" Fawn doesn't miss a beat. She's a much better liar than I ever have been.

"Perfect. Fawn, you're amazing. So, let's discuss the plan a bit more deeply." I automatically get up. Usually, I have no part in the discussion. Fawn figures all the details out and then relays them to me later. But this time is different.

"No, Adelaide," Fawn says. "Sit back down. I want you to hear this too."

I plop back down in my chair. It scoots back with the impact and squeaks, which makes Mr. Green frown at me again. "Has she been sworn to secrecy?"

Fawn reaches across the table and pats my hand like I'm a five-year-old. "Yes, sir."

"My mission is of the highest importance. Our reasons are not important, but our goal *is*: we are penetrating the mind of Prince Adam."

The *prince*? I freeze a bit.

"The crown prince is in a coma with brain damage, probably from a botched past Memory Jump. We need you to pull him out of it," Green says.

"Botched?" Fawn interrupts sharply. "That wasn't Adelaide."

"I wasn't saying it was," Green snaps back. "Let's focus on the present situation. It's very important that Adam survives. He is the only heir to the throne, and he must be ready for Crowning Season in one month when he takes over the title of king."

He continues explaining the plan, but my head spins with information.

If I were brave, I'd question him. I'm not a doctor; it sounds like they need a medical professional, not a Memory Jumper.

But, of course, I don't comment.

"Very few people know of the prince's serious condition. As far as the masses know, he's been overly busy preparing to be king."

Fawn leans across the table, rapt by his words. "So we have three weeks?"

"Two and a half. I'll reveal the specifics of the plan closer to the date."

"No problem." Fawn's twittery voice cracks a bit, but I'm the only one who notices.

"All right then. Any questions?"

Can I not do this? Is it okay if we just leave things the way they are? Are you a madman?

Fawn answers. "No."

I gulp. I must ask. "Um...I thought the King and Queen hated Memory Jumpers?"

"They're desperate," Green says quickly. "We've...collaborated with them."

Fawn turns to me. "You'll be safe, I promise."

She grabs my hands, squeezing too hard. "Would I ever do anything to hurt you?"

My face is empty, and Fawn drops my hands from her grip. She and Green exchange a few more details, Fawn escorts him to the teleporter, and he leaves. When she comes back into the kitchen, the questions tumble out of my mouth.

"Aren't you a bit worried about what will happen if we don't pull this off?" I question her. "I don't want to be responsible for messing this up and having the government fall—"

"Addy, you can't think that way. Failure isn't an option."

"But I—"

"I know what's best for you. Don't forget that, ever. This is going to be *terrific.*"

She sees the worry in my eyes, swipes her hands around my face, and pokes my nose. "Don't worry, love. Braid my hair?"

I give her a little smile before she pinches my cheeks. She nods approvingly and sits on the couch as I do a Dutch braid on her. Then she leaves to gather more clients.

I hide in my closet and call Mason. His form appears, and I lower my voice to talk. "How's the hacking coming?"

"I've got it," he says proudly. "I'll be over in twenty minutes. My aunt needs my help with my floor cleaner. It was a prototype and keeps bumping into walls."

"Okay." The fact that one of his inventions is failing kind of freaks me out, but I tell myself to trust him.

I turn the Communicator off and go to the pottery room to look at my materials for the outer space jewelry. The beads will work great for the necklace, and Buddy and Perkins found some clear wire for me to suspend the beds on the earrings.

The signal comes earlier than I expected, and I let Mason in.

"You did it?"

He lugs a big backpack on his shoulders; I wonder what's in there. "Yup! I hacked into your wifi and downloaded the program onto the security cameras."

"So, if I do this, Fawn will never see it?"

I stick my tongue out at the camera pointed directly at me, its single black eye staring emptily at me.

"No, she won't." I head towards the living room, and Mason follows. "She'll see you doing homework, cleaning your room, reading, and doing all those other things you say you do."

I pause in the doorframe of the living room. "Mason, you're a genius!"

He shrugs. "Well, I don't know about *that*. But my robot is getting *so* close to being finished. I can't believe, after all these years of wanting to be a *real* inventor, I'm so close!"

"You *are* a real inventor," I say as we take a seat on the couch. "You've been a real inventor for a long time."

"I'll be a real inventor when I've done something good for the world. When I've helped *you*." Mason sets his backpack at his feet. "Wanna see your Piece of the World?"

"I thought you were done bringing those."

He kneels down on the floor and unzips the backpack. "Nah, I like seeing you smile. Besides…I think you need me to entertain you. You *know* you do."

I roll my eyes at his false bravado.

Today's country is Italy: a blue wooden gondola. I want to cry. It's just like the one in my daydreams. I hold the gondola up to the light. It doesn't take much imagination to visualize that I'm in it, sailing through the canals of Venice.

And Mason is there too.

As he tells me how he got the gondola, he picks at the plant on the table. It's wilting a little bit, even though it's not even real. Fawn got it, and a new vase, to replace the vase she threw a few weeks ago. Sort of an inaudible apology to me.

But the vase isn't mine. She can't undo the parts of me, visible and invisible, which she's broken.

She's like that; explodes, then hides the pieces and pretends everything is normal and okay.

We chat for a little bit and then he leaves an hour before I expect Fawn to get back. I don't want to take any chances.

I set the gondola in one of my drawers in my room. It's where I've hidden everything Mason has brought me. I don't have much furniture, so I had to move all the notebooks I had in my drawers. Now they're stacked up at the back of my closet (apparently, my closet holds anything: me, boys, notebooks…).

I go back to my pottery room to craft, pulling out beads and painting them to look like planets. I use the tiniest paintbrush I have and make everything dainty. It gives me a thrill, and my brain turns off, and I can just breathe.

It's moments like these where I feel almost normal. Almost sane.

EIGHTEEN
ADELAIDE

It's another afternoon of Memory Jumping for me. The woman in our living room right now is getting married next week and wants to forget her abusive father. As she explains the situation, her face looks absolutely, masterfully unemotional. I recognize that look.

She's all-around square-shaped, square faced, and square bodied. Her makeup is flawless; her lipstick stays neatly inside the outlines of her mouth, and her brown eyeshadow gently melts into gold.

She wears that same white that a lot of other people in town wear; she'd be a blank slate if not for her artistically put-together face.

"I just want to feel like a normal person," she says. She's been babbling for a solid twenty minutes, so much so that I've nicknamed her *Baggage*. Surprisingly, Fawn's really good at playing psychiatrist.

Baggage finally stops jabbering, and Fawn looks at me. She has special plans for this Jump. Fawn wants me to attempt to bring her into Baggage's mind once I've done the job.

To Baggage, I say, "You ready?"

"Yeah."

I Memory Jump. The familiar feeling envelopes me, and I am sucked into her brain. The doors materialize. They are drab and slightly disorganized. She's not kidding about emotional baggage: it's totally messed her memory up. Thankfully, the memories central to her father are at the beginning of the hallway. From them leak inky ribbons of black, invading other doors through the smallest of cracks.

I really do feel bad for her. I'm glad I'm helping her in a way. I delete every recent memory labeled with something about her dad. I check the memories first just to make sure, but so far everything is good to go.

When I've deleted all those, I call all the other memories to me that involve Baggage's dad. It's a bit like turning yourself into a human magnet. They all flood at me. When brains are labeled according to the main person in the memory, it's easy to do jobs like this. But, in Baggage's case, it would've taken me forever to file through each memory.

I do my job. Some of the memories are terrible. The further back they are, the better they are. Some are even happy memories. I'm almost about to delete those, but I figure I'll leave them. She deserves to keep the happy memories of her father.

Memories are so personal. I've relived so many, taken empathy to a new level.

In a way, I'm just a walking container of memories.

Sometimes I wonder how good life really is outside of my world. There are some pretty messed-up stories I've had to deal with.

My life could be so much worse.

After I'm done, I exit. My heart pounds, not as intense as it has before. Baggage is a bit dazed and Fawn manages to convince her to accept a drugged drink. She's out ten minutes later.

"Ready?" Fawn picks at a piece of lint on her shirt. Well, *my* shirt. I complained once about it being too big and Fawn commandeered it from my wardrobe.

Would it really hurt Fawn if she just said *good job* once? Just once?

I reach out for her hand. "Yeah. I have an idea about making this work; maybe if we're linked? Like, holding hands?"

Fawn hesitates for a second, as if touching me will render her paralyzed for the rest of her life. But she grabs my hand and wraps her feminine, skinny fingers around my own thick, short ones. "It's worth a shot."

I Memory Jump. The doors drip into existence...but Fawn isn't with me. I growl and then exit Baggage's mind.

"Didn't work," I say.

"I know," Fawn snaps.

"Do you have any ideas?"

Fawn shuffles. She has no idea what to do. She may have all those psychology books; she may have pored over them until her eyes busted out of her head, but Memory Jumping isn't exactly science. I'm truly the brains of the operation. "No."

I run a hand through my hair and my hand meets the butterfly pin in my hair. A bit of courage pulses through me. "Well...I have an idea. But you won't like it."

She stares at me from under her luscious lash extensions, emphasizing her look's intensity. "Tell me."

I inhale—*bravery in.* I exhale—*bravery out.* "I think I need a mental connection with you. Like, a mental presence. So... what if I Memory Jump into your mind and then try to Memory Jump from there?"

Fawn's forehead swoops into a dark valley, her arms into a furious fold. "I don't want you in there."

"Why not?"

"Because, you're a snoop, and you'll snoop."

I frown. "You know I hate the personal aspect of Memory Jumping. I don't snoop. I'd walk through blindfolded if I could."

Fawn sniffs. "I don't believe you."

"I don't have any other ideas, I'm sorry." I'm basically begging. "Mr. Green is just gonna be super ticked come Friday."

Fawn snarls and glares at me like I'm doing this on purpose. She probably believes that. "I guess it's our only option. But *swear* you won't dig around."

I gulp. At first, I never would've dreamed of poking around. But, now that she's made it so obvious there's something in there, I'm terrified I'll lose my mind and break my promise.

My hands clench. I can't. Fawn always finds out. It's like she has cameras everywhere, including my brain. I lower my head. "I swear."

"All right. So help me, if I ever find out…"

I cringe. "I'm not going to look."

Fawn takes a seat on the couch next to Baggage. It's like she thinks I can't Memory Jump unless my victim is on that magical couch. I stand up this time and squat down just the tiniest bit. I feel like this Memory Jump will need a bit of extra effort. I gingerly place my hand on her forehead.

I was wrong. It isn't made of ice. My hands meet flesh thumping with the smallest bit of warmth, the hardness of her skull strangely human.

Fawn shivers. My hands are probably cold. That or she

hasn't had any human contact since she came out of the womb.

"Don't touch me," she snaps. "I thought you didn't need to do that anymore."

I don't. I just wanted to know if she's made of flesh or stone.

I drop my hand and close my eyes to target the center of Fawn's brain. With a click, I connect and slide through time and space. I land in Fawn's brain, almost surprised I made it. She must've taken down whatever has blocked me from entering her mind for all these years.

The doors materialize in front of me, and I am terrified to read the labels or take time to let them all appear. The curiosity inside of me tears at my sanity, trying to get me to give in and explore.

I stand in the darkness, surrounded by secrets that could save me. My only thoughts are those telling me to close my eyes and search for Baggage's mind. I do so.

Thank goodness, I find her brain. It's not as sharp as usual, but it's still there. I send myself to her brain but, before I do, I try something. As I shoot towards her brain, I force myself to swing a bit to the left. Then more, more, more. It works, and I lasso around Fawn's brain and shoot us both into Baggage.

The blackness isn't empty when I open my eyes. Fawn stands there, a smug grin on her face.

She takes a look around. It's as if she's calculating every-thing quietly, turning it over in her head and analyzing all the bits and pieces.

"This is…interesting," she says. I relax a bit, which surprises me. I didn't know I was so wound up. Colors flash around us, a thrashing aurora borealis.

"Okay, can you get her out of unconsciousness?" Fawn asks.

"Oh, um…yeah." I worry a little bit that I might fail under the pressure of Fawn watching, but I just roll my shoulders back and begin. Memories are *my* world: I pretend I've written her out of existence here, and I immediately feel at peace.

A bit of light blue flashes in a corner but I wasn't prepared; it's too late to try to catch the color.

The colors I gather are a beautiful range of aquas. Kind of like a mermaid tail. I smash them all together and release Baggage from unconsciousness. The doors drip back from nothingness. There's not a door in sight with the girl's father in it.

This is the kind of Memory Jumping I enjoy. Baggage gets a second chance at life now and maybe a happy ending. With special thanks to me.

There's a slight jolt, and I remove Fawn and me from her brain. Fawn surprises me once we're back by wrapping me in a hug. It's so anomalous to have her showing me any kind of love, I stiffen up and release myself from her grip.

Now that I have Mason, I feel invincible, like I'm wearing a comfortable sweater that blocks out any amount of coldness.

"Why won't you let me hug you?" Fawn snaps.

"It's been a long day, and I just—"

"I don't know why you do this, Adelaide." The vulnerability in her voice sends shards of ice through my heart. Fawn's big, animal eyes pierce right through my skull, unpacking every secret and worry and desire. "You've shut me out. We used to…we used to be friends. You used to like me."

The words hang in the air. Memories of Mason shoot through my vision, strengthening me.

"What happened?" Fawn whispers, mournful.

I feel too many things, emotions crashing around in my body like a herd of elephants. And I'm afraid. I don't want to feel.

I'm afraid it's a trap. Afraid I'll say the wrong thing, be too honest. "You stopped being my mom."

The words aren't angry. They're laced with sadness. Fawn and I are at a funeral: the death of our relationship. The only thing that ties me to her is duty and fear.

There is no love.

I retreat to the kitchen, thinking about baking something to calm my nerves. But I'm too emotional right now.

I hit the wall—I need something to keep my brain away from all these confusing thoughts. My hands sting, but the pain makes me feel like I'm real.

I make myself a cup of tea, refusing any of my usual flavors and bravely grabbing a bag of rooibos. Something different. Something bold.

My hands shake. Making tea won't make the pain go away.

I'm so tired of my life. So tired of my lack of a life. I'm watching everyone else live, fixing everyone else's lives, while I'm stuck in a never-changing jail cell of oppression.

But I can't do anything.

I can't.

Mason says I can. But he has never been in her icy presence.

I retreat into my room, keeping the LED lights dim and moody. I throw myself on my bed and just cry for a good, long time.

I may not know what living feels like.

But I sure know how to die.

NINETEEN
ADELAIDE

It's been four days.

Fawn left after our strange interaction…and she hasn't come back.

Good, I keep telling myself. *Maybe she'll never come back.*

I have enough groceries; Buddy and Perkins bring them. I clean the dishes, make my own food, and do my schoolwork. I make pottery and jewelry, but I'm running out of supplies and I have no way to get online to sell my crafts. I don't have a penny to my name. If Fawn hasn't paid for next week's groceries, I'm doomed.

Could I possibly leave? I rub my neck, the bump from the tracker still there. Tears pull at my eyes for the gazillionth time. And yet they never fall. It's like I've lost the ability to cry.

Mason comes every day. He makes things better too. Yesterday he brought me jewelry from Egypt: a necklace and a scarab pin.

USELESS FACT #501

Ancient Egyptians invented toothpaste.

The day before, the theme was America. Mason found a little flag, beautiful and bright shades of red, white, and blue. I love the history of America: so many good, smart people came together to attempt a government devoid of corruption of power.

Today when he arrives, I like that the visit is beginning to grow familiar. I like to expect good things. I like Mason in my life.

"Enjoying life as a free woman?" he asks as soon as the teleporter doors open.

"Define 'free.'"

"Fawn-less."

I give him a small smile. Fawn's shadow follows me everywhere. Maybe I don't want to admit the truth to myself. Maybe I don't want to accept that Fawn…that Fawn is a monster. It's easier to wake up every morning that way.

We walk to the living room. It's always nice when there isn't an unconscious body lying on the couch because then we can sit there instead of in the hallway.

I tell him something I've been wanting to ask for a while. "I'm worried…I'm worried you're going to disappear somehow. Forget to come one day."

I watch him carefully, ready to read any telltale signs. Signs of what, I don't know. What am I looking for exactly? I have a small idea, but I'm afraid to admit it. "How could I forget? Until I finish that robot and get you out of here, as I promised, you're stuck with me."

Stuck with me. I like that phrase. Stuck with me, like peanut butter and jelly.

Mason's eyes keep resting on the butterfly pin in my hair, which I've worn like it's a sacrament. Maybe his feelings are hurt since I'm not wearing the scarab.

Mason hands me my brown package for the day, which

makes my face light up. I tear into it and forget about Fawn for a little while.

"Oh my goodness, it—" Sounds come from above. At first, I can't believe it. I've learned to associate that sound with Mason.

But now…

Mason sighs, trying to act like the situation is funny, but I'm sure he's just as scared as me. "I'll get in the closet."

I can't decide whether to laugh or scream, so what comes out is this obnoxious, staccato beginning of a chuckle. "Good idea."

As he runs towards my room, I smooth down my shirt and close my eyes. No matter how many times Fawn has been to The Outside, I doubt she could say *she's* had a guy in her closet.

When the teleporter door opens, Fawn running out doesn't surprise me. But Mr. Green following her close behind does.

"The stakes have risen," Green says quickly. For once, he doesn't look at Fawn in order to talk to me. His eyes pierce into mine. "We've run out of time: We need to get to the castle immediately."

"Like…right now?"

"That's kind of what immediately means," Green snaps. Fawn keeps her eyes lowered; she hasn't made eye contact with me yet. She's wearing an aggressive black jacket with crisscross mesh and sharp edges.

"If the prince dies…" Green never finishes his sentence. Instead, he straightens up like a stick. His words are sharp, too. "We need to go *now*."

Words. So many words. None of them are making sense, just floating around in an abyss of meaninglessness.

Fawn grabs me, and I forget to have the decorum to not

flinch. How did she get behind me anyway? I don't look at her.

Fawn grabs my arm and pulls me toward the teleporter. She leans close to my ear, and I want to run as far away as fast as I can. She lowers her voice and whispers in my ear. "Please. Just do this. Do this thing for us, you and me."

I swallow, confused by the mixture of emotion in her voice, allowing myself to be pulled into the teleporter. She almost sounds tired?

As Fawn speaks, Green smiles. An actual smile. Glory, hallelujah, the man's mouth goes in an upward motion. He types in the capital's zone number and we transport.

As the teleporter shudders, my heart drops. *Mason*. He's still in my closet. Did he hear what happened?

I force those thoughts away. I can't afford to dwell on them right now, considering everything I have to do in the next few hours. Once we reach The Outside, I'm pulled so quickly along I can barely even take everything in.

As usual.

We exit the machine, and I look up at the sky. It's a strange, sickly gray. There are no clouds, not a bit of texture. It's just this empty, foreboding gray slate. It makes my stomach hurt a bit, like it's telling me I'm headed for doom.

"We have to go in the back way, obviously. It's faster and won't raise questions." Green tells us. Yeah, I *obviously* knew that because they tell me everything. I don't even have time to ask what *the back way* is before he darts in the opposite direction of the city. Fawn and I follow him into a wide expanse of trees, more of a forest than anything I've ever seen.

I wonder how far away this *back way* is. Turns out, about a ten minute journey. I enjoy it thoroughly, taking in the way the sun falls through patches of cookie-cutter leaves that carve abstract shapes on the forest floor.

Green stops at a thick wall of stone near a stream. The wall wears a cape of fuzzy green moss. A secret door hides behind the moss, a rich shade of green only possible in either nature or a chef who's trigger-happy with his food coloring.

Green leads the way into the darkness. I can see nothing and my stomach hitches again, but Fawn shoves me in the small of my back, and I step forward, a prisoner.

We climb down a staircase, dirty and cobwebby and shadowed. A suspicious dark substance covers the steps. Blood? Fungus? Something worse? My stomach is about to lose its contents.

"Servants' tunnels," Fawn murmurs. Green nods. "Ingenious."

"Yeah, the king redid some of it after the insurgence because it wasn't totally secure," Green adds. "It definitely was worth it, though. We could almost charge admission and offer tours through here."

Fawn laughs, really girly and cute. That is *not* her normal laugh. She's milking him, and I'm almost proud of her.

As we walk, just enough light shines that we can see. We weave around until the ceiling above us becomes transparent and...watery. It's the stream I saw outside. Fish even swim by, casting little shadows. It's beautiful.

We continue walking for such a long time. Green chats with Fawn, trying to get her to share details about her life. I zone in and out of the conversation.

Why do I keep thinking about Mason? I'm so confused by this. The thoughts that used to be made up of books and random facts are now all taken up by the paradise-eyed boy.

Then I almost stop in my tracks. I try to remember those books I read: the ones about a girl and a boy that meet and—

Could I be in love?

I almost laugh. I almost cry.

There's no way. Mason is the first boy I ever met. And besides, even if I did love him—even if he loved me—it would never work. Fawn would never…I glance at her. She's moved from behind me to stand up front, next to Green. The light from the sun diffuses through the water above us and casts eerie streaks of pulsating white across her face.

I want to do something crazy. I want to grab Green's gun; to tell Fawn and Green to go back to our home, to never come after me. I want to get Mason and run away with him, to go outside every day and look at the sky. I want to *live* underneath the sky. I never again want to be parted from it.

My heart hurts. My stomach takes turns with it. The tears come. I know the truth now.

The isolated, permanently lonely girl has fallen in love with a boy who's as free as the sky. Maybe it's only because he is everything I can't have.

I can't put words to it. The only simple answer is that he makes me feel like I finally started living. For so long I've simply been existing; I didn't know anything else.

I know we've reached the castle because everything abruptly changes from dirty darkness to castle-like slabs of dark gray stone. My thoughts fly out of my head. Silly, foolish thoughts.

Adelaide can never be free.
Adelaide can't mess up.

> *Clipped my wings,*
> *Clipped my wings,*
> *"You don't need those silly things…"*

We climb up a set of stairs. This one has a banister, but none of us touch it. Maybe I should lick the banister so I can get some disease and end my painful being.

I'm surprised at this thought. I don't like it.

We reach an alcove. The stones melt into pure, unlined white. Marble?

Green speaks. "Stay close. I'm going to be in front. Follow my lead."

Green darts out from the alcove like a muscular ant with a gun. Fawn follows, like a reflex, leaving me all alone in the shadows. Not for long, though. Her arm darts around the wall and grabs me. Her fingernails dig into my flesh.

I'm being pulled against my will, Green way in front of us. I pretend I'm tripping to keep it like that. I keep my eyes on the ceiling as we continue ahead.

We climb up yet another staircase.

I was not made for this level of cardio.

This must be the castle. The ceiling is high, made of glass arranged in artistic, geometric patterns. The floor is white tile, and I peek over to make sure Fawn isn't wearing high heels that'll give us away. She isn't. She has her practical black sneakers. I wonder, assuming this project goes well, if she can buy me some better sneakers. Sneakers that don't seem like they were designed for a toddler.

The walls are stark, empty white, embellished periodically with well-behaved shrubs in blue glass vases. At the end of this hallway is a huge white door with a little keypad.

Fawn slips her hand inside the dent. She pulls something out of her pocket—it looks like a silver pencil—and touches the door with it. A beep sounds and red lasers flitter over her hand before the door slides open.

Green walks in first, then Fawn.

I follow her.

Inside the doors is a bedroom. The walls are blue; the bed hovers midair, silver and blue, with a stream of smoke coming from the bottom.

A crowd of people dressed in white surrounds the bed. A priest stands at the ready in the corner. Green approaches one of the white blob people.

"She's here," Green says. It's like he's Moses. The White Scrubs Sea parts to reveal a boy lying on the bed, eyes closed. He's hooked up to all kinds of wires and monitors, with hair the color of toasted graham crackers. A woman and man stand close by him. They don't fit in with the white scenery, and I figure they're the king and queen.

The king immediately looks at me, but the queen watches her son's face. My heart stills—*the king is the man from Mason's memory*.

"Your Majesty," Mr. Green says with a polite bow. I continue staring at the king; thankfully his attention is on Green. "This is Adelaide and her mother, Fawn. Adelaide is the girl you heard about. She can get the boy out of his coma."

The king looks me up and down. It's as if he's calculating my intelligence, and I want to hide behind something. His face is very smashed-looking with a stubby, snobby nose and a permanent grimace. His towering height adds to his terror, as does his silence.

It's his wife who finally speaks. She has a calming, hostess-like presence with graceful hips and skin that's definitely seen the sun more than once. I recognize her as the woman from Mason's memory and I'm both excited and terrified for Mason. Could these people really be his parents?

Could I have actually done something right for once?

Mason was hoping to save me…but maybe I could save him instead.

TWENTY
COLETTE

N o.
No.
It can't be him.

Paul Green.

I'd know him anywhere. I know his face better than my own. When our eyes meet, my fears are confirmed. I beg him to not say anything. Did he know I would be here?

Wesley demanded I be here for this, and my heart burns at his cynicism. How could he not think this would hurt me?

I want to run screaming from the room. But I must maintain my composure. So, instead, I focus on the people with Green. Jealousy boils inside of me at the sight of the woman standing at his side. Everything about her is sharp, deadly beautiful. Her eyes hold no light. She wears nothing special, yet the way the fabrics cling to her is something any woman would pay dearly for.

But then I see the other woman. Well, the girl.

She's so young. Just eighteen or maybe nineteen. Around the age of my son.

But that's not the first thing I notice. The first thing I notice is the so-familiar look of emptiness in her eyes, with fear hidden just beneath. It takes my breath away.

She has a terrible, jagged mistake of a haircut, offset by a pretty blue ribbon in her hair. The shade of blue would be a bit too bright for Wesley's liking—it's a brave color. I smile on the inside.

"She's here." I don't see who makes the statement, but the tone of the room changes. The beautiful woman and Green look at the young woman. She must be the Memory Jumper.

I wonder if she is scared for her life.

Green walks forward, and the nurses scatter from the room. The Memory Jumper follows close behind, his blue-bejeweled shadow. I glance over at my son, willing to use any means necessary to save his life. I beg his forgiveness for thinking death is better, for I know now that is not true. If this Memory Jumper can use her powers for good despite her nature, I know my son can become a good man despite his father.

Green bows, and my heart dips with him. "Your Majesty." He says this to the king, not to me. He hasn't looked at me since he walked into the room. He introduces the girl as Adelaide, and the woman as her mother, Fawn. I wonder if Green is her father. He goes with the woman very well. Like a nice sweater set. Something you'd see at a store or on a poster.

Wesley hasn't replied yet. Adelaide tugs at my motherly heart, and my husband's rudeness moves me to speak first.

"Thank you so much for coming, Miss Adelaide." I want to wrap her in a hug. Her face is so honest; she gives me a scared smile, and I smile back. "We really appreciate you trying."

"Of course," she replies. I am comforted: she will do all she can to save Adam.

The healthcare workers leave the room at Green's request, leaving a mess of humans behind. A broken boy, my stoic husband, Green and his secrets, the young Memory Jumper, the simmering woman, and myself. Certainly not a room I'd want to be locked in.

"Do your stuff," Green says to Adelaide.

"Go on, Addy," Fawn says with festering darkness. The familiarity of the tone makes me bristle.

Adelaide closes her eyes. Suddenly, any discomfort or shyness melts away. Her shoulders rise, and she settles into herself. She breathes deeply, pauses and—

TWENTY-ONE
ADELAIDE

I close my eyes. Prince Adam's brain is cold. It barely calls out to me. However, it glows slightly with a very rare brand of kindness. He's the type of guy who would give a chunk of his income to a charity; the type of guy that would throw himself in front of a bullet.

I also pick up on his unfortunate habit of lying. I'm surprised at how much I know about him immediately. Usually I'm not this intuitive. Maybe Mason's positivity is starting to get to me.

I ricochet myself into his brain. It's dark, which at first isn't surprising. But when flashes of light don't appear after a good ten seconds, I start to freak out.

I see Fawn's eyes in my mind. They warn.

Then, a tiny spark. Seriously minuscule. I get ready for what I hope will be the next one.

There it is! I jump at it and grab it. A few more seconds pass before another spark appears. Then a good twenty seconds go by before a purple light explodes right in front of me.

I smash what little light I have together. "Wake up, wake up, wake up."

I shut my eyes again. Concentrate. Breathe. Find. This is what I do. I search for the lights, try to see if I can anticipate the next flash. That's when I see it: barely-glowing orbs appearing around me. They weren't visible until I closed my eyes.

I grab at the lights and, as I shove them together, they combine to become brighter and brighter. The light bursts out from their central location and douses everything in brightness. There's shaking, and then—

Doors appear.

Chills trickle down my spine.

I did it.

I actually did it.

I send myself out of the prince's mind. The bedroom reappears. I stare at the floor and hunch my shoulders ready to leave. I've already stopped celebrating my accomplishment.

But then one of the monitors picks up a heartbeat. It grows stronger and stronger, thumping up and down. Prince Adam's brain is warm again, and when I shut my eyes, I can see it.

Green looks like he's in shock. I frown at his surprise.

"You are amazing," the queen says. I almost fall over. She grabs my hands in hers and looks at me with adoration. Her eyes are wet. "Adelaide! Bless you."

Although she is overcome with emotion, her husband shows nothing. He stands by his son's bed with a grimace.

"Send the doctors back in," the king says into a band on his wrist. Within seconds, the doors explode open. They see the heart monitor, steady and sure.

Someone whoops. The eight or nine people in the room

wearing white jump up and down, slamming their hands together to make a terrible racket. Clapping.

For me.

Nobody's ever clapped for me.

"You did it!" one shouts.

I may explode with all the attention. Fawn addresses the people. "Please! We really appreciate your kindness, but Adelaide isn't used to so much noise."

The thunderous compliments turn into raindrop whispers.

"We need to clear the room," says one masked nurse. "Give the prince some air while he recovers."

Fawn whisks me away. I don't even feel my legs walking. I'm still overcome with the strange experience of being thanked; of being adored, even. The queen stays in the room, but the king and most of the nurses leave.

"Is there anything else you require of Miss Adelaide or Fawn?" Mr. Green asks the king.

The king stares at me with a look that goes right through me as if I were a piece of saran wrap. As quickly as that, my feeling of euphoria disappears.

"No. That's all." The king leaves like he can't stand our company any longer.

Green turns to us. "Thank you, Fawn, Adelaide. I'll be in contact shortly with another task."

"And I'll expect the payment within a week." I can't believe Fawn is so straightforward.

"Of course. But this is just the tip of the iceberg," Green says. I note that he's lowered his voice, glancing to the side. He doesn't want anyone to hear this part. "That was a trial run. There are a lot bigger tasks to accomplish."

"Of course. We're ready for whatever comes our way." Green tries to high-five Fawn, but she makes a face at him. It makes me want to laugh, seeing this big, buff guy with biceps and camo pants shrinking at Fawn's glare.

I know how he feels.

We sneak back into the secret tunnel and get back to the house. Fawn parks herself in the entryway, chatting with Green.

I find Mason, sitting in my closet, playing some kind of game on my Communicator. I can barely keep myself from exploding with the news about who his parents are.

"You're still here? Why didn't you leave?"

"Those two guys came in immediately." He must be talking about Buddy and Perkins.

I wince. "I don't think you'll be able to get out of here tonight."

Has Fawn kept a boy in her closet overnight? I don't think so. *Fawn-0, Adelaide-1.*

"I'll call my aunt and just let her know I'll be home tomorrow." He tosses his Communicator into the air and catches it right before it hits the ground, my news about his parents' identity rattling inside my brain.

"Mason, I really need to tell you something." But then my confidence shrivels. What if those people aren't his parents? His being a royal is a huge assumption. "But first…can I just check your subconscious again?"

"Why, checking up on those skeletons again?"

I grin. "No, just…just let me, okay? It'll be super fast."

"Sure, I don't care." I barely blink before I enter his memory. I'm getting faster and faster at this. I wave my hand, and the last door slides towards me. I have a memory of where the door is and decide to see if it's right. I stick out my foot and—connect with something solid. I grin. Who says I have a bad memory?

I practically skip down the stairs, the glow around me lighting my way. I file through shelves and stacks of memories to find the one I need.

It's still fuzzy, but I'm so certain. The woman's face appears; I know the shape. I know. I didn't forget.

A mural spreads out from behind the queen's face, probably painted on the nursery wall…looks like a tree. I decide I'll transfer this to long-term memory and ask Mason to remember it by using the tree as a kind of bookmark.

I grab the memory (it's warm in my hands) and carry it up the flight of stairs. I open my hands and swipe down to create a door. I open the doorknob and throw the memory in, where it expands and comes to life.

When I'm back in reality, I ask Mason to think really hard. "I may have information about your parents! But I need your help: I took your earliest memory out of your subconscious and put it back in your memory…dig deep. Think of trees."

"Trees?" His face scrunches. "Does this have to do with the Christmas tree smell thing?"

"No," I chuckle. "Forget the Christmas tree."

"My earliest childhood memory is…in a forest?"

"No! Be more…abstract," I command. "Just search."

He raises his eyes to the ceiling.

"Okay…okay. A woman." I nod, encouraging him on. "It's all black and white but…looks like I'm in a cradle. At least from the perspective."

"Yes! Describe the woman."

"Well, there's no color."

"That means nothing. Describe her."

"I don't know, I'm not—"

I widen my eyes in exasperation. "Mason, *describe her*."

"Okay, okay! Let's see…nice face. Big eyes. Pretty."

"Keep going."

"Um…sure of herself. Super happy. Kind."

"And what's behind her?"

He closes his eyes now as if that'll sharpen things. "Swirls…texture almost. Coming out from next to her, behind her. It's…is it a tree?"

"Yes!" I rock forward on my knees. "Do you want me to tell you who I saw that looked just like her? While I was at the palace?"

"Sure."

I look into his eyes, searching for any kind of premonition. Seeing nothing, I continue ahead. "The queen. The queen looks like the woman in your memory."

TWENTY-TWO
COLETTE

L ast night was yet another dinner with yet another rich couple droning on about politics. I thought it was a small mercy that I developed a migraine thirty minutes before they arrived.

"Wesley, dear…I have a migraine." My eyelids fluttered open and shut, pounding in beat with the drum in my head. "I do not think I can come to dinner tonight."

Wesley's back was turned to me, but I could feel him stiffen. "You don't like these people, do you?"

The pounding multiplied. Why did he always take everything so personally? "No, I—"

"You don't have any friends, and this is why," he snapped. I could barely hear him through my mental sludge, and the cruelty didn't register.

"I have to go lie down. I'll come down if I feel better but I —" I couldn't even finish the sentence. Navigating to my bedroom would be enough of a chore.

I spent the rest of my evening in my bedroom. My head was on the softest, most luxurious pillows available in the country and yet a little gnome inside of the fluff seemed to keep kicking my temple.

I fell asleep and didn't wake up until 10:00 the next morning. Wesley was in an awful mood; I should have anticipated it.

I found him in his study, burrowed deep in maps of the kingdom. He likes the ones on paper, despite all his counselors begging him to switch to more modern technology. He always said there was something about being able to mark or scribble on the paper that captured his attention more than *space lasers*.

"I'm sorry I missed breakfast," I chirped to contrast his sourness. He said nothing to my apology, only burrowed his head deeper into his papers. "Will you take lunch in the dining hall?"

Silence, once again. I waited patiently for his answer.

Finally: "...No."

Rejected by my husband. I smiled on the outside, turned away, and plunged into the hallway.

Just make it to my invention room. Just make it to my invention room. There I could fix things. I was so good at fixing problems that I was never allowed to have any problems of my own. I was always the super glue...but what if I was the thing that needed fixing?

TWENTY-THREE
ADELAIDE

After my big announcement to Mason about his parents, he doesn't say anything.

"I know it's crazy, but…but your story about your aunt…it would make sense."

Mason frowns. "I appreciate what you're doing but…well, no offense, but you hadn't been outside before this month and…one of the first women you see, you think she's my mom?"

I'm disappointed by his response. "I know it seems far-fetched, but—"

"That would change my whole life. Adam would be my brother."

Oh my goodness. I hadn't even gotten that far. "You have to trust me. I may have never been outside, but I've seen thousands of faces in memories." I shift on the couch. My leg is falling asleep; I put my legs in front of me and readjust my weight.

"Which one of you is older? You or Adam?" I ask him.

"What do I care?"

"You could be a king!"

He makes a face like he was offered a bologna sandwich. "I don't want to be king. I want to be an inventor."

"Well…would you want to be reunited with your parents?"

He shrugs. "This is a lot to swallow. Let me think about it."

I glance around the tiny closet. "This closet isn't very comfortable, by the way."

"It's fine."

I sigh and leave the closet to grab a blanket folded up in a corner. "Here you go. That'll have to be your bed. Did you need any dinner? Coffee? We can continue this discussion once you prove I'm right."

He doesn't respond to that. "Dinner would be great. I haven't eaten since lunch."

I nod.

"I also really need to use the bathroom."

"Okay, last time this happened I almost had a heart attack."

"Fawn isn't here though, right? Just those henchmen? I've been holding it for four hours already."

"Okay, okay." I stick my head out the door and look left and right to check for Buddy and Perkins, even though I haven't heard Fawn come down, and there are four other rooms humans could be in. "Let's go."

I move in a way that could be termed *creeping*. I know I'm paranoid, but I'm just sure that Fawn's ears are perking up and picking up on the fact that I have a refugee.

"Hurry," I whisper. Mason slips inside the bathroom and shuts the door. I feel weird standing right outside, so I put a little distance between myself and the bathroom.

I hum Mason's folk song to calm my nerves. From somewhere in the house, the twins yell at each other. *Beeps* and *boops* drift through the hallways occasionally; they must be gaming in the living room.

The signal comes from above. The teleporter whirs a little. My heart does too. Seriously? Just for once, what if things actually went my way? Would that just ruin everything?

"Mason, time to finish up!" I whisper aggressively. Out loud, to the twins, I screech, "Would one of you hit the teleporter button?"

The signal comes again. Now is not the time to make Fawn mad, what with all the stress of overthrowing a government and lying to people.

"Why, what are YOU doing?" Perkins yells back.

I hiss: "Mason, you have about ten seconds!"

I yell: "I'm INDISPOSED!"

"Have you been reading *Pride and Prejudice* crap again?" Buddy yells.

What the actual heck? "Okay, would you please just be helpful and—"

I see Perkins in the hallway, waddling over to the teleporter.

"Just stay in there," I command Mason.

"I guess it is a nice change of scenery—"

"SHUT UP!" I run over to the teleporter and join Perkins. He's pressing the button as I walk into the entryway.

I throw him an exasperated look. "You are the *least* helpful person. Ever."

Mason yells from down the hallway. "Adelaide! Adelaide, I went in the wrong room! I'm—"

The doors part and I say a prayer.

"Hey, Fawn!" I shriek, loud enough that Mason and every rabbit within ten miles can hear.

Fawn brushes past me without even looking at me. "What's up with you?"

I accept the terse answer. I need to divert her so Mason can go back to my room. I don't even know where he is—pottery room? Fawn's room? "Would you, um, help me open a can in the kitchen?"

Fawn stops walking. She's dead quiet. You'd think I told her I loved her.

"It's tomato sauce. I need it for the...pizza bagels."

"Not that crap again." She knows as well as I do that my pizza bagels are killer. But do we have mozzarella? Hopefully Fawn won't come to the kitchen to realize I just made it up that I'm making pizza bagels; but no, I need her to come or else Mason's cover might be blown.

"Can you...can you help me?"

Fawn looks at me as if I'm stupid. She gives a mean-girl smile. "I think you're perfectly capable of using a can opener. You're smart."

"I broke the can opener."

USELESS FACT #2002
Can openers replaced the common hammer and chisel method of opening a can, and were first invented around the 1850s.

Fawn shakes her head, incredulous. "You broke the can opener—what? How do you even do that?"

"I dropped it."

I glance towards the hallway. Mason will be safe. He'll be okay, even if I'm not.

I run to the kitchen to buy myself some time. I pull open a drawer and grab the can opener. Where should I put it? I open the trash can and throw it in.

Fawn clomps into the kitchen, her heels sharp as her face. "Where is it?"

"I threw it away."

She stares at my right eye, then looks at my left as if searching for something. Her face furrows.

"This is ridiculous. Figure it out yourself. Dinner is in twenty minutes." Then she leaves.

I glance around the kitchen. I take in the white. White is the color of purity. But how much hatred, how many cruel words have these walls seen and heard? Even our walls lie. Even our walls look better externally.

Hope for a better future has always kept me going, no matter how fake that promise was. But now, I have real hope.

Maybe I am going insane. It's been so long since I've felt real happiness. As I pull out the bagels, heat the tomato sauce, find the oregano, and sprinkle the cheese, my mind is fully on another subject.

I imagine all kinds of beauty. Scenes of oceans, lakes, and swamps. Of snow falling, of birds flying overhead.

I'm not cooking for Fawn and me. I'm cooking for Mason and me. For the world and me.

I give Fawn her food at 6:00 on the dot, then retreat to my room with three pizza bagels. I half-expect Mason to be gone when I open the closet door, but there he is.

"I come bearing gifts," I say. Mason laughs, the pink blanket around his legs. It looks funny cocooning him. "Glad to see you made it out safely."

"Let's just hope Fawn doesn't decide to do some spring cleaning in your wardrobe."

I laugh and sit down next to him. Mason takes one of the pizzas. He finishes the two bagels in the time it takes me to get through five bites of mine.

"You're amazing at cooking," Mason says.

I grin, a little embarrassed for reasons I don't know. "It's *just* a sandwich."

"There's no such thing as *just* a sandwich. One sandwich can change the world." We break out into laughter, and it's the warmest, most meaningful laughter I've ever shared.

Our smiles don't mean just anything, but rather every-thing. It's a smile that says it's gonna be okay and that you understand the other person almost perfectly.

And, most importantly, you're glad for it.

TWENTY-FOUR
ADELAIDE

The man is a rat.

A real-life rat.

His shoulders are so disgusted by the weight of his evil head, that they refuse to hold it straight up. His oily hair is parted down the middle and sticks to his cranium with the weight of his sin. He keeps his head lowered, looking up at us with fidgeting black eyes.

"I know it doesn't appear to be a good situation," he says without even trying to appear honest. He's lying through his teeth. I just know. "But Grammy's health has been off and on through the years. My family…we're suffering. I can't land a job because of some previous family issues that have nothing to do with me. If we could just get her inheritance—"

"No worries, Octavian," Fawn says. My mouth is open in disgust at what he wants me to do. His grandmother sits on the couch, whimpering and staring at one person: me. Like I have a choice in this. She wears a doily-like beret on top of her head and white orthopedic old woman shoes.

"If we could just make it seem that she's gone batty, we

can keep her in the hospital for a while until they proclaim her a vegetable and then, regrettably, we'll have to pull the plug." The woman doesn't hear a bit of the plan this man has in store for her. Her wild eyes scrape over me like I'm a savage performing a sacrifice.

Why doesn't he just *ask* her for a loan until he gets back on his feet? Fawn is so blind. He doesn't have a family; he doesn't need the money. He *wants* the money. I don't have to peruse his memory or anyone else's for the truth to be clear.

"All right." Fawn nods and laughs as if this is any other job. "Thank you for letting us help you, Octavian. Adelaide, do your stuff!"

But the floor has grabbed my ankles and bound me in some kind of unseen frozen shock. I can't move; I don't even want to breathe anymore.

Fawn's laugh rises a pitch. "Addy?"

I can't do it. I can't.

I've seen the look in that old woman's eyes too many times. I tremble now, violently.

"Is she having a seizure?" Octavian hisses, stepping back a bit as if a seizure is contagious.

"No, this is part of the process." Fawn stomps across the living room, and her fingernails scold me. But I almost can't feel them on my shoulder.

It doesn't matter.

I can't do this anymore. I just…

The world whooshes back. I realize where I am, what I'm doing. What I'm supposed to be doing. My momentary bravado vanishes and cold drenches me.

"Adelaide…" The whisper is deadly. It tickles the instruments in my ear and makes them cower in fear.

The weight of what I have to do is too much. Octavian glares at me, his greedy fingers clenching and unclenching.

The old woman's eyes are closed now, and she moves her lips in a silent prayer.

Now I know what it feels like to have the weight of the world on my shoulders.

Lightheadedness knocks on the door. I allow it to enter, and it appraises the situation. My legs waver and my arms feel as if they aren't attached to me. The darkness pulsates, and I want to cry for joy at an escape.

"*Adelaide.* Don't you *dare* do this to me. To us."

I'm in the middle of two moving mountains, in a valley of moral decision. One mountain is the ever-present fear that I've accepted. The knowledge that I can never change my life.

The other moving giant is the courage I threw away years ago.

The combination of Mason's presence in my life and the twins' Envisioning has awakened the courage in me. It isn't strong, but it's gaining ground.

I stand there, in my valley, cold and small and feeling very much like Adelaide.

And I choose neither.

My legs give out, and as I'm falling, the black captures me and brings me up on the wings of an eagle. I feel as if I'm flying for three seconds.

And then—

Nothing.

Fawn is gone. I'm in my bedroom. My arms ache, and something on my head thrashes violently.

My foot hits the icy floor and I grab some socks to combat the cold. I try my door, but it's locked. So Fawn's locked me in here.

Mason can't come over today. There's no one to let him down. I don't want him to know how Fawn is treating me, anyway. I run my fingers through my hair; the stunted blades of hair are all over the place and ridden with knots. My butterfly pin clings to my half-up hairstyle. I tighten its hold and fix my hair so I look presentable and then put on a smile. Then I walk over to my desk. The chair is my favorite; Fawn claims it was vintage. It's been in disrepair for some time, but I can't bear to let go of it. The cushion is burgundy and torn badly, with bits of the yellow inside coming out. I shove the chair guts back into the seat and take a seat as I pull my Communicator out of my dress pocket. After I tap twice, it shakes and then grows to normal size.

I call Mason. I'm so shaky. I *really* need something to eat.

"Adelaide?"

"Hey, um…you can't come over today." My stomach growls loudly, and I shift in my seat like that'll make it stop.

Mason doesn't say anything.

"Adelaide?" I drag my eyes over to the Communicator. Mason sits there, his hologram suspended in the air. He doesn't smile.

"What?"

"Did Fawn hit you?"

My hand shoots up to the still-aching area on my forehead. That's a mistake, because the pain flames stronger in response to the pressure. I act like I don't notice.

"No."

"Adelaide." He looks furious.

I don't even have to look to know that Fawn did leave her mark of disapproval.

"This has to stop."

I shrug, but fear tingles up my spine. Fawn rarely hits me;

her threats are almost always verbal. "It's nothing. I passed out, anyway."

Oops, mistake. I shouldn't have said that.

"You passed out while she was hitting you?"

"No, no. I passed out before."

"Why did you pass out?"

I check my shoulders and arms to find a handful of bruised splotches. I grab at my too-short sleeves. No matter how hard I tug, they won't hide the marks.

"I'm coming over right now." I open my mouth to speak, but Mason interrupts.

"But Fawn might still be here."

He shakes his head, then pauses. His eyes grab mine. "Then she's in a world of trouble."

I'm speechless.

"Listen, you have to know: if Fawn finds you, she'll wipe your memory."

"No, she'll force *you* to wipe my memory," he corrects. "And maybe that's the wake-up call you need. Because you won't do it."

Every time I think of standing up to Fawn, it's like my train of thought hits a brick wall. Everything turns black and nothing makes sense. It's like going against her is genetically impossible for me. I can't imagine a world that isn't like the one I live in every day.

"I hope you're right."

"Okay, I'm going to head over now." He disconnects and the hologram disappears. I'm so excited he's coming, but mad he won't listen to me and leave well enough alone.

I see my favorite sweater tossed over my desk chair and glance down at the telltale bruises on my arms. I can't let Mason see the rest of the marks, or he'll drag me to The Outside even if I'm kicking him the whole way up.

I pull the sweater on, a chunky white cable knit cover-up.

A short while later, clumpy man's footsteps thwap across the floor.

"Adelaide?" It's Mason. I want to hug him, but the door blocks me.

"Yup, I'm here."

"Okay, hold on; I brought my stuff and I'll get you out of there." I sit down in front of the door, legs crossed, eyes watching the door for my hero. Random noises come from the other side as he messes with the keypad guarding my door. He works patiently, the keypad chirping like it's upset. Variations of the noise continue. I want to check on Mason's progress but don't want to annoy him, so I stay silent.

Finally, the door swings open and reveals Mason, wearing dark wash jeans and a grin. Relief washes over me, and joy buzzes through my bones.

"You're the best!" I squeak. He runs over to me and gives me a hug. My head hits a little below his shoulders. I've never felt safer, and I never want to let go. I tear up without meaning to, and I hurry to collect myself before he lets go.

My stomach gives a snarky, very loud grumble. Mason lets go of me and laughs.

"Okay, message received: let's go get you some food."

TWENTY-FIVE
ADELAIDE

Mason darts to our kitchen like this is his house. A small smile finds its way onto my lips, despite everything. When I get to the kitchen, he's flinging the refrigerator door open. He finds a loaf of bread.

"Will Fawn get mad if you eat that?"

I lean against the doorframe and cross my arms behind my back to stretch. "No, I'm in charge of the kitchen. She doesn't really notice what goes on in here. Besides, she doesn't believe in bread."

"Like…believe that bread exists?"

I like how easily we joke around. I never thought being with someone could be as natural as breathing. "Precisely. It's an extinct species."

He opens the plastic surrounding the bread and pulls out two pieces, then realizes he doesn't have anywhere to put them. My smile grows. I arch my back and stretch. Muscles that I didn't know existed pop in my legs and back.

"Plates are—"

"No, no; I'll find them. Just stay there." He scavenges

through all the cupboards, finally finding our stack of four plates. He grabs one and places the bread on it with precision, making sure the crust edges match up perfectly. He finds some jelly and wordlessly holds it up.

"Sure, sounds good to me."

He goes through the same process to find a knife. He scrapes at the jelly jar, which I'm sure jiggles and cowers against the sides. He smacks the sides of the jar and finally urges the jelly to ooze out. It plops onto the bread.

He finishes with gusto, brandishing the butter knife in the air like he's a top chef making me a steak dinner. I accept my sandwich and eat it.

"How long have I been in my room?" I ask. The jelly to peanut butter ratio in this sandwich is massively off, but I won't tell Mason.

"I haven't heard from you since yesterday, so everything must've happened last night. Which means Fawn left you in your room overnight."

"What time is it?"

"Almost 7:00." No wonder I'm hungry.

I sigh. He makes me two more sandwiches. I eat one and insist he eats the other one.

He wants to stay with me, even though Fawn could be coming home at any moment. "I want to make sure you're safe. Get your mind off everything."

I feel as if I'm in a dream. Maybe Mason never even came over; maybe I'm hallucinating.

"And...remember that conversation we had? About leaving the robot here and fooling Fawn?" His excitement makes me grin. "I'm almost done. In the next few days, you could be a free woman."

"Mason, that's...amazing!" My smile is fake, and I know it. And he knows it.

"Don't tell me after this event you're still unsure if you should leave?"

I bristle. "Leaving is *terrifying*. There are people ready to hunt me down, ready to kill me because of my powers.

"And logically…where will I live? How will I get an income? I barely even know where I am. Should I trek through the forest for a month, hoping to get as far away from her as I can? What if I'm kidnapped?"

I shove my plate aside, done with the meal. I want to be done with this conversation. "I can't even remember basic details in everyday life. I'm ditzy and a klutz and…I don't think I can be on my own."

Mason frowns. "This is so…frustrating. I want you to want this—freedom—so badly."

Tears build in my eyes. "I'm scared. Either way, whatever happens…I'm scared. But at least, here, nothing is unknown. I know what I'm dealing with. Out there…I've seen a lot of things in peoples' memories. I *know* living outside isn't just a fairytale."

The words of Mason's song come back to me:

> *All that flying does is show you*
> *All of the wealth of foolish kings.*

All my life, Fawn has taught me that freedom—living life outside, up above our safe house—is just a mirage.

"What can we do?" Mason asks quietly, eyes haunted. "Ideally, we'd go to the authorities—but your existence is illegal."

The silence is so awful. I'm hurting him, dragging knives against his heart every time I say no. *Be brave, be brave,* I will myself. Maybe I can tell him what he wants to hear; I'm good at that. I'll tell him I'll let the robot pretend to be me, that I'll leave with him.

I open my mouth, hoping some answer will fall out, but then—

"Adelaide?" *It's Buddy. And Perkins is right behind him.*

The twins are here, holding bags of groceries.

And they see Mason.

I stand in front of Mason and shield him like he's a little fairy I have to protect.

"Guys! Um, this is Mason."

"Hey," Mason says, voice breaking a little.

The twins just stare at me.

"Don't tell Fawn," I beg. They look behind me, trying to get a peek at the boy I've smuggled into my sheltered life.

"Adelaide…" Buddy starts. Then, he comes to me and wraps me in a hug. I'm so scared and relieved and emotional, that I start sobbing. Perkins adds to the hug, and I'm surrounded.

They pull away, and I rub at the tears on my face.

"We're *so* glad you finally have an ally in all this," Perkins says.

Buddy sticks out his hand to Mason. "Nice to meet you, sir. My name is Buddy."

I snort. "Short for Buddington."

"Whatever, Adelaide."

Mason shakes his hand and nods. "Well, I'm Mason. Thanks. You saved my skin."

Buddy lets out a coarse laugh. "Yeahhh…you have no idea."

I shove Buddy for that comment. Perkins shakes Mason's hand with much enthusiasm.

"I'd say I hope to see you around," Mason laughs, "but that would probably mean bad things for me."

Perkins chuckles and sets his grocery bags on the floor. "True, true."

I realize something. "Wait...how did you guys get in here?"

The twins suddenly both look extremely suspicious. My skin tingles, and I look behind me to see Mason inches away from me.

Forget it, the magical moment is over.

"Um..." Perkins tugs at his t-shirt. It's navy and has the Rolling Stones logo on it. "Crap. This isn't good."

Buddy sighs. He runs a hand over his head like he expects hair to be there. "We didn't expect you. Last we heard, Fawn needed groceries and she was taking you to The Outside. We come through this secret entrance whenever you're not here. Fawn always led you to believe we were already here, but... there's another way."

Why would she hide the entrance from me? Has she always believed I would be brave enough to run away? Must she have her claws in every part of my life?

I can't breathe; it's like this massive weight is on my chest. My head spins with all this information. "Why would she keep it a secret?"

Perkins shrugs. "It's just another way of controlling you."

Buddy continues. "Listen, we're just going to drop the groceries off. If Fawn ever finds out about this guy...we'll go up to bat for you."

I smile and hug both of them again. "Thank you. But... just be careful. You don't know the Fawn that I do."

Perkins smiles. "We can handle her."

"Are you guys going to be okay?" I ask. "Like, what if Fawn finds out?"

"What exactly is she capable of?" Perkins asks, rifling

through the bags (probably for some "contraband" he purchased for himself, like candy).

That's what I'm afraid of: I'm not sure I know. There's this dark cloud hovering on the horizon, the unknown warning me to watch my step. "She's a very angry woman. She's insulting and strategic." I try to think of other examples, but my mind goes blank. It's all the years of little pokes and pricks and prods, all adding up to *now*. "She breaks you down to your core, until you feel ashamed and exposed."

"I've heard her," Mason admits. I watch the twins' reaction to him, but their faces are hard to decipher. "She is *vicious*. She calls Adelaide names, yells at her, blames her for things that make no sense…"

Buddy leans against the counter and shakes his head. "How has Fawn hid it so well from us?"

"I think she's a narcissist," Mason says. "They're very good at putting on a façade, except around their victim."

Buddy shakes his head. "I'm so sorry, Adelaide. I wish we'd known sooner. This *sucks*."

"But we can take care of ourselves," Perkins says. "And so can you. And it's about time you realize that."

Perkins throws a bag away in the trash. Shivers run through me.

"We thought we were your only friends in the world, Adelaide." Buddy's words make my world so much bigger. It makes my heart sing. "You were so smiley as a little girl, so happy. So free, even. You didn't know any other world existed outside of this box. And you were so talented."

"And so intuitive," Perkins adds. "You could look at a person and immediately tell their personality. It was uncanny."

"And…" Buddy glances at Perkins. "You had an amazing memory."

"Photographic, almost." Perkins begins to open a box of ice cream bars, but Buddy slaps his hand. "Yeesh, I was getting one for you, butthead."

"Don't talk like that in front of the woman," Buddy snaps back, but it's all in good fun. They grin and punch each other like two little boys.

"I had a good memory?" My whisper cracks.

"Of course," Buddy says.

I'm so confused. It's like Fawn has been showing me the color green and telling me it was red. Up is down, right is left...my life feels like a lie. And I don't know who I am anymore.

Am I just a projection of Fawn's insecurities? Have expertly woven lies become a tapestry of my character, my reality?

"We want to show you something. Fawn's Envisioning has been changing more drastically." The twins reach out for my hands, and I accept.

"What are they doing?" Mason asks, but I can't explain before blackness covers my vision. I lose my grip on my physical body and suddenly, I'm floating and empty.

A gun.

The barrel stares straight at me, threatening and icy. Hands drip into view.

Again, the nails give it away.

Red.

Fawn's face terrifies me until I see the strange lack of harshness. There's uncertainty in her eyes, and her lips tremble.

Then I'm shot back to get a view of the person she's aiming at: *me*.

I stand confidently in the Envisioning, eyes aflame, stance

firm. The anger scares me; it seethes from my face, out of control…like Fawn.

The scene wipes away and changes. There's darkness and danger…like the dark blue of a burning fire. The gun is flying through the air; a gunshot sounds, screams and roars echoing all around me. Hands wring Fawn's neck until her face is gray —hands that are mine. The screams and the roars are mine as well.

Fawn collapses to the floor. I climb over her, triumphant, almost mad with fury.

But, suddenly, Mason stands across from me. His face, too, is gray. He stares at me emptily, as if he doesn't know me. As if I'm just another stranger.

He slumps to the floor, and I scream. My heart rips out of my throat, my soul shakes.

He's dead.

Then I'm back in the kitchen, trembling and trying to control my breath.

"What was that?" Mason asks.

I hate that Envisioning. The other was empowering and hopeful; this one filled me with dread. "An—an Envisioning."

Mason's eyebrows shoot up. "Wow. You guys are *so* much cooler than I am. Envisioners, Memory Jumpers…All I can do is use a drill."

His comment pulls a grin from me. "At least you're legal."

He shrugs. "*Boring.*"

"Hey, Adelaide," Buddy says. "We'll show you the secret entrance. Mason, we'll be right back."

The twins and I head to the little closet. The exit is tucked in the very back of the house, in a little closet I thought Fawn only used to store our *emergency equipment* just in case we had to evacuate. It's like *Chronicles of Narnia*, except there are two rotund, bald men climbing into my house with bags of groceries through a hidden door in the back of a closet.

The closets in this house hide so many secrets.

Buddy looks at me like I'm a caged lion. "Adelaide, anything you need to tell us about that Envisioning?"

I shake my head. "That wasn't me. Fawn has ruined my life but…I'd never kill her. And what happened to Mason?"

I stare into their eyes, begging for answers. "How do I change this reality?"

Perkins sighs. "You know how this works. Only you can change it. We just transmit the visions. We don't control them.

"We were stunned to see such a…violent Envisioning, front and center. It's just kind of worrying."

Buddy pats me on the shoulder. "And now that we know about Fawn…"

"Are you physically safe?"

The glint of scissors flashes in my brain; I feel Fawn's shoves, her nails digging into me.

Warnings scream through my brain: they could lose everything if they know the truth.

Lie.

"Yes, she doesn't touch me." The sweater I put on before they came covers the truth.

Perkins frowns. "I think you should tell her she can't treat you this way, though. No one deserves to be put down constantly. It's inhumane."

I force a smile. They don't know, they don't understand. And I can't expect them to. "Maybe."

"But back to the Envisioning, let's make sure it doesn't come into being," Perkins says. "There are so many possible *good* alternate realities. Seek those. Look for the good."

I hug the twins. They are the only two people in the world

who took an interest in me pre-Mason. My only friends for so long, even when I didn't know it.

When they leave, I just stand there, staring at the door I didn't even know was there.

When I get back to the living room, Mason is fiddling with the wall. He's found the remote for it and is looking through all of the scenes. They're just meaningless blurs in my eyes, interpretations of the world I'm missing, shadows of what could be. Kind of like how I create memories that never even existed, manipulate moments that never could have happened.

He looks up at me.

"So…" His voice cracks a little bit, like he hasn't spoken in a while. "We were talking about you leaving."

My heart thuds again like it did before, and I'm afraid it's going to burst out of my chest and run away for the high hills.

"Is it really the logistics of it that's keeping you from leaving?" Is it? I'm so lost, so mentally stuck, I don't even know anymore. "What if—What if I came with you?"

My heart stops. "But what about Kendror? Being an inventor?"

He closes his mouth, eyes staring intently into mine.

"I need to know…Mason, what am I to you?" I whisper, afraid I'm wrong. Afraid that I've ached to be loved for so long, and I'll only be disappointed.

Maybe I didn't even know what love was. Maybe I still didn't.

"Adelaide—you're better than Kendror." He looks at me differently now, like I'm a different person; like I'm a puzzle he finally found the missing piece to. "I'm in love with you."

The words make everything click. I've been living life with a dislocated shoulder. Maybe a dislocated heart. But, with those few words, I've found my voice.

I've found my freedom. I've been made whole. "I love you too."

He leans in, and then everything blurs together; all I know is that Mason is kissing me. It's like visiting The Outside for the first time, but a thousand times better.

He grabs my hand; it opens like little flowers touched by the sunshine and I intertwine my fingers in his. How is it possible to feel so alive, and yet so dead?

"I don't want to lose you," I whisper, tearing up already at the thought of him disappearing.

"I'm not going anywhere," he promises. Maybe he's something I can believe in.

"Then you need to know who I am. I've—"

He doesn't know the ins and outs of what I do. How I've deleted memories of people against their will; how terrified, innocent people have begged me not to bend to their oppressor's wishes. How I've wimped out every time. Would he think I'm a monster?

My lip quivers and I'm afraid I'm about to explode.

"I've done—I've done terrible things."

"What?"

His eyes are killing me. His presence is all around me. I'm exploding. Exploding in stars, flaming stars.

Yet he doesn't say anything. He gives me one of the things I've always wanted: someone to listen.

"Fawn turned my gift into a curse. And I haven't stood up for myself. Other people have been hurt in the aftermath." Finally, I can admit that to myself. It doesn't make me feel better though. In fact, now I feel as if I have *two* holes in my chest.

I felt better living in a lie.

"Whatever you've done, you can start over. Every day you can start over. But *you* have to choose it." Mason says, gesturing at the door in the closet. "Unfortunately, I can't drag you out of here against your will. That'd be very Fawn of me."

With juddering hands, I sweep the hair away from my neck. I run my finger down the back of my neck and search for that bump; that terrible, condemning bump.

"Feel this."

He gingerly places his thumb on the spot I point to.

"Fawn put a tracking device in me when I was little. I can't ever leave." A curtain of tears blocks my vision. "It's *inside of me.*"

Mason is just a mass of circles and blurs. I collapse into his arms and cry even more, even though I feel as if I can't cry anymore. My brain hurts from crying so hard, but I can't stop. "No matter—no matter h-how f-f-far I run…she w-will always —always find me."

"You're going to be okay." Mason's words are like a golden key, shining gloriously. A key that will unlock my prison. I know I shouldn't believe him, but I do.

My crying turns into little, random shakings of my chest. And then he's just holding me, and honestly…I feel as if I'm already free.

He squeezes my hand before letting go. He stands up, so tall I almost have to look straight up. I bet he can see right down my nose. How attractive.

I am a druggie. Addicted to freedom, to Mason.

"Pippa is a nurse. If I bring her tomorrow to remove the tracker…will you leave?"

Yes. *Yes.* The curtains are gone. There is nothing holding me here. Mason will make sure I have all I need to survive in the real world. Fawn will not be able to hurt me so long as he is with me.

I grab his hands and stand up. Hands that will lead me to safety, to something better. "Yes. Yes, I'll leave."

He grins down at me and hugs me, but I feel him freeze. He grabs me by the shoulders and pulls away, a searching look on his face. "You're serious? You've really thought this over? You aren't going to change your mind, right?"

I pause for a second, but I can think of no other options. This is what I want. "No. No, I'm done here. I'm done being trampled. You make me feel like a real human, valuable and worthy; I want that, every day. And I want to help you come back here one day and be an inventor."

He chuckles. "One step at a time, Miss Bravery. Okay, I'm going to leave so I can talk to Pippa about your tracker and get some stuff together."

"Do you really have to go?"

"Yeah, I do." I know he can't stay. But at least I tried. I feel…disappointed. I don't know if I like feeling things. "I'm coming back tomorrow, I swear."

I can't say anything. The words won't come. Mason leans forward; I'm so numb I don't even realize what's happening. His lips meet my forehead and colors twirl in front of me. I still can't move, and all my emotions are so tangled.

He pulls away. I don't want him to. And then he's walking away. I don't even have the energy to follow him.

So I just stand there.

Alive.

Oh, so alive.

ADELAIDE'S USELESS FACT #1042

Adelaide is in love.

TWENTY-SIX
COLETTE

"L ast year's ball was...lackluster." For such a dull man, my husband has an extraordinary vocabulary. He used to dazzle me with words like *laconic* and *ostentatious* while on dates at the most extraordinary libraries in the country.

But this is an indirect insult. I planned Wesley's birthday ball last year, choosing every last painfully boring detail. I'd done it in an attempt to win his favor which, as usual, failed miserably. In fact, it seemed to bring about the opposite effect: he loathed me for weeks.

"What do you suggest to make it better?" I ask, for he is never in the wrong.

He has no answer, of course. "I don't know. Just come up with something better. Lillian's party for Jeffrey was superb."

Perhaps because they had caviar, golden plates, and a chandelier made of thousands of intricate diamonds. But they were the rulers of Great Britain, not our infant country.

"I will try, my dearest." That was all I could do, anyway.

"Ma'am?" A maid is at my side.

"Yes?"

"A letter for you." She hands me a dirty white envelope.

"Thank you," I say as I accept the letter. There is no return address, only my name. I tear the top open and pull the note out, written hurriedly on loose-leaf paper.

My hands grip the paper.

Colette,

I'm done playing games. I want my son to know the truth about who he is. Your husband's attempt to cover it up led to Adam's brain damage, I'm convinced of that. Releasing the secret in his memory will make sure he doesn't suffer any other negative side effects.

I'm bringing that Memory Jumper back to the castle in two days to restore Adam's memory. Be in Adam's room at 2:00 p.m.

If you cause problems or attempt to sabotage the procedure, I'll tell Wesley—and the country—about our relationship. You will be humiliated and your husband will shun you. It's an easy choice.

Green

I glance up from the paper as my fingers tremble. I slowly lower my hands to my lap on the off chance that Wesley would notice my strange behavior. Luckily, he's distracted by his newspaper.

When Adam was fourteen years old, Green broke one of our agreements: that Adam could not know who his real father was. Green snuck into the castle, told Adam, and tried to kidnap him.

He was caught by our guards, and we had yet another round of arguing, fighting, blackmailing, and agreeing.

Wesley said the only way this charade could continue was if we removed the memory of Green's revelation from Adam's mind. We compromised by hiring a Memory Jumper to lock the memory up. As a further layer of security, only I was allowed to unlock the memory should we ever choose to reveal the truth again.

"What if I just tell him again tomorrow?" Green sneered. I hated the rage in his eyes, so unfamiliar and cold.

The Memory Jumper told us that the truth may interfere with the locked memory, and there could be terrible consequences.

"Memories are very fragile," she told us. "There's a reason why we have a Memory Jumper rule book. We can't just do whatever we want to peoples' brains. There are many consequences when reality and memories don't match up, or when belief and truth conflict."

Guilt overwhelms me. It makes sense that Adam's strange illness was due to Memory Jumping. But the Memory Jumper had been so careful, so thorough…

We have The Tour today, plus four hours of speaking to the citizens. I won't have a free moment to process this information until tonight when I'm in my room.

Panic rises in me, but I shove it down.

"Pretend you're an actress," I coach myself. "You didn't get that message. Or maybe you did, but you're glad to hear from an old friend. Just don't let it get to you."

The next few hours are pure torture. Green's words race through my head, and my sins weigh heavy on my soul. I'm sure Wesley can see right through me, and I wish I were invisible.

In two days, Adam will turn twenty-one. I turn my eyes toward the ceiling, in prayer. I can't burst into tears right here, right now.

Of course, Green would want to ruin Adam's birthday by revealing this secret. Green also is aware that Wesley will be away, a rare occurrence. He is touring a military base, and it is encouraged to keep women out of the camp because it is too harsh of an environment.

In the solace of my room, I reread the letter. I churn every word through my mind, trying to figure out his intentions. Surely he won't hurt Adam; he has always seemed interested in, even covetous of his son.

Would he hurt me? Doubtful. He's more calculated than that. Unfortunately, I no longer care what becomes of me. Death doesn't scare me.

I'll have to keep the guards away. Easy enough on my son's birthday. I'll tell them I just want a quiet day to ourselves.

And what to tell Adam? I freeze at the thought of revealing my affair. Would it be better to prepare him before-hand? I'm not used to making decisions on my own. I almost crave Wesley's unflinching commands so I don't have to think for myself.

If I tell Adam, I'm not sure he will keep it from Wesley. I doubt his loyalty to his father would be broken by my request for silence and secrecy. I have no other option: he must learn about my deeds the moment the Memory Jumper opens his memories.

Then I will truly be alone.

TWENTY-SEVEN
ADELAIDE

F awn returns at about eight that night. The signal comes like the thunderous anger of mythological gods.

I'm in my room. Mason locked me back in before he left so Fawn wouldn't know I left. He also checked the cameras to make sure they show me in my room all day.

Buddy and Perkins came back this afternoon with some other purchases (Buddy forgot the detergent on their first trip), so they get the teleporter. I don't hear much, and I almost convince myself I'm out of the woods until Fawn's heels echo down the hallways. They come closer and closer to my room. The doorknob rattles as if she forgot she locked me in, and then she grunts, and there's a pause. Nails jabbing glass. Beeping—a happy chirp. The doorknob trembles before flying open.

I'm curled up in my bed, my back facing the doorway. I thought it would be better that way, but now I'm not so sure. It's like being scared of the monsters that roam at night: would you rather be facing them so you can reach out and strangle them if they dare to show their face, or would you rather deny their existence because you can't see them?

I turn over a bit, Fawn clacking over to me. She grabs my shoulders and I stiffen, a scream rising in my throat.

"Oh, Adelaide." I blink against the light tendrils shooting from the door. Her hair falls over her face as she leans over me. I pull myself up to a sitting position.

"Why do you punish yourself like that?"

I tilt my head. "What?"

"Hey, hey. It's okay." She gives me a hug. But, unlike Mason's hug, Fawn's hug only hurts. And she doesn't let go when I say *ow*. "You need to forgive yourself. I forgive you for what you did."

My tears border on the edge of fury. She's the one who needs forgiveness. And she knows it. Her hand circles the bruise on my face.

"I have some cream for that." She sighs. "We'll have to cover it with foundation, but that's no problem. Rest up. You have a big day tomorrow!"

"What are we doing?"

She gives me an empty smile. Then she leaves, slamming my door shut. I listen for her to lock it, but she doesn't.

I sit there in the darkness that has taken over my life.

Fawn and I sit at the kitchen table for breakfast the next morning. Fawn cuddles a cup of coffee with a water bottle close by. She says coffee is bad for you and that water is way better, but she still drinks coffee. It's like she believes she's absorbing the water by association.

"You're not the first Memory Jumper to mess with the prince's mind, you know."

Is this a trap? I don't want to talk or think about Memory Jumping anymore. Yet the curiosity takes over. "Really? How many other Memory Jumpers are there?"

Fawn's eyes lower and her mouth hops up and down like she's searching for the right words. "Well, there *were*. You lived in a community full of Memory Jumpers at one time. Every day, hundreds of people came to request their services. The Memory Jumpers wrote a code that made a lot of types of Memory Jumping illegal.

"But, when people asked for those things and Memory Jumpers refused, they became irate. A bunch of them got together and burned the community to the ground."

I mentally plead for her to continue but don't dare to say anything.

"The king and queen used Memory Jumping to remove a memory from the prince's mind. Now, they need to put it back."

This is the most Fawn has ever told me about Memory Jumping. Sounds like she knew a lot more than she'd let on. "So…we *aren't* illegal."

Fawn's eyebrows dart into a furrow. "Well, I mean, we *are*. But the king and queen have given us a kind of immunity, in case they ever need our services. Regular people don't know about it, so they are still dangerous.

"And, if we can complete this mission, we'll have plenty of money. Money is security, Adelaide. Maybe we can move!"

I don't believe her. For the first time in my life, there's not even a tendril of belief budding inside of me.

"You said I need to unlock a memory? What memory?" I ask.

"It's a golden sphere, marked as 'Adam's childhood memory.' Most likely in his subconscious." Fawn says. "You will bring the queen into her son's mind, and she'll unlock it. She's the only one that can."

My face falls. "But…why?"

"Don't ask those questions, Addy. You have no right to the answer. It doesn't matter." She leans towards me. "All that matters is the payment. Right?"

I wonder what that code against corrupt Memory Jumping included. Probably a lot of things Fawn makes me do daily. "Right."

I write Mason, telling him about my last Memory Jumping assignment.

We should be back by 3:00, I write. *But I'll keep you updated.*

Green shows up around 10:00. Gone is his camo, replaced by black cargo pants. He wears his bandana around his neck like he forgot he doesn't need to hide his identity anymore.

"How are you doing, Fawn?" he asks politely. "And Adelaide, how are you doing? Ready for this mission?"

I love how he calls them missions. He has such a big head; he must be reliving his glory days. "Yes, sir."

Ready to be finished.

Ready to come back.

Ready to leave.

We head out and find the secret passageway. This time around, I feel a bit more confident, less like I'm not supposed to be doing this.

We enter the castle. It's decorated beautifully, probably for the upcoming Crowning. Green garlands curl along the walls and expensive-looking flower arrangements sit on tables spread out in twenty-foot intervals.

Servants bustle around; my instinct is to hide from them, but Green walks by them with no emotion.

When we get to Prince Adam's bedroom, I'm glad to find him standing up next to his mother. He wears all white, except for his shoes which are cobalt blue sneakers. The king is nowhere to be seen.

My first thought is that Adam doesn't have his mother's eyes. His eyes are dark brown, so dark brown that they're almost black. They're not unkind like the king's.

Adam walks toward me, a smile on his face. "Are you the girl that saved my life?"

I like this greeting. "Yeah, I am. I mean, yes."

"It's much appreciated," he says. His mother nods her agreement.

The tears in his mother's eyes are unexpected. "This is an early birthday present, love."

Adam looks back toward her. "Thanks, Mom—wait, why are you crying?"

The queen shakes her head. "Nothing. No reason. Just *so* proud of you and the man you're becoming."

He walks over to her, taking confident and heavy steps like his father. He wraps her in a hug. *Why didn't I get a mother like her?*

The queen looks at me and swipes at the tears falling over her lips, holding tight to her giant son. "Shall we begin?"

"Sure, if you're ready," I say. She nods, lips trembling ever so slightly.

First, I Memory Jump into the queen's mind. The doors are each decoupaged, covered with various patterned papers and stickers. So, she's creative. A light hangs next to each door, pristinely clean and tastefully picked.

I close my eyes and find Adam's brain. It's familiar, now bright with consciousness. I circle around the queen's brain and my own, then fling us at Adam.

Adam's mind bleeds into view.

"This is stunning!" The queen gasps as she stands beside

me. I notice how elegantly her hair is braided; I wonder if her mother taught her how to do that.

Her amazement makes me happy and I find myself grinning. This is the only part of the world that is my territory. Even still, it's ultimately owned by other people. The thought wipes the grin off my face.

"And you get to see this all the time?" The queen places a hand on my shoulder. I'm so used to Fawn's pinches that I flinch. "Oh, I'm sorry, dear."

I smile. "Um, it's okay. And, yeah. It's really cool."

I'd say I love what I do, but I don't like lying if I can help it.

"Marvelous." The queen has forgotten why we're here.

"Excuse me, Your Majesty, but…"

"Oh, sorry, dear! My husband says I'm always on a different page. I got sidetracked for a moment." She turns to face me, eyes on everything else. "The Memory Jumper who helped us all those years ago encased Adam's memory in a golden sphere. She stored it in a closet of my subconscious. It's labeled…let's see here, what did she say?"

"Fawn told me it was *Adam's childhood memory*."

"Yes, that's right!"

I close my eyes and see the trail where I encircle my mind and the queen's and send us into Adam's memory. I focus on keeping that trail alive, but also send out a second line into Adam's mind.

We arrive, and I quickly absorb everything. The doors in Adam's mind are heavy and steel, organized in no particular pattern. The labels are crooked and sloppy.

"This is Adam's…brain?"

"His memory, yes," I comment. "Brain is a physical part of the body. Memories aren't something you can hold—well, if you're a normal person."

The queen stands enraptured. "Oh, dear—if seeing this makes you a not-normal person, I'd rather be not normal any day."

She's absolutely precious. So innocent and bright-eyed. She doesn't know what she's saying.

"Okay, I'm going to go find that memory. You good here?"

"Yes, you do what you need to."

I start my job. I drag my hands and the doors fly by me. When my hand seems to hit a wall, I stop and find myself at Adam's earliest memory. It's a less menacing door, made of wood with simple, childish letters carved into the panels.

I approach the side of the door and feel around for the subconscious. Not here. I move a bit farther away and keep nudging the area around me until my foot kicks something hard, and a staircase appears.

I descend into the darkness, which feels less dark than usual. I remember what the twins said about my ability to read personalities. Here, enveloped in the memories and mind of Prince Adam, I relax and attempt to read his personality… however I'd do that.

I continue down the stairs as words come to me. Kind. Unselfish. Emotional.

The steps flatten out to form a floor. I glance around to decide what I'm up against. Rows upon rows of shelves are stuffed full of random memories. I envision the golden sphere and trust my instincts.

I go straight ahead quite a few steps, then turn right and left. Part of me is always scared I'll get lost in these caverns, but this is my domain. I belong here.

I'm drawn to a splintered, crudely-shaped shelf. It's only hip-height and drenched in darkness. If I were to reach for something, I have a feeling my arm would keep going further back than should be physically possible.

Everything on the shelves looks broken. I scrounge around, finding that there is a back to the shelf. I unearth a stuffed frog toy missing both arms and one leg, two baby teeth, and a wooden box that's locked.

Finally, I find something round and metallic. I wipe at the gunk covering it, curious at what the filth could possibly be. It's only a projection of the mind, but to a Memory Jumper, it's still gunk.

The metal is slightly gold underneath. I keep brushing at the object until my fingers meet a raised surface that's pentagon-shaped. It has a border and, engraved in the middle, a simple crown made of three triangles. When I move the sphere, the crown wavers and disappears.

I flip the circle upside down and engraved on the bottom are the words *Adam's childhood memory*. This is it.

I turn around and find my way back to the steps, continuing to shine the sphere. I almost trip on a step, because I'm not paying attention.

I reach the queen and hand her the sphere. "This is it."

The queen stands there, staring at the object. She doesn't say a word. Maybe I shouldn't have shined it?

"Is this the right thing?"

She nods. "Oh yes, that's right." She takes a step closer. "You do know what Paul is doing, don't you?"

I only wish I did. "No ma'am, actually I don't. My employers don't tell me much."

She takes a deep breath. "That's probably for the best."

"I'm sorry. I'm really, really sorry. I don't know what's going on, but…I'm sorry."

I don't know her story, but I'm determined to reunite her with her son. She has a kindness about her that contrasts with her husband's prickly personality. Her quiet courage is thoughtful and speaks only when it has something good to say.

"You have such innocent eyes," she says, breaking my thoughts. I stare at the ground, a foggy bit of gray and black. It whispers across the tops of my feet. "There's a whole universe inside of you, my dear. Hold that tight."

All of my responses have a double meaning. They'd only encourage her to ask more questions, dig deeper, and here in my safe place, I'm worried I'd let all my secrets fly. I can't afford that.

TWENTY-EIGHT
COLETTE

"You should probably take this," Adelaide says.

I watch her face, soft and wise. If I had a daughter, I'd want her to be just like this young woman. She carries herself like an older adult, even though she must barely be seventeen or eighteen.

I glance at the sphere. Only I can open it, a safeguard we put in place upon its creation…a safeguard made against my will.

I tremble, biting the skin inside my lip as if it will anchor my soul. My hands gravitate towards the golden pentagon which, at the angle I see it, is crown-less. My thumb hooks underneath the pentagon and pulls. The halves of the sphere collapse inwards, leaving just a glowing ring. Voices whisper, some louder than others, ebbing in and out of hearing range. The glow spreads further and my hands burn; I drop the orb. The light is so bright I have to look away. I cover my eyes with my hand but still see the brightness, its heat flickering at my skin.

It grows brighter and brighter. I can't help but wonder if

this is supposed to happen. Maternal anger seizes me: I can accept mistreatment aimed towards me. But when could I no longer make choices regarding my son? It sometimes seems he is my only ally, but when he finds out the truth about me, he will hate me.

I fall to the ground, my hands covering my face.

Adelaide asks if I'm okay. "It didn't do anything to you, did it?"

I'm not embarrassed to be sobbing in front of this Memory Jumper. Maybe because humiliation is so normal for me now, or maybe I'm just thoroughly numb to emotion. What a relief that would be.

I wipe my face with the back of my hand like a child. "Yes; yes, I'm fine I think. I'm sorry. I'm just—I'm just—just—"

I can't finish. I'm choking on life, drowning in the injustice of it all.

"Let's get you out of here," Adelaide says. I close my eyes and a shivery, swirling feeling overwhelms me.

When I open my eyes, we're back in Adam's room. The anger has taken full control by now. Oh, I can feel all right.

I glare fully at Paul for the first time since he's re-entered my life. My voice boils. "Is this what you want?"

"Mom?" Adam says, hesitant. He must be putting everything together as we speak.

"Shut up, Colette," Paul says. Shards of memories come back to me: sneaking away with him in the night, in the late afternoons. His beautiful promises, his cleverly-worded compliments. "This is getting to be too much. I'm so tired of your drama, your lies."

I was just a game. A game he won.

"He deserves to know the truth," Paul says.

Adam yells again, but the exact words are foggy. My eyes remain fixed on Paul.

At that moment, I break.

I always held myself back. Dignity, poise, acceptance—these were the guidelines that kept me in possession of the life I had. But was it the life I truly wanted? My reaction was to stay silent, to become invisible.

But my son was worth fighting for.

It was too late: he knew the truth now. But it wouldn't be too late for me.

A mother-bear shriek hurls out of my throat, and I launch myself at Paul. That was silly of me; he grabs me, holding me tightly. A sickness grows in my belly at his familiar touch, all disdain and no desire.

"Now, now, Colette," Paul says calmly, pulling me even closer. I let out a whimper and wriggle like a fish on a hook. "Let's be calm. I've kept up my side of the bargain as have you."

"You liar!" I gasp, fury trembling in my voice. "You snuck in here and told him who you were all those years ago; you almost destroyed the whole thing. I had to clean up the mess and now you're here complicating things again."

"Don't you dare blame me for this! It was your idea to cover this all up with Memory Jumping all those years ago, and you ended up *hurting* my son."

"Our son!" I scream into the room. The nausea crescendos and bile rises in my throat. The world spins in circles, an endless tornado. I melt to the floor, my face on cold tile. "Stop! No more." My arms go limp, Paul lets go. "Just go."

There's silence for a moment—then Paul's woman companion says a sharp, "Let's go."

I raise myself up, rocking back and forth. Adam yells, "Mom, what's going on?"

I return my gaze to Paul, not ready to confront my son.

"*You.* I swear, if I ever see your despicable face in this castle again, I will not hesitate to call every guard in the vicinity. I don't care who finds out anymore.

Paul sneers. "You're such a sad, lonely woman." Shivers run down my spine. "My, how you've fallen from grace."

He slips out of the room, out of my life. Just like he did twenty years ago.

And just like twenty years ago, I am left with a son, a broken heart, and no answers.

TWENTY-NINE
ADELAIDE

We get to the secret passageway and I pause, but Fawn pokes me again, and I continue forward into the darkness. Behind me, the queen fumes at Green. "I swear, if I ever see your despicable face in this castle again, I'll—"

I shoot forward, wanting to wipe this situation, this day off myself. I'm disgusted that I had any part in it. I had thought I was helping the queen, but…I am ending my Memory Jumping career as a villain.

I'm glad the passageway is darker here, because tears fall down my cheeks, and I don't try to stop them.

The longer they fall, the harder it is to control the sobs that want to tear out of my throat. I force myself to breathe in and out, deeply and slowly. The tears come harder and harder, but I have to keep control of myself.

When we get back to the house, Fawn and Green stop in the kitchen, but I head for my room. My body seems to know I'm close to relief, because the sobs start to become uncontrollable again.

I dart into my room and close the door. I'm not even scared that Fawn will come yell at me for whatever reason. I'm leaving her, closing my door, isolating myself, not waiting to reflect on our mission…I couldn't care less right now.

I collapse onto my bed and there, muffled in the pillow, I sob.

I am a monster.

I hug the pillow to myself, squeezing my anger and disgust out.

If only it were that easy.

These memories haunt me. Every time I close my eyes, I hear the queen's stomach-clenching screams and Green's insults. And as I replay them, over and over, more and more memories drown me. Who am I to be free?

"Adelaide!" I wake up to Fawn's yell. Is it tomorrow yet? Is Fawn gone yet? Can Mason come save me?

I climb out of bed and run into the hallway. "Yes, ma'am? Where are you?"

"Living room!"

I scream on the inside, but my feet move towards the living room. *Tell me you're going out. Tell me you're leaving for the night.*

I arrive at the couch. "Yes?"

Fawn's grin is plastic. "Sit down."

I plop down.

"This is it: the end of the job. After tomorrow, you and I won't live in fear anymore. We'll move. We can leave this place."

Fawn, living in fear? Ha! What a joke. She creates the fear in my life; I figured she wasn't scared of anything: demons, murderers, con men, assassins. Her mind is made up of a combination of all of those, after all.

I have a far better plan. I want to smile, because for once I feel like I know something that she doesn't.

Fawn stares at me like my head is supposed to pop open and rain confetti on her and Green. I know she's giving me false hope. Whatever she's doing will have no benefits for me.

"Come on, Adelaide," she snaps. "Seriously? No reaction?"

"I just don't understand the plan."

"There's a whole soap opera going on at the castle, and I'm absolutely *living* for it," Fawn laughs. Her joy brought about by other people's pain makes me sick. "So, get this: Adam? The prince? He's *Green's son.* But *with the queen.* Oh my gosh, can you believe it?"

She really thinks I haven't picked up on that?

Fawn continues. "Green has had it *up to here* with the monarchy; they're blackmailing him, he's blackmailing them, it's a hot mess.

"Green really thought Adam would just up and leave with him when he found out the truth. But…he didn't. Adam's just a momma's boy." Fawn has a gift for telling stories that make the characters out to be absolute Neanderthals.

"So, Green has this super detailed plan…eh, it's not important. You'll probably be best off not knowing the details. But we're basically going to reunite Green with his son. You can feel good about that, right?"

Fawn's idea of justice is so off. Adam clearly doesn't want to be with his dad. Where will his mom fit into the picture? And the king?

"We're going to make another visit to the castle. When I tell you to, I need you to Memory Jump into the nearest soldier; then, from there, you need to Memory Jump through all the other soldiers' minds."

I'm a simple, disrespected tool, used for purposes I was never intended for.

"What?"

"I have more experience with Memory Jumping than you'd think; I know it can be done." Her tone is so derogative. "It's called Conglomerative Memory Jumping. You'll pile all their minds together and then wipe them clear."

You can't keep telling me to do impossible things.

You're just using me to get what you want.

Why would I want to do this for you when I still can't be free?

Little prickles of irritation dance throughout me. Irritation that I'm not used to. I'm so ready to be done with all of this.

Fawn has offered me too little, too late.

"You've been different lately," she comments. "You seem a little tense."

More like *happy*.

"I need you to be in your best mental game for this Conglomerate Jumping," she says. "Listen, it's going to be a lot. I won't lie."

Imagine that.

"But I need you to remember something: these people you're Conglomerate Jumping on…they hate you. They hate *us*."

"You could live in freedom every day though," I say. "You're *normal*."

Fawn actually looks uncomfortable. Her eyes lower. "Well…not exactly. Um…listen. Hiding down here has been a combination of things. But you and I, we're not so different. I'm—I'm also a Memory Jumper."

Layers of fake excitement sit atop her revelation like cheap frosting. My heart drops out of my chest: why has she been using me for so long then? Why hasn't she Memory Jumped? Why has she *used* me?

"For your protection, I had to completely lose my identity as a Memory Jumper. That way, I could be a second-party vendor of your services. I could protect you better." Her lies are slathered onto her life, cheap frosting. "You *have* to keep this in mind during this mission: These people have limited our lives for so long."

These people? Really? Because the only person I've seen holding my leash has been her. "We've had to live here in secret. I've had to risk my life to go above ground."

For the first time, Fawn actually sounds apologetic. She sounds…sad, even. Are those tears in her eyes? They glisten unnaturally, not in glee. "All these years, I've been protecting you from these Memory Jumper haters."

Chills dart through my head; across my shoulders; down my spine. They jolt through my thighs and down my legs. Tears well up in my eyes.

She must be lying. Or maybe she's been lying for so long that she actually believes she's protecting me. I think about the things she does to me, the things she says.

I don't care if there are soldiers out there looking to spill my blood. Fawn's been spilling mine since I was a child. She's made me feel soulless. Turned me into a porcelain doll; no, a weapon of mass destruction. One that she takes into peoples' lives and…and uses to destroy.

"But now, we can be free." She really believes what she's saying. I fear the look in her eyes because it's the look of honesty. "Green wants his son back, and I want justice. And then we leave."

I want to hit the pause button and demand an explanation. But she leaves no room for a question-and-answer session. "Green is taking over the throne. And we're going to help."

With my boat and oars, I fled
To the sea...

All I hear are the voices in my head begging me to be brave, begging me to stand up and fight.

"We're heading out tomorrow," she says. I look deep into her eyes, past the knowledge that I don't really have a choice. The Envisionings come back, moving me forward. Away from fear, toward the light.

...and then I said,
"Got my wings, got my wings,
How I love these silly things!

I open my mouth and boldly, breathlessly, say, "No."

I watch her like she's a lion that skipped breakfast. She shakes her head and kinda chuckles. "You're funny."

But my staunch face makes her drop her cheer. Her nostrils flare and she raises her head in fury. She comes at me, and I flinch. Next step: after saying *no*, run. But I'm not there yet. I'm taking baby steps. I can't move.

Even though I see the pain in life...

She shoves her face in mine and pulls out a poisonous, "What did you say?"

...I now know the answer why

Can I say it again? Do I dare? "No."

"You sick, demented, selfish—"

All the bitter folk
End up sad and broke:
They just focus on the dark."

Her fists rear back.

She's all over me, and I can only cry.

I've been fighting mental deadness for so long, I'm almost surprised her blows hurt. I shove her, and she only grows more angry.

I scream at her to stop. I beg. But she refuses.

Her massive hands connect with my nose at an amazing speed. She pushes me and roars at me to go to my room. "Don't ever cross me again!"

I flee willingly, tripping on my own feet.

Once in my bedroom, I shoot onto my bed and grab my pillow like it'll save me. I place a hand on my chest in an attempt to slow my heart down, fully knowing that won't work.

I write Mason: *We have to leave. Soon. It* has *to be today.*

Fawn's nightmarish lullaby plays in my ear: "Don't. Ever. Cross. Me. Again."

Clipped my wings,
Clipped my wings,
"You don't need those silly things…"

THIRTY
ADELAIDE

Mason immediately calls me.

"What happened?"

"We have to leave," I sob. "We have to leave now. She needs my help to…to hurt a lot of people. And I'm tired of it. Mason, I told her no."

He smiles, and I can't help but wish he were here with me so I could lean into him and feel safe. I need him here with me, in the flesh. "I'm so, so proud of you, Adelaide. Hold tight. Is she still there?"

"I…I don't know. I've been crying, I haven't heard anything…"

Mason frowns, face filled with determination. "Let me hack into your security cameras. I'll check the past hour."

I shake my head. "Green has a final mission for me. He wants to take over the *government*, Mason. They're going to stage a coup. If I leave, they'll both hunt me down for sure."

"Okay…okay. Let's think about one problem at a time."

I sniffle as he gets to work. Then I start shivering. Flashes of heat and cold wash over me. Something is *not* right. "I'm all hot and cold and then hot again—"

"It might be shock," Mason says. "It's going to be okay, I promise."

I shiver for a few more minutes while he does his computer magic.

"She left!" he yells, making me jump. "Fawn stormed out right after you guys fought."

"Please come," I whisper, shutting my eyes.

"I'm going to leave right now. Do you need anything? Um, food, water—"

"Just a bag," I say. "Something to carry my things. We'll figure it out from there. I'm scared she'll come back."

Once he hangs up, I gather my things. I peel the photos off the wall, pick out two books (*Emma* and my book of fun facts), and grab a couple of dresses (not the ones Fawn made me).

Then I stare at everything. I wish the room could be totally cleared out when Fawn comes back, but I can't carry everything. I wince at the bookshelf full of my friends, my confidantes. I must leave them behind.

I think about my pottery room. I have five mugs on the shelf, two plates, three bowls, and a couple of orders to fulfill. I never even got to sell my solar system jewelry.

Now I get to go out and create my own galaxy.

I'm too tired to be sentimental, too disgusted to wish I could bring more with me.

Mason writes me: *I'm about to teleport. Be there in a couple of seconds.*

I head to the teleporter for the last time. The signal comes.

The teleporter doors slide open.

Mason practically falls out of the teleporter. I drop my measly possessions, and I'm wrapped into a hug that seems to ground me. It's like I'm finally a part of the world for the first time in my life. I cry out of fear, joy, and who knows what else.

When he pulls away, his face is fierce. "She's a monster."

"I just need to get out of here. The sooner the better. I'm so scared, I—"

"Hey, hey, don't think about that. We need to get your tracking device out. Then we'll leave this place. Pippa is coming in five minutes."

"Okay." But there's something in his voice that tells me there's something he's not sharing. Sure enough, he fidgets and adds to his sentence.

"Well…we were just going to try to turn the tracking device off and leave it in your neck. But…listen, Adelaide. Your best shot—our best shot—is to actually remove it."

Black eats away at my vision. The room spins, and I think I'm about to pass out. "Like…surgery?"

"Don't worry, she's bringing an anesthetic. You won't feel anything."

I don't know if I believe that.

"How long is it going to take?"

"Less than an hour."

"I don't know when Fawn is coming back. I don't know if—"

Needles. *Blood.* Stitches and chunks of skin. I clench my wet fists together.

"I don't trust Fawn's mental stability, and you leaving is going to tick her off to no end. If I turn it off, she might be able to figure out a way to activate it again. And I don't know what she would do if she found us again. So this has to be done now."

"Hey, you okay?" I refuse to look at him and he captures my hands in his. "Look at me. I'm going to be right here. It won't hurt a bit, I swear. The needle is just like a pinch, and then for everything else you'll be numb."

I finally look at him. His shock-blue eyes wouldn't lie to me; they brim with honesty.

"Adelaide?"

I can't believe we're actually doing this. I tap my legs, nervous energy shooting through them. I wish time would stop. I wish I was already done with the surgery.

I go over the plan in my head again. They'll take the tracking device out. But what happens when Fawn comes home and doesn't find me?

"How's the robot?"

"Not finished," Mason says. "But that's not important. Once we get this tracker out, we can disappear. It won't matter that she knows. We'll just have to move quickly."

A signal comes from above and I want to scream. Fawn is back and—

Wait, that's not Fawn. The signal is different. Too many taps.

"It's okay, it's Pippa. I gave her a different signal so we'd know it's her." I'm too scared, too emotional to speak. Mason goes to bring the teleporter down. I go get some paper towels for the blood.

When I come back, I find Mason chatting with a woman of average height with curly burgundy hair. She has milky blue eyes, an exhausted but honest smile, and freckles all over her arms and bare shoulders. She wears stylish pants with a geometric silver pattern. Her shirt is a simple sleeveless tube top with a white scarf hanging on the front. It's the huge white case that she's holding that makes my breath hitch.

"Pippa, this is Adelaide."

Pippa walks up to me, grabs my hand, and nods in

approval. In her mid-forties, she is surveying and thoughtful, fascinated by other people. "Nice to meet you, dear."

I smile at her. "It's so nice to meet you! I've heard so much about you."

Pippa's eyes flit towards Mason, and a hint of a smile plays on her face. "Same here. Mason has told me a lot about the girl who lives underground."

Mason averts his eyes, and Pippa and I both share my first laugh of the day.

Then she's back to business. "If you want to sit down somewhere, we can start. Do you have anything for—"

"I have paper towels," I interrupt. I don't want to hear the word *blood*.

Our small party sets up camp on the floor of our dining room. I sit on a classy spread of paper towels. Pippa takes out all of her tools and I turn to face the opposite direction of her. Mason sits down next to me, scooting close and wrapping an arm around me. I don't admit I'm scared, but I'm sure it's all over my face.

"This will be really fast," Pippa promises. "This first part will just pinch a bit and then your neck will be numb."

I nod. Mason lets go of me so Pippa can reach my neck, but he holds my hand instead. I can't look at him because Pippa holds my neck captive. His presence is like a second covering, and he tells me more about his robot. None of the words make sense, but the familiar hum of his voice soothes me.

The pinch comes—okay, that's not that bad—oh wait, *ow*. It melts into something more than a pinch, like a violent sting. I move my lips in silent prayer.

"The *YKK* on your zipper stands for *Yoshida Kogyo Kabushiki-gaisha*." I glance over at Mason to see that he's reading random facts off of his Communicator. I relax ever so slightly as his voice lures any remaining nerves out of me.

"Keep going," I whisper.

"Cookie Monster's real name is Sid."

"What is a Cookie Monster?"

"I'm sorry, Adelaide," Pippa says, "but could you try to stay still?"

"Oh, of course."

I close my eyes and just listen to Mason's voice.

It's impossible to hum while holding your nose.

A dragonfly has a lifespan of twenty-four hours.

A goldfish has a memory span of three seconds.

A dime has 118 ridges around the edge.

When Pippa is done, I keep my eyes closed until she and Mason have cleaned up anything and everything that would make me think of the surgery. I open my eyes and the first thing I see is Mason. He puts his big arms around me, and I smile.

Pippa gathers everything up and asks if we need any more help. We say *no* and I thank her.

"So…you're…letting him go?" I ask. My parental figure is so overbearing and controlling. Pippa is in direct contrast, willing to trust her adult son's decisions.

Pippa looks at Mason, pride bursting in her gaze. "He was never mine from the start. And he knows that now. He's free to do what he wants, and he knows that. All I ask is…you two let me know when you're safe. And where you are."

"Of course." Mason wraps Pippa in a hug.

She nods. "You make sure you follow through on that promise, boy. Bye, Adelaide. Nice to meet you."

Pippa wraps me in a hug as well.

"Thank you for giving Mason something to fight for," she

whispers. She looks at Mason once more. "Well, I guess this is goodbye. Good luck, guys."

She hugs Mason one more time. I quickly locate her brain and Memory Jump in. I collect memories of Mason and strengthen them, bringing them to the forefront of her brain so she can return to them often.

I jump out, and neither of them notices my interference. It feels good to help.

Pippa leaves, and after the teleporter doors shut, Mason turns around and looks at me. A smile grows on his face, and I match it.

"I can't believe we did it," I say, then throw my arms in the air. Mason rushes at me and picks me up by the waist. I shriek, scared for a moment that Fawn might somehow hear me—but she no longer has any power over me. I can run as far as I want, and she'll never find me.

I'm free.

When he lowers me, he's so gentle, not as pent-up with excitement as before. When I look into his eyes, they're soft and loving. The freedom I thought I could never have.

And then, Mason kisses me.

I'm so happy, I could explode. I pull away to hug him, and I kiss him again.

We're free. Really free.

We laugh as loudly as we want.

We go to the entryway, and I grab my things which are now in a lopsided pile.

Then I grab the hand of the boy I love and we head toward the teleporter.

"I love you," Mason says, out-of-breath but honest.

"I love you too."

USELESS FACT #7640

Your pupils can expand by as much as 45% when looking
at someone you love.

Then there's a gunshot. My heart stops, my brain explodes. It's not because I've been hit; it's because that sound doesn't belong here in this dream. No, not in my *reality*.

It's the twins' Envisioning.

But Mason and I are leaving.

It's game over.

No more, we won.

"Adelaide Victoria Constance." It's a level higher than Addy. A name so sacred, it's only been uttered once before when I first Memory Jumped in her brain.

It's been saved for this moment, seething in anger.

All the breath in my lungs escapes in one explosive gasp. My shoulders collapse and anger rises in my throat, vicious and unafraid.

I spin around and see something that sends me off the cliff I've been hanging onto for so long.

It's Fawn.

She's back.

And she's mad.

THIRTY-ONE
ADELAIDE

I seize Mason's hand and throw myself in front of him.

"Don't you *dare* touch him," I hiss.

The gun in her hand doesn't scare me. I saw it in the Envisioning, the scene familiar. It only adds wood to the flaming fury inside of me. I take a step towards her. Mason's hands attempt to pull me back to safety.

"Get away from him," Fawn demands. Her bottom lip trembles.

"No, he's coming with me. I'm leaving." Those two words seem to send a crack running through the surface of the earth. I swear mountains are toppling over; oceans are draining into an endless cavity.

"Adelaide, stop this."

"No," I snap. "I'm free. Free of *you.*"

Fawn puts the gun back into her jacket. I clench Mason's arm as her face drops. She looks down at the floor, biting her lip like she's about to cry. "Oh, Adelaide."

What is she going to do?

Mason tugs at me. "Adelaide, let's go. Please."

"Don't you want the truth?" Her eyes glaze over. They don't look at me anymore.

She takes a deep breath. "The more you Memory Jump, the more you become lost in your own mind. Adelaide, Mason is just a figment of your imagination. You've been so alone, which I apologize immensely for because it's partly my fault. You subconsciously created him. He doesn't even exist."

Behind me, Mason yells. "What? Adelaide, that's stupid. She's lying to you, don't believe her."

Of course I don't believe her. Mason is the best thing to happen to me.

"You're a liar!"

"Adelaide, please," she says sorrowfully. "You're very, very ill. And it's all my fault. I made you Memory Jump too much. Must I prove it to you?"

Mason pulls at me, and I hear him push the button for the teleporter.

"Buddy! Perkins!" Fawn calls. There's a pause for a moment; a second where nothing moves, nothing breathes. Then Buddy and Perkins walk into the room.

"Buddy! Perkins! I'm leaving!" I shout. The empty look on their faces makes my stomach tumble. "I'm doing what you said, I'm being brave." But there are no jokes. No smiles. No hugs.

They stand there, scowling at me, eyes cold and hard.

"What…what?"

"You altered your reality," Fawn explains again. "You made them into your friends. Didn't you ever wonder why they seemed so much like those people from Alice in Wonderland?"

Tears roll down my cheeks like little trains on a tragic mission.

"Tweedledee and Tweedledum," I answer obediently.

243

"Yes. From *Alice in Wonderland*," Fawn says the name of my favorite book. My childhood escape.

Fawn's face breaks. Something inside of me claws desperately; I think it's the bravery.

It's trying to leave.

"What I can't stand, though, is you made me out to be a villain. It started when I didn't let you out, but don't you see that was for your own good? I know what happened last time people knew about the existence of Memory Jumpers. They destroyed us. I was just trying to keep you safe."

Mason throws himself in front of me, eyes wild. He's so tall, he blocks Fawn from my view. "Adelaide, don't believe a word she says. I'm real. This is all real! I don't know what she did to Buddy and Perkins; they're real too, though! They're good and kind and they love you!"

He brings his lips to mine but I'm dead. I'm empty. I don't kiss him back. He doesn't exist. More tears fall down my cheeks.

I want to die.

Mason gives up, rests his face on my forehead. He whispers, voice broken and sad: "Tell me that's not real."

I just shake my head. It's all I can do.

"What about the Pieces of the World?" Mason asks. "If I'm real, then they are too."

There's no recognition in Fawn's eyes. I tear away from Mason and run to my room. The tears fall down in torrents. I haven't really escaped. I've only bound myself more tightly.

I fling the drawer open, the one I kept all the Pieces of the World in.

It's bordered with black-striped paper and holds piles of books.

No Pieces of the World.

I made it up.

I really did make it all up.

Oh my gosh. Oh my gosh. *I'm insane.*

I fall to my knees and shake. I'm afraid I may hit something, I'm so out of control, but at this point…do I care?

A hand slips around my shoulders. I grab it and beg it to pull me out of the water I'm drowning in.

"You can't give into the manipulations," Fawn says. "We used to have Memory Jumpers go insane in the community like this; you see all kinds of things."

Mason stands beside me, begging for me to not listen to Fawn. Yet his words are fringe on the edge of my mind, and I force myself to zone him out.

"They only get worse," Fawn says. "You'll be lost in your own mind forever. Please, I—my mother. She loved Memory Jumping and she practiced every day. Soon she was roaming around our little community, talking to nonexistent people. She'd even make up new breeds of animals. And me? She thought I was her dead sister."

She sobs at the memory. "I don't want you to become like that."

I close my eyes and see Mason; Mason, and only Mason. He's so beautiful; he doesn't exist. Why would someone as wonderful as him love me?

I look at Fawn. The earth changes; the walls grow dark; chains entwine me; the colors leak out of everything. I'm losing my mind.

"Make it stop."

Fawn gazes into my eyes, more tears falling down. She lowers her eyes and nods as if upset she must take away the only hope I have.

So I let the darkness take me.

This darkness is part of my mind, I realize. I almost consider fighting it, but then I remember who I am.

I am Adelaide.

I don't fight.

I don't yell.

I'm not brave.

The black pulls me into itself, icy as hate and dead as my soul.

I don't even care if I ever come back.

I've never felt so cold in my whole entire life. It's like I'm not even human anymore. I haven't eaten. I've barely moved since yesterday.

I breathe, yet I am dead.

Fawn tied Mason up and put him in the closet with the secret passageway. At first, every time he heard movement, he would yell and try to convince me he really exists. But now he is silent. Has he faded away? Maybe I'm healing.

Ever since I discovered that I'm going insane, that Mason never existed in the first place, I've felt as if I have crossed the finish line and now have nothing sending me towards my goal.

I don't even have a goal any more.

"Adelaide! Almost time to go!" I turn the light off and go find Fawn. She's in the hallway transferring the contents of her purse into a black backpack.

She glances at me and frowns.

"Smile," she begs. But I can't. I've been broken. "You've been a ghost. I know it's hard, but…we must be brave."

The word is like a slap in my face.

> *You may soar beside the clouds,*
> *But all this foolishness allows*
> *Is a higher view*

Of this cruel world
That we blindly call our home.

The song brings me back to all kinds of memories. Fake memories, ones I made up to console myself. To deal with the loneliness I felt every day.

Could I be the girl with the clipped wings? The foolish, stupid girl who wants to fly but doesn't realize what darkness awaits her? I once had hoped that things could change. I believed Fawn had clipped my wings. I believed Mason taught me how to fly.

And that moment. That moment right before Fawn found me…that moment when I was laughing with Mason, free and alive.

Was that my moment?

Fawn's explanation of our plan for today replays in my brain. Every detail makes me shudder, but I truly feel like an emotionless tool now. She can have whatever she wants. I have nothing left.

"We have to make Adam disappear," she explained to me last night. "It's a big task, but I'll help you. Green wants his son, without interference from the crown. So we're going to Conglomerate Memory Jump on the guards, the king and queen, and all of Kendror so there's no memory of Adam.

"We'll also have to convince Adam that he never was the prince and he's always been with Green."

I stay silent for a moment. Then I ask: "Does Memory Jumping cause brain damage?"

"What do you mean?"

"The queen mentioned it while I was in Adam's brain. Does what I'm doing cause brain damage?"

Fawn laughs, nerves bubbling up. "No. That's ridiculous. If you know what you're doing, and you're careful, it—"

I interrupt. "When we leave—when we finally get out of this place, I never want to Memory Jump again."

Fawn watches me. I was so broken, yet so sure.

"Okay," she agrees. "If you do this last thing."

"I just want to get out of here."

Fawn gives a small smile. "Just think, as your final act of Memory Jumping, you'll be bringing justice for so many people. That's *very* noble of you."

I barely slept last night. Now I sit in the living room, turning the wall screen on to see the sad representation of The Outside.

I know what it's like out there. Out there where the sky bleeds on for eternity. I've never seen such colors before in my life; indescribable, a painting of majesty. It's what life would look like if you could see it: colorful and bright, so small yet so big at the same time.

"Be brave." Mason's words tremble through me, and I shiver. Why should I be brave? I'm going insane. The boy I love doesn't even exist. If I go through with this, I'm guaranteed a golden cage. I'll be the exotic bird in the corner everyone simply takes care of and then ignores. I wonder where we'll go, what Fawn will do.

I'll be safe. But I won't be loved.

But love is better than safety, right? Love will bring me danger, but I'll be really and truly alive.

What is Fawn's idea of justice? That word had passed her lips, sharp and vindictive. Was that a part of my delusion as well?

I could die tonight. If not physically, then mentally.

I remember Mason's eyes. They sure seemed real. And that moment. All the moments that we shared together.

What am I doing?

Maybe I am going crazy.

Maybe I am alone in the world.

And yet the decision to leave wasn't fake.

That bravery I felt, that wasn't fake.

Maybe all it took was another lie to actually show me the truth. Maybe Mason was more like a part of my brain, or even a bit of my conscience, showing me all the reasons to seek true freedom.

And I decide right then and there.

I'm going to be brave.

THIRTY-TWO
ADELAIDE

I find Fawn in the kitchen, rummaging through the fridge. "Good morning, Adelaide. Are you feeling okay?"

"No, actually. I feel terrible. I—I can't do this anymore."

Fawn turns, holding three plastic baggies with sandwiches. I look her straight in the eyes. What is there? Fear? Anger? Pain?

"What?"

"I can't be a part of this." My hands shake so hard, but I'm not changing my mind. "I'm really sorry, Fawn. I just...it doesn't feel right. Mason might be fake, but my convictions aren't. Every time I Memory Jump for evil purposes, part of me dies."

Her mouth twitches the tiniest bit.

"You can't wimp—you can't give up now, Adelaide. We're so close!"

I sigh, figuring she'll understand. "Please, Fawn. I don't want to argue anymore."

Her face turns the brightest shade of red I've seen on her.

"Don't you *dare* wimp out on me, Adelaide."

She sure does seem like a villain right now. She said the manipulations even edit how I see *her*. I try to see through the fake, try to find the real Fawn who I've suppressed.

"Help me, Fawn," I plead. "I'm scared. I don't know what's real and what's not."

Her anger melts. She breathes out, watching me. For a moment, I see her: the mother. The mother I always wanted.

"Okay," she says. "Let me make a cup of coffee, then we'll go over some methods for removing the manipulations."

Where do I go from here? After fighting so long against her, the opportunity for a stalemate is…worse?

I have nothing to fight for anymore.

Fawn hums happily to herself. I don't remember her ever humming before.

And she's humming Mason's song.

Clipped my wings,
Clipped my wings…

She pours coffee into a thermos. Shivers cross my shoulders, and all I want is a big sweatshirt to cuddle up in.

"I'll be right back, gonna go grab a sweatshirt." I go to my room, which no longer feels like a safe haven. Every part of the world now feels like an alien terrain to me, without Mason. Without my sanity.

What is real and what isn't? Can I truly become lost in my own mind?

The walls are empty now. I really must've removed the photos from my wall in preparation to leave.

The stitches on my neck hurt. I rub my fingers over them. Could I have made this up?

Then I remember—my Communicator. I walk into my

closet and check the farthest corner, under my laundry bin where I used to hide it.

It's there.

Which, wait...if Mason doesn't exist, how would I have gotten this?

I think...

I sprint back to the kitchen, forgetting my sweatshirt. Rage and warmth are building up inside of me again.

"You lied to me, didn't you?" Fawn jumps, spinning around to glare at me. "Did you lie about me being insane?"

Fawn grabs my hand. I jerk my wrist to get out of her grasp as her fingernails dig into my flesh. "Tell me the truth! For once in your miserable life, tell me the truth!"

The aggressive words shoot into the air, deafening. I've never yelled at Fawn before, and the effect is explosive. She lets go of me and steps back, fear shading her eyes before being replaced by anger.

"I did this all for you. I did it—I was trying to do what was best."

"*This?*" I scream. "*This* is what's best? You've made me *hate* myself. Hate my life."

I want to destroy her for what she's done to me: she's persecuted me, taken away years of my life, used me, abused me. Not only that, but she made me believe that Mason didn't exist and that I was losing my sanity. And that's truly unforgivable.

"Listen Adelaide: the world is harsh. And you have to be a little harsh to survive. You'll learn this in time. But clearly not today."

Fawn's eyes are murderous.

She kicks me in the stomach and I lurch back, scared momentarily. But I'm ready to fight. I'll tear her limb from limb if I have to.

I see the Envisioning. My hands around her neck, her face gray. Her body collapsed in a heap on the floor.

No, I won't do it. Killing Fawn in anger would be completely wrong. All I want is for Mason and me to get out of her life.

She doesn't expect me to fight, so I use that to my advantage. I run at her and go for her middle, shoving her with everything I have.

Fawn falls backward, cursing at me as we collide and fall to the floor. Rage simmers in my throat, begging me to knock her out forever: to scratch and pull and choke. But I rein it in, gritting my teeth.

I roll away from her as soon as we hit the ground, then run to the closet and yank the door open to free Mason.

"Adelaide! Oh my gosh, Adelaide, I thought—I thought—"

His arms are tied up, but his legs are free. I grab him and we spin around, only to be nose-to-gun with Fawn.

But Fawn is too fast for me. She shoves me in the forehead with the butt of the gun. The universe inside of me explodes, tilts…

When my eyes open again, everything throbs like I fell down Mount Everest. Worst of all is my head, and I wonder if Fawn gave me a concussion.

I'm in the closet with Mason. My hands are tied together, but my legs are free.

Mason sits propped up against a wall, tied with rope, and tightly at that. His right eye is swollen shut and his lip is spliced and badly bleeding. Duct tape covers his mouth. "Oh my gosh, Mason, I'm so sorry…"

253

I peel the duct tape off gingerly, wincing with him as it slowly releases his skin.

As soon as the tape is off, he starts talking. "Don't worry about me. She's not done with you. You need to—"

Mason's voice disappears. I've zoned out. I'm seething with anger. Everything turns red and I scream into the air.

I *want* to see the woman who has ruined my life.

I want to let her feel the pain she's inflicted on me and now the boy I love. It takes everything I am to not turn the Envisioning into my reality.

"Fawn!" I summon her, my own personal demon.

There's silence. The floor shifts. The last bit of fear inside me runs through my veins, but the bravery I've uncovered cancels it out.

The queen was right. There is a universe inside me. And right now, it's on fire.

Fawn opens the closet door. Her smile doesn't glint as brightly as the gun in her hand. She flicks it up a bit, brandishing it at me, looking for the terror she cultivated in me.

"You're going to complete this mission," she snarls, "if it's the last thing you do."

I grit my teeth and try to control myself. I have to get my hands free.

"Do you want your boyfriend to still have a beating heart when we're done?"

"Don't bring him into this," I seethe.

"But, Addy, he's the whole reason you're acting like this." She gives me a sympathetic look—*sympathetic*. That makes me really mad. "You would have gone through with The Plan if it weren't for him."

Fawn laughs. It's a sharp sound that bounces around my room and pins me right in the heart. I struggle in my bonds but they don't yield. She tied them so tightly I'm sure the blood can't even flow to my hands.

"We could've had everything: a whole country. Freedom. Adam would be king, who knows what would happen to Mason. But why should you care?"

"I'm not going to help you," I say. "Mason is the rightful ruler. There are too many innocents whose blood will be shed. I don't want to be a part of this."

"Don't forget who saved your pathetic life," she barks. "I took you down here. To save *you*; to save *me*."

"You didn't save me," I hiss. "You've been killing me for as long as I can remember."

Her whole face stays still except for her right eye, which twitches.

"You. Are. So…" I start, but can't find a good enough word.

Fawn's face is devoid of emotion. She cocks the gun.

"Now, you're going to fix all this mess you've made." Her tone is dangerous. But I *feel* dangerous. "First, you're going to go into Mason's mind and delete every memory of yourself. Make it so that you never met him."

Every bit of adrenaline leaks out of me. I shake. "*No.*"

She shakes the gun. "Do it. Or I'll kill him."

"You wouldn't!"

I turn to Mason. My breathing is staggered and tears run from my eyes, a stampede of sadness.

Mason leans towards me, and our foreheads touch.

"*Adelaide.*" Fawn's voice is warning.

"Just do it," Mason whispers. I don't ever want to see the light in his eyes go out. "Have you ever heard that saying? 'I'd love you even if I lived a thousand times?'"

Mason's words from the Envisioning come back: "*Who are you?*"

I nod, chest heaving. I choke on tears, on sobs, on not wanting him to forget me. Those words were for me.

He won't remember me.

"Just trust me." He gives me his Mason smile. "It'll be okay. You have to help me remember."

I push his hair back from his forehead. It's tinged with red and I'm scared of what I'll find. Flopped over his forehead, his hair hid a nasty, bloody gouge. Anger drips through me again.

"Adelaide…" Mason says. He can read me like a book.

"Adelaide!" This time it's Fawn. "Do it!"

"Don't forget me," I tell Mason.

"I promise."

Then I Memory Jump.

I stand there for a moment. The Christmas tree scent makes me want to cry. I want Fawn to just leave us be.

But I begin.

I tear doorknobs off, anything that has to do with me. They drip away, drizzle into nothingness, and my tears send them there. His beautiful mind, so interesting and complex. I'm destroying it.

Colors burst and the Christmas tree smell dissipates. His mind shakes a bit like he's fighting me. I'm so proud of him for trying. The moments seem to turn into hours. My tears are the size of bricks.

So many things sweep through my mind. Meeting Mason for the first time; going to The Outside; game nights with Buddy and Perkins.

Is my mind preparing me to die? I stop the memories.

USELESS FACT #769
When you die you have 7 minutes of brain activity left, which is your brain playing back memories in a dream sequence.

Memories.

I'm a Memory Jumper. Who cares if Fawn is one too; my mind forms a plan, an ingenious plan, one against Fawn. And for the first time in my life, there's not even a tiny bit of doubt in my mind.

I have a plan. An ingenious plan, one I—ditz, useless, forgetful, broken, sheltered—created all by myself. It has to work. It must.

I tear myself from Mason's mind, only to find him looking confused.

I was right.

The light is gone.

My devious plan begins. I fall to the floor, trembling in passionate anger.

Fawn grabs me by my hair and pulls me up as I wince. She might rip it out with her bare hands this time. "If you fight back again, I will kill you without even blinking."

She tosses me aside. "We leave at 6:30 tomorrow for the palace."

Redemption is coming. I just have to endure a few more hours.

THIRTY-THREE
COLETTE

What was it like to be in love?

What was it like to be wanted?

I can't remember anymore.

Wesley and I were an expected marriage. Although I'd barely known him for three months when he proposed, I'd seen flashes of a man worth loving. He gave without bounds and made beautiful promises, sweet in the possession of a young woman who knew nothing of the world. Who knew nothing of lies. Who decided to trust, because that's the virtuous thing to do.

But Wesley wasn't on the same page.

As soon as we were married, he turned. The rocky façade emerged, and never again could I break through. He seemed to hate my very existence; I was everything he loathed.

I'm on the floor of my bathroom, heaving. Memories of every mistake I've ever made are playing in my brain, and I wonder if I'm dying.

I took too many migraine pills, and I'm not sure why.

"Why didn't you tell me?" Adam's questions come roaring

back into my mind. He's never looked at me with so much hurt, so much disdain.

My words were so pathetic. I had no answers.

Deep down, I know the pills were a halfhearted attempt at relief. I didn't care if I fell asleep or poisoned my blood or whatever too many of these pills would do.

I had lost Adam. He was my sole reason for living. I was a trellis, desperate for him to follow my lead and become an intelligent, kind young man. But now he would never forgive me.

Am I crying? I think so.

I hear myself laughing amidst the tears.

Years of anger and mistreatment and hurt and confusion boil over. The word *treason* knocks back and forth in my head, and fireworks explode in my insides.

I drop the pill bottle, the world swirling around me.

Four words fall out of my mouth, and they feel so good.

"Down with the king."

THIRTY-FOUR
ADELAIDE

'll be back, I'll be back, I promise Mason.

I stand in the kitchen with Green and Fawn, watching my adopted mother wolf down her omelets with a combination of savage cuts with her fork and large mouthfuls hastily chewed. I stare at her, then Green. I'm so excited to be rid of these disgusting people. They make me squirm.

"Let's go," she says, picking up a surviving pepper and popping it in her mouth. We follow Fawn out to the teleporter. Green begins a conversation with her. She snorts and laughs as the teleporter slides up and then teleports, like a normal person; not the person I know.

We climb out and enter The Outside. I'm still holding my shoes in my hands and Fawn throws a fit as Green flips on a flashlight.

"Put your sneakers on! You can't walk with bare feet in the forest! It's dark out, you'll step on something!"

I clench my fists and dig my fingernails into the flesh of my palm. I throw the sneakers on. "I'm sorry."

We walk in silence, so I just take in the colors of the early morning. Colors that I'll be seeing a lot more of.

Soon we're at the secret passage. My heart burns. I walk in the darkness of the shadows. The light doesn't touch me, I don't reach for it. The darkness is all-encompassing, and I feel safer here. The darkness is what I know. Fawn and Green have stopped talking; perhaps they've realized the insanity of their mission. I can only hope we're caught, except then I won't be able to ruin Fawn.

We get to the entrance of the castle. My head spins and my heart pounds. I dig my fingernails deeper into my palms. I will my heart to beat as fast as the automatic *ow ow ow ow ow* commentary in my head.

Don't lose heart, don't lose heart.

"Remember what I told you, Addy?"

"Yes." *No.* It's Mason's words that play themselves on repeat in my brain.

"Green, you ready?" He pulls the gun from his belt.

"Yes, ma'am."

Fawn reaches to her own beltline and pulls out a menacing, shiny pistol. She aims it at the sky, her wrist cocking back with comfort. "Me too. Let's go."

We run into the alcove. Fawn moves with confidence, Green and I following. Her ponytail swings like a pendulum as she holds her pistol with both hands, finger on the trigger.

"Adelaide, now!"

I lock eyes with a young soldier, his hair a militaristic, buzzed stripe down the middle of his head. I make eye contact with him as I circle around his mind; it's strong, young. As I shoot myself in, I find the strength to slow down my catapult.

I have time to look at him. Really look at him. He wears all white with gray combat boots. His eyelashes are thick and almost girlish; I wonder if he is ever teased about them. He's the first one to train his gun on us, but the only one with fear in his eyes.

I wonder who his mother is. Whether he wanted to be a castle guard all his life. If he has a girlfriend.

What his favorite memory is.

I Memory Jump, using his memory as my main operating base. I'm safe in there, where time stands still and no bullet can hit me. My stomach reels violently and there's a curious pain near my hips. I shoot out reels from my safe place in his brain.

I see the castle guards so clearly, focusing harder than I ever have. There in the darkness, the palace fans out, pale and flimsy but still there. There are three brains across the hall, and I circle around them. Every circle makes my heart hitch; my breaths grow heavier and heavier. It's like I'm breathing for five people.

I expand my search. I dart through the castle, into the throne room where a soldier flirts with a maid; his memory is mine now. There are a few men in the garden, a couple at the front entrance of the castle, and dozens more at various other entrances.

One stands watch in front of the queen's bedroom.

It's like being underneath a thick, stretchy blanket and trying to push your arms out away from you. The fabric gets harder and harder to extend, harder and harder to keep even that which you have.

But I hold on, using my own sweet memories to keep me going.

Mason. My first time in The Outside. Late-night talks with Buddy and Perkins.

My reach expands. I'm out on the roads of the city, a clash of cobblestone pavement and one-wheeled devices that move a person to their workplace. Guards are scattered throughout, some near booths, some working crowd control.

I capture all of their brains. Not a single one escapes me.

I tremble. My muscles threaten to spasm, but I can't lose my grip. I push harder and hear a terrible, terrible sound; half groan, half scream. I realize it's me, and I let it grow louder.

Even guards off duty don't escape me. There's one in his home with his family. I shriek and barely notice I've fallen to my knees.

I open my hand and pull back, willing every single memory in the minds of these men to flood towards me. It's like I'm in a vat of peanut butter, or maybe syrup; I can hardly move.

Maybe this is why people were scared of Memory Jumpers. They knew we could do things like this.

I slam my hand down, weaving together a memory: Fawn, strong and menacing. Her presence is a curse, her eyes a combination of hidden hurt and cutting words. The whole kingdom is on alert for this woman, according to the king and queen: but be patient. Don't let her out of your sight. Play along with her until the perfect moment, then snag her.

I swear that the ground underneath me is giving way.

It's over too quickly.

THIRTY-FIVE
ADELAIDE

Colors pierce me from all sides, and I'm in a tunnel shooting faster and faster towards some unknown destination. My feet hit the ground and send a judder through my body because it was too much, too fast. I fall forward, and my jaw connects with something cold and smooth. My hands rush to my face to protect myself.

My eyes fly open. I'm facedown on a white floor, sucking in breaths like I was in a vacuum. Air, air—I need more air.

"Did you do it?" Fawn asks. Her voice echoes around me.

I wheeze, which Fawn must take as a yes. I push myself up and roll onto my back. Black swims in my vision, dotted with beautiful colors. It's the sunrise from this morning, invading my vision, but the pinks are bloody. "You're gonna be like this for a while. We're going for the king and queen."

I splutter. My diaphragm spasms, sending me up and back down to the ground. Even if I wanted to speak, I couldn't. Everything hurts, even my lips. Or maybe I can't even feel them. I honestly don't know.

I roll back onto my stomach. Stars spiral through my

system, jagged and sharp. My arms are on fire. I think I broke the laws of time, physics, space, matter, everything.

I need to calm myself down. I breathe in and out while counting slowly, my chest trembling less and less.

I don't know how long I'm there before I finally feel like I'm back in a human body. My eyes are still closed, and I think about falling asleep right here.

"You!" My eyes dart open. "You're the Memory Jumper!"

I can't catch a break. A face appears above me, distorted because you aren't supposed to see humans from this perspective. Big nose, symmetrical eyebrows, upside-down fury.

It's the prince.

"Yes, I am." I gasp. "And right now, I'm here to save your parents. You know Green? Your real father? He's lost it; he's here to take you and erase the memory of you from everybody in this city."

"*What?*" His face hardens. "Is my mother in danger?"

"I don't know what Green plans to do with her," I admit. "But it involves messing with her memory."

"Okay. Tell me what to do."

"Can I borrow your arm?"

He helps me up, and I keep a steady grip on his arm. The castle darts around me. I might fall back down.

"Let's go," he says

My legs give out, and he has to fully support me. My eyes drip, my legs drip, I drip. I'm melting. Like a witch.

"Okay, here's the plan. I've already Memory Jumped on your castle guards and alerted them to Fawn; if any of them see her, they have orders to capture her. Now, I'll Memory Jump on Fawn and Green, getting rid of their muscle memory so they can't walk. Do you have some sort of jails or cells we can put them in?"

We hobble along at an excruciatingly slow pace "Yeah, we

have dungeons below this castle, from the insurgence."

The prince drags me along, which is probably necessary but definitely not preferable. He slaps a keypad on the wall and a door slides open: it's an elevator.

"Come on," he insists. I climb in and the doors close. This elevator is so different from my teleporter, with lights on the top and glass on the sides so I can see out. I gasp at the scene: roads and buildings and shops and dogs and people. It's life. Life, sprawled out before me. People running and walking and chatting and selling.

And I'm saving them. Right now. They don't even know it. A burst of energy shoots into me like a caffeine shot.

The teleporter shudders and stops, then the doors slide open. Another white hallway with solemn plants.

Adam breaks into a jog again and I follow. His eyes are on the door at the end of the hallway. He swipes at the keypad on the side and the doors open.

We burst into the room. Fawn and Green screech at the king who's kneeling on the ground, hands behind his head. Somehow the king still looks ticked.

But it's the queen that makes my heart sink. She's on the ground, crumpled like a doll, eyes closed. A terrifying thought flurries by: is she dead? Am I too late?

"Perfect timing," Fawn spits. "It's time to Memory Jump on these—"

Green sees Adam. "Wait, this wasn't part of the plan. Adelaide, why is he here?"

"Fawn, put the gun down," I say, keeping my eyes on the queen. *Please be alive, please be alive.*

"Fawn," Green says in a warning tone. "You two need to start Memory Jumping *now.*"

I'm on an absolute high. I didn't know I was capable of this. I focus on Fawn; her eyes are staring at me so sharply, almost as if she knows I've snapped. "You've been bullying people my whole life. Hurting them. You've been so twisted you don't even know how to love anymore. But no more."

I cast out my mind to Memory Jump on her, to render her useless. This is it; I'll—

I see nothing. Where are the brains? Usually this is so easy. I second-guess myself; maybe I can't do a hero speech and Memory Jump at the same time…

But then I see Fawn's smirk. She puts her gun back on her belt and crosses her arms, throwing her weight to her right leg. "You can't Memory Jump for a *long* time, Addy. A consequence of Conglomerate Jumping."

Shivers run down my spine. "I don't believe you."

"When I saved your life as a baby, I took out over twenty men with Conglomerate Memory Jumping. It's against the code but I couldn't have cared less." She struts towards me, a lion playing with its prey. "I couldn't Memory Jump for a month."

"You're a liar!"

She lunges at me and curls her arm around my neck. Adam yells and runs at her, but she takes her gun out again and waves it in the air.

"You are absolutely uncontrollable," she yells. "I've sacrificed my entire life for you!"

It's everything I can do to keep myself from biting her. All Fawn does is lie. She's been lying for so long that she believes every grimy thing she says. I reach out for the glowing, comforting presence of memories.

Maybe it took her a year, but she isn't Adelaide.

I pull at the surrounding area, begging the memories to come to me. The faintest flicker comes from Fawn, and I continue searching.

"Don't waste your breath," she hisses, but the fact that she knows I'm trying to Memory Jump on her gives me more determination.

I'm a Memory Jumper. Fawn thought after today, I'd be on her leash for the rest of my life, never to Memory Jump again.

But this is who I am.

I am Adelaide. And I am free.

I unclench my fists and relax. I find the center of my brain, the core, and direct it at Fawn's brain.

Fawn's brain puts off a strong force field, which is nothing new. But I have to get through. I *have* to. I can't let this kingdom, this country, fall. I can't give Green the throne, can't let Fawn drag me to some new place and set up the same old life with the same old rules and the same old restraints.

I can't leave Mason in that closet with no memory of his life.

I can't be afraid anymore.

My brain pounds as I sharpen my entrance and tunnel through her barrier. I hear screaming from somewhere, but it's muffled and from a different world. Perhaps it's me, perhaps it's Fawn. But it really doesn't matter right now.

Colors mesh together in inky, oozing tremblings. They shiver around me and drip into door shapes. I don't even wait for them to fully form. As soon as I see the door handle, I tear it off. Fawn's brain shakes, as if it knows I'm in there and is attempting to scare me out.

But I'm mad.

And I'm brave.

I rip off another door handle and watch the door burst into sparkles and disappear. I'm a handle-ripping fiend as I sprint down the hallway like a madman. There are so many doors vanishing, the twinkling all adding up together into a glittering waterfall of memory.

There's something I can't shake, though. All those things

she told me about the Memory Jumpers…was all of that true? I search Fawn's dark mind as it convulses and twists, trying to remove me.

And I find what I need.

I watch the memories. I see the burning building; the tiny baby; the boy, Brandon. So she did save me.

There's no insane mother, but there are instances of Fawn Memory Jumping. She is indeed a Memory Jumper. I burn, thinking of how she could've bore the burden of our work. Instead, she gave all the dirty work to me and collected the money.

I watch her deleting Buddy and Perkins' Memories.

Finding the Communicator, slapping Mason in disgust.

She cannot take these people away from me. I will take *her* away instead.

The quakes begin to slow in frequency until they stop altogether. And I destroy these sick, twisted memories.

Then I transfer myself out of her memory. I'm lying on the ground.

My eyes dart open, but they burn. Ache streaks through me and I fight to focus on the world around me. I identify Green, sprinting away from the conflict.

Don't let him get away, my brain screams. *Go after him.*

But my body won't move. My legs and arms are wooden, burning matches.

"Green! Green!" Adam calls after him. He hesitates as if deciding whether to follow him or not.

I close my eyes, tears streaming down. My brain explodes with a migraine, but I'm forgiving myself.

Green will live to fight another day, but I stopped him for now. I can track him down later.

Now that I'm safe, I can now fight for others. And fight I will.

THIRTY-SIX
COLETTE

T he world lies heavy on my eyelids, dark swaths of texture and light. Through the sludge, my son calls to me.

"Mom, Mom!" His voice is wild, and a slight pressure pushes on my sides as if he is embracing me.

I can't tell if the pills have done their job, ushering me into the afterlife, a world where my son forgives me. I don't want to believe I'm still flickering in between life and death if this is merely a mirage—I can't deal with any more disappointment.

I am no longer afraid of the dark. Before, I was numb to it. But now, it seems more like a friend. Life was not kind to me—perhaps death will be. That's all I can hope for.

My breath slows.

My eyes close.

This is bliss: nothingness. I melt into it.

Yet death will not take me tonight. It has overlooked me, and I find myself grateful.

When my eyes open again, I am in my bedroom surrounded by the same nurses and doctors who had been tending to my son. Adam sits on a chair in the corner, staring at his Communicator.

As soon as I stir, he is at my side. "Mom!"

My hands reach for him, and then my baby boy is in my arms. Pieces of myself snap back together like a puzzle, and a sudden burst of energy overwhelms me.

"My sweet boy," I whisper in his ear, never wanting to let go. "Where is your father?"

Adam pulls away. His face is blank. "He…he's been in his room. Won't come out. We all…we all had a rough day."

I wince, knowing my lies and selfishness are at the root of it.

"But listen, Mom—I know Dad is a harsh guy. I wish you'd been honest with us, but I'm not angry. Please know that." His words are the pills I needed but couldn't buy. I close my eyes, soaking in his words. "I love you, Mom."

My heartbeat is stronger now. I have a purpose in my mind: the good of my son. And that alone will keep me going.

But Adam has more to say. "The Memory Jumper has requested an audience with us as soon as you are well enough."

I'm afraid she knows too much. But it's time to come clean, for the sake of my son…for the sake of my *sons*. I've been a shadow for too long.

I nod. "Of course."

The guards escort the Memory Jumper into my bedroom, and Adam persuades Wesley to retreat from his room. It stings that he wasn't there for me when I awoke, but I really shouldn't be surprised.

Adam sits with me on my bed, while Wesley settles into a chair close by. The guards escort the Memory Jumper into the room. She is suddenly a ray of light, her eyes no longer dull black orbs. There's a glint that didn't exist before. Her steps have a lightness, her shoulders sit higher and back.

She has a voice.

Perhaps I do too.

"Adelaide," I say. Our souls feel intertwined, and her joy is contagious. I want to scoop some of it up for myself and save it in a container for a rainy day. "I don't even know what to say…You were so brave. I'm so proud of you."

The girl grins brightly. "Of course! I knew it was the right thing to do. But, um…I do need to tell you something. And I don't think the king or prince should be here."

"Are you kidding me?" Wesley sputters. I swear the man was raised by cavemen. Fear settles in my heart—what if Adelaide is here to blackmail me?

"Dad…" Adam warns.

"Please, sir," Adelaide says kindly yet firmly, staring at him confidently. "I just need to tell her something. It will only take a moment."

Wesley glares back at her for a moment. Perhaps he isn't used to being talked back to, because he suddenly looks shaken.

"Fine," he yells as he storms out of the room. Adam follows him, tossing a grimace behind him in our direction.

When they've left, I offer my hand out to Adelaide in an invitation for her to come closer. She smiles that same stardust smile and walks toward me.

Adelaide tells me about a boy. A boy who helped her be brave; who builds things and fixes things and makes her laugh.

And then—

"You cheated on your husband." The forsaken words. They make the air electric and I flinch at their magnitude, their truth. "You cheated on your husband with a man named Paul, Paul Green."

Tears bead up in my eyes and shame drenches me in scarlet.

"Don't worry, ma'am! I'm not here to shame or blackmail you. I just want to tell you that I know who your lost son is: the one you had with the king. Mason is…Mason is wonderful. He's everything your king isn't. Do you know he built an AI? It's amazing!"

Her words rush out in a garbled mess, and my mind races to resolve all the details she's spewing out. My son…she knows my son? I could meet my son? My heart freezes, equally terrified and overjoyed.

"Are you okay?"

A question trips out of my mouth. "How do you know my son?"

She shakes her head. "It's a long story. But there was an accident and he's lost his memory. I'm not powerful enough to restore it, but we can help him."

A quietness descends over the room. Nothing moves, nothing breaths.

"My son—my firstborn. He's okay?"

Adelaide nods. "Yes ma'am. He is."

I sigh in relief. But another question hangs in my mind, and now that she knows the truth…Adelaide is my confidante. "Where…where's Paul?"

"I honestly don't know," she says. "But we're all in danger. He wants to take Adam from you, using whatever method necessary. He's failed once, but he will try again."

"We need to find him," I choke. I raise my eyes to the

heavens. "I have to fix this: I have to come clean with him. And…I think he needs to go away for a while."

Adelaide nods. "I may know where he is."

THIRTY-SEVEN
ADELAIDE

Colette stands behind me with her husband just above the place I've called home for so long. Ten of the king's guards have gone down the teleporter leading to my home, hoping to find and arrest him. He is officially a traitor to the crown…and he's attempted a kidnapping.

The king clears his throat while we wait. "So…what is this? Some kind of hobbit hole?"

"This is where I lived."

"What, so you're a mole?"

The queen flinches at his sarcastic remark, but I ignore him. "Colette, did you have something you wanted to tell your husband?"

Colette's eyes drop. "Um…well…Wesley…I've asked the guards if I can have an audience with Green. It will be safe, they'll have him tied up."

"Why are you asking me? Do whatever you want," the king says. I share a look with the queen—I've heard *that* nonsense before.

"And one more thing." Colette's voice trembles. "I need to do this...alone."

"What, so I'm just supposed to stand over there by that tree like an idiot, waiting for you?"

"Please."

My thoughts are with Mason. Is he still downstairs? Is he conscious? Confused? Scared? As soon as the guards say it's safe, I'm running down there one last time to find him.

Muffled grinding and whirring signals the teleporter's arrival, and the teleporter stops to take a moment to bask in this suspenseful moment. I'm sure Colette wants to tear the teleporter doors open, because I do too.

When the guards emerge, my heart stops for one beat... before Green's bald head appears, shiny and slick.

"Paul Green," one guard snaps. "Before we take you away, your queen wishes to have an audience with you."

I give Wesley a look, but it's his wife's gentle yet firm gaze that gets him to stalk off. Four guards maneuver Green closer to Colette, his arms bound behind his back, his eyes full of disdain.

"What do you want to say, Colette?" Green spits, refusing to look her in the eyes. My insides burn at his disrespect.

The queen gasps through silent tears. "I'm sorry. I'm so sorry."

I want to lecture him; to tell him I know the truth about him now. But I stay quiet.

Her broken voice must crack his heart; Green shakes his head. His words are hurt, covered by anger. "You won't let me see my son."

"I was wrong," she sobs. "I thought it was too complicated. I don't know how to fix all this. But violence isn't the way to go."

Green shakes his head. "I came back to kill Mason to ensure the throne for Adam. But...I couldn't."

I'm furious with myself for not figuring he would take such drastic steps.

"I just want to have a relationship with my son." The queen's eyes are that of a haunted woman, stuck in memories of realities that can never be changed. "Please, Paul. Let's just fix all this."

Green lowers his head. "I'm so tired of fighting. I'm so tired of losing."

Colette takes a cautious step toward him. "We'll figure this out. You'll get to see your son."

I can't hold myself back any longer. I approach the nearest guard, a man with a heavy beard and watery, sleep-deprived eyes. Someone's been working extra hours...perhaps he's expecting another child? I begin to Memory Jump to verify if I'm correct, but a sting darts straight through my brain and I stop.

I may need to take a break from that for a while.

"Excuse me, sir. May I go inside now?"

The man nods. "The perimeter has been checked and cleared. You can go down."

I turn to Colette, who's watching the men lead Green away.

Time to forget this chapter of our lives.

Time to reset. To rebuild. To plant new flowers and water them, waiting for the spring when good things can finally bloom in our lives.

With the company of the queen, we enter my house one more time.

It's so white, so barren, so cold. I don't enjoy the experience in the least.

"Colette, would you mind waiting here? He may be a little confused…I don't want to scare him." Colette barely has time to nod before I run to my room, feeling as if my feet are moving in slow motion.

I turn the lights on to defeat the darkness swallowing everything. Mason lies at the foot of my bed, arms bound, eyes half-open like he just woke up from a long nap. I fall down to my knees and smile, the look in his eyes so hurtful. There's no recognition. Part of me had hoped somehow he'd reset. It takes everything in me to not fix his terribly mussed-up hair, to not touch the bruises on his face.

What do I say? How do I encompass what I'm feeling at this moment? Only two letters fall out of my mouth, and they're barely audible: "Hi."

Mason's eyes squint further. "Do I know you?"

I run my hands over the coarse rope binding him. "There's been an accident and you've forgotten some things in your life. You don't remember me, but I'm your friend. And I'm going to help you remember."

He shakes his head. "Why am I tied up? I'm so confused…"

"I'm going to get you out of here." I fight back tears. I can't explain how much I hate this. "Hey, I'm going to introduce you to someone else. Your mom. Remember her?"

"Someone told me she's the queen, right? I don't know if I believe that or not—can't remember."

"Yes, she's the queen. Can I introduce you to her?"

He nods slowly. "Yeah."

I go back to find Colette pacing around my entryway. Her eyes brighten at my approach.

"Mason is such a special guy," I brief her. "I was threatened and had to delete his memories of me, but he's still the same."

She gasps. "Is he hurt at all?"

"No, he's fine! I just need to get some scissors from the kitchen; Fawn tied him up."

We grab scissors before heading to the bedroom. They're the same scissors that my captor had used to cut my hair, scissors used to control and mentally bind are now used to free.

We go back to my room. "Hey Mason, I got something to free you. And…this is your mom."

It takes everything I can do to not hug him, to be a part of this moment with him. But I don't want to scare him. So I just cut his bonds as Colette reunites with her son.

She gasps from behind me. Tears fall, and she looks as if she could melt. She whispers his name. It's a holy, reverent moment. I feel bad being here.

I finish my cuts and step back awkwardly.

"I'll be right outside—" I begin.

"No," the queen says. "I want you here. It's fine."

"Someone…someone told me you're my real mom. I can't remember who told me."

I grin from behind Colette. I'm still there, in a tiny way.

Colette leans in gingerly, reading Mason's expression before she engulfs him in a hug. My entire body warms with the beauty of the moment.

And I realize so many things about freedom that day.

Freedom is so many things.

And it's beautiful, whatever color it wears.

It's loud, refusing to be silent. It gives a voice to the small, to the silent, to the simple.

I sneak back outside. There's a sturdy breeze, and I close my eyes to feel it truly sift through me. It breathes life over my soul, over my bones, over my confidence and bravery. My hair whips around, a little lower than my shoulder blades.

My eyes open again.

I see the sky. *My* sky.
I see the world. *My* world.
And I'm never going to let it go.

EPILOGUE
COLETTE

I didn't expect to lose my son so soon.

But in doing so, I gained a daughter.

Mason easily fell in love with the Memory Jumper again, and it's no wonder. I could never forget Adelaide's darkness when I first met her: the half-smiles, the empty eyes, the way she seemed more shell than human. I was looking at a reflection of myself.

And yet once Adelaide stood up to Fawn, and once she had something to fight for—Mason's memory—she truly blossomed. Her heart grew strong, not like iron which cannot change or bend, for the heart *must* shift on occasion. Humans break, but humans also heal. No, her heart was an oak tree, blossoming up and out and into the world to bless those in her midst with shade and soft breezes.

And her branches mingled with mine. Her bravery was contagious. She spoke her mind and encouraged me to do the same.

It's been six months since everything changed—since I talked to Green, since I met my firstborn son for the first time.

I live in peace, knowing I did what was right in the end. And knowing that, while I do not have Wesley's love, it is not my fault. And I now have the love of two more beautiful young people.

I want to speak up, to tell Wesley he is cruel and selfish. My voice may still be quiet, but every day it gains intensity. It is melodic and thoughtful, and Adelaide fuels me, my living example of what I could one day become.

Because of the Memory Jumper, maybe, just maybe...

One day, I will be brave too.

MENTAL HEALTH RESOURCES

Domestic abuse is common yet misunderstood. Abuse doesn't need to be physical to be valid and reportable. Many suffer from mental, psychological, emotional, or financial abuse. Paired with mind games like gaslighting, victims are systematically brainwashed into believing that their relationship with the abuser is normal.

Labeling a situation as *abuse* can be scary, but I promise it will only help. If you believe that you or a loved one may be a victim of domestic abuse, please view the following resources:

- **National Domestic Violence Hotline:** thehotline.org
- **Live Your Dream:** liveyourdream.org/get-help/domestic-violence-resources.html
- **Womens Law Hotline:** womenslaw.org
- **The Hope Line:** thehopeline.com/partners/focus-on-the-family
- ***Something Was Wrong* (Podcast):** Listening to other people's stories helped me notice patterns in abuse. Please note that the podcast is for mature audiences and can be triggering.
- ***Gaslighting: Recognize Manipulative and Emotionally Abusive People—and Break Free* by Stephanie Sarkis, PhD (Book)**

ACKNOWLEDGMENTS

This book is a patchwork of so many things, and I have many people to thank.

Firstly, all praise be to God, without Whom I truly believe I would not be here. God, thank you for putting me through such hardship over the past couple years. Each trial and each tear breathed something beautiful into this novel; without the hurt, this book would have no heart or soul. Thank You for giving me something to live for, and reminding me every day to keep smiling.

I'd like to give a special thanks to the team at Lost Island Press. Shira, thank you for believing in my book and pulling for it to win! And an infinite thanks to Mel Torrefranca—what you are doing is absolutely amazing. You are building an empire and giving publishing a new (and better) face, and I am so proud to be a part of that. Thanks to everyone from cover designer (Aleksandra) to proofreader (Hannah). Anyone involved with Lost Island Press has my sincere gratitude.

Mom, thanks for raising me to love writing. Thank you for reading my silly stories even from such an early age, and for saying that storytelling flows through my blood. You always believe in me, no matter what adventure or hobby I am involved in. I love you more than words can say, and I am truly the way I am because of your influence.

Thank you to Diana Cockrell for being my writing mentor. I felt so weird being the only kid in writing class who actually *wanted* to be there, but it looks like it ended up paying off. Thank you for reading my stories, for encouraging me, and even beta reading a very early draft of this novel. I hope my writing makes you proud!

Thank you to Julia Ryan and my *excellent* sister, Rachel Brown, for originally reading the entire manuscript and encouraging me to keep writing! I needed someone to believe in this concept, and you were there for me. You always have been.

Thank you to all the girls I counseled at summer camp in 2019. Many of your stories broke my heart; I was in the midst of writing this book, and I saw Adelaide in so many of you. No child should have to go through the horrendous circumstances some of you so willingly shared with me. And yet your bravery and strength at such a young age spurred me on to give Adelaide the ending she deserves. Thank you for trusting me with your pain; I hope this novel inspires other girls to keep fighting as you all do.

And lastly, I must thank the reader...especially the reader that made it to this paragraph! If you're anything like me, the fact that you're reading this means you fell in love with the story and want to savor every word associated with it. Adelaide's story is so much bigger than I am. Rewriting the classic tale of Rapunzel has opened my eyes up to the world of psychology and abuse, and I pray this story gives strength to the mistreated. I want it to be a Mason for the weary: something that comes into your life and whispers, "Hey, you deserve to be free and happy. This darkness isn't forever." And for everyone else, I hope this story encourages you to partner with the people around you living in fear. If we band together, we can create an amazing community that cannot be crushed by cruel, domineering people.

ABOUT THE AUTHOR

Amanda Michelle Brown is a blogger, author, podcaster, and graphic designer who loves nothing more than a BBC drama and an oat milk latte. Amanda wrote her first novel in middle school with a green pen (complete with illustrations). You can often find her planning her next crazy project, haunting libraries and thrift stores, or telling stories about her day that *may* be a little exaggerated.

amandamichellebrown.com

ABOUT THE PUBLISHER

We specialize in dark young adult fiction. Amanda Michelle Brown won our 2021 Lost Island Writing Contest with the submission of her debut novel *The Memory Jumper*. Explore quizzes, merch, and free bonus content on our website.

You can support Amanda Michelle Brown and Lost Island Press by reviewing this book online. Use the hashtag *#The-MemoryJumper* and mention *@lostislandpress* on social media platforms for a potential shoutout.

lostislandpress.com

ALSO BY LOST ISLAND PRESS
SIMILAR DARK YA BOOKS

Memory Minefield by Mel Torrefranca

My Brother's Spare by Shira Behore

Capsule by Mel Torrefranca

Leaving Wishville by Mel Torrefranca

Lightning Source UK Ltd.
Milton Keynes UK
UKHW012301101022
410270UK00010B/269/J